OUT OF REACH

A SAM POPE NOVEL

ROBERT ENRIGHT

For my girls,

CHAPTER ONE

The clouds that dominated the sky had grown darker and darker as the morning progressed, and their promise of rain was becoming a reality. A constant drizzle had begun to fall, coating the entire city of Glasgow in a cold, damp blanket. The famous city was, as ever, alive with activity, with the welcoming inhabitants going about their daily business. The wide streets were lined with magnificent buildings, all of them now filled with the latest popular shops and other high-end boutiques. The traffic-filled roads that ran through the city like a network of corridors spiralled out from the city towards other focal points, such as Glasgow Airport and the macabre-looking Necropolis. The picturesque cemetery was a tribute to gothic beauty, like a number of the buildings that dominated the city itself.

It was a wonderful place to live, with the locals happy to share a smile or a friendly word, but aware enough to allow someone to keep themselves to themselves.

Sam Pope had fallen in love with the place the second he had arrived.

He had no idea why he'd chosen Glasgow, but when he

had set off from Derbyshire, he hadn't had a clear destination in mind. After the brutal few nights of battling some of the most dangerous hitmen the world had to offer, Sam knew he needed to keep moving. Not just for his own safety, but to keep his word to a young detective who had actually been able to track Sam down. Detective Constable Saddler could have made his career.

The man to bring Sam Pope to justice.

Yet, once Sam had explained the severity of what was happening, and why there had been gunfights in Derby, all the detective did was remind Sam that there were good people out there. People who knew that despite the fact that Sam broke the law, he wasn't a criminal.

It had reminded Sam that there were people worth fighting for. That his fight wasn't for nothing.

After being allowed to leave by the young detective, Sam had laid siege to Dana Kovalenko's home in Mayfair, London, fighting the vengeful woman who had blamed Sam for the death of her brothers. The fact that they had run a sex-trafficking empire didn't alleviate her anguish, and she threw everything she had at Sam. A ruthless gang of thugs and some of the deadliest men in the world had fallen to Sam before he was able to put a bullet through her skull and walk away.

It ended the hit on his head, but it came at a cost.

It had fully exposed his return from the dead, with the press and countrywide police forces now confirming his return after his faked death two and half years ago. His battles with Daniel Bowker and then the destruction of Slaven Kovac and his empire had lit the fuse of their suspicion. The continuous blood baths over those few days all but confirmed he was alive and well, and Sam knew he would be hunted, especially by the enthusiastic new commissioner, Bruce McEwen.

But at a greater cost, he had betrayed Adrian Pearce's trust.

After the heinous assault on their friend, Sean Wiseman, Pearce had begrudgingly accepted Sam's return to being a vigilante, in spite of his hopes of his friend finding peace. When Sam had surprised him at the Bethnal Green Youth Centre, he had done so with an ulterior motive. By asking Pearce, a former detective and a man with a strict moral code, to aide him in his quest for Kovalenko's blood, he had damaged their friendship.

Probably irreparably so.

Pearce had done as Sam had asked, and provided him with a gun, but the man had made it no secret that their friendship was over.

That was four months ago.

Four months since he'd walked out of the Marlow Heights building, leaving the walls splattered with blood and Dana and her henchmen dead behind him.

Four months since Jacob Nash, one of the hitmen sent to kill Sam had in fact helped him, allowing his own disillusionment in the world to turn him against his employers and fight alongside Sam. The last Sam had seen or heard from the large, tattoo-covered American was as he raced to the bottom of the building, ready to lead the police on a high-speed pursuit to give Sam the time he needed to get away. Considering the powerful people Nash had worked for, he doubted he would ever see the man again.

Four months had passed since Sam had stepped out of Mam's Café in Spondon, having left her enough money to cover the damages to her eatery and to put her mind at ease. She had unwillingly given his identity to a dangerous hitman, who had confronted Sam in a brutal hand-to-hand confrontation in the Derbyshire train depot. Sam still had the scar across his cheek from that night, although he had shattered the man's skull and broken his neck with a brutal stomp of his boot.

Sam was built to survive.

With the amount of pain and destruction he had put his body through, he often wondered if he was unbreakable.

It had been four months since he'd stepped off the train at Glasgow station, realising that he had never been to the Scottish city, and he allowed its gothic beauty and irresistible charm to welcome him with arms open. As had become a ritual for him, Sam had located a local internet café, scoured Airbnb for a long-term booking, and paid for it in full. A former associate and a good friend, Paul Etheridge, had passed on a considerable fortune to Sam to continue his war on crime. Sam had appreciated the gesture, knowing that he'd changed Etheridge's life forever the moment he walked back into it. The two had served together in the army when they were younger, but Etheridge was never the elite soldier that Sam was. While Sam's skills took him around the world and saw him recruited into the off-the-books Project Hailstorm, Etheridge had left the armed forces to become a tech millionaire. After selling his company, Etheridge had aided Sam up until he broke Sam out of a prison convoy and then went dark. The man was out there somewhere, and Sam could only hope he was happy and safe.

The fortune, which was in the eye-watering seven figures, had long remained untouched, and Sam only dipped into it when he needed to either repay someone for their kindness, or to open doors he couldn't himself. Etheridge had created an entirely new identity for Sam, who had been known as Jonathan Cooper for nearly three years, and had been able to falsify secure, online records to ensure that Sam Pope's savings and military pension were wired through to his new persona, completely undetected by the best digital security on the market. Considering Etheridge had built the security himself, he'd been able to bypass it.

Sam lived within his means, which meant the Airbnb had been a modest, studio apartment overlooking one of the high streets, and most weekends, Sam would lie reading in his bed, while the drunken cheer of a busy night would echo outside his window. He had only intended to stay in Glasgow for a couple of weeks, but then one night, everything had changed.

The night he met Melissa Hendry.

Sam was approaching his forty-second birthday, and the idea of romance had long since left him. After his marriage with Lucy had crumbled after the death of their son, the idea of sharing his heart with another person felt like a cruel prank. The only time he'd felt someone call to his heart in such a way was Amara Singh.

The fact that she was the lead detective tasked with bringing him down had been a stumbling block, but over a few months, their lust for one another had culminated in one evening of passion, and the agreement that in another life, they could have been happy together. She had gone dark, recruited to a shady government agency, and Sam hadn't heard from her since the night they were both offered the job.

The next day, Etheridge had broken Sam out of a prison van, and in the space of that week, Sam lost Singh, Etheridge, and a dear old friend, Mac.

The fight had cost him everything.

But he had to keep fighting.

But meeting Mel had stopped it in its tracks. He hadn't picked Glasgow to look for trouble. He was smart enough to know that he wouldn't just walk into a situation that required his skills. It usually required a bit of digging and the bravery to confront those who felt above the law. When he arrived in Glasgow, he was hoping for a few quiet weeks to clear his head.

Then, he walked into the Carnival Bar, twenty minutes from his apartment on the edge of town, and everything changed. The modest bar wasn't the biggest, with fifteen tables, a pool table and a large screen for the sports. It had lunch and dinner menus, along with signs promising the best coffee in the city. At night, the liquor licence allowed it to operate as a watering hole, but with hardly any staff and the footfall more attracted to the larger bars and clubs near his apartment, it was never busy.

A few locals ventured nightly to watch whatever sports were showing, but the main business came during the day. Melissa had opened the bar seven years ago, finding comfort in running her own business after her marriage had broken apart when her husband had cheated on her.

A decision that Sam had explained seemed totally baffling.

Mel was thirty-five years old, and her brunette hair was always pulled back into a messy ponytail. A local lass. Her accent was thick and deep, yet she maintained a cheeky charm with everything she said. It was no wonder her customers loved her, and after the devastation of her cheating spouse, she had thrown her heart and soul into her passion for food and entertaining. While the Carnival wasn't the hub of activity that many other bars were, she did well enough to get by, and more importantly, to show her teenage daughter, Cassie, what could be done with hard work and application.

Sam had stopped in for a non-alcoholic drink, been ribbed by Mel for it, and the two soon hit it off.

Within the first week, Sam had been in five times, and after the sixth time, when the bar had closed, Mel told him she knew who he was and refused to call him Jonathan anymore. They had kissed, which had led to Sam being taken upstairs to the well-decorated flat above, where they'd spent the night together.

Since then, Sam had found himself envisioning his life in Glasgow, and through an old school friend, Mel had got him a job at the local haulage yard, which was a thirty-minute bus ride from his flat. If Sam wanted to build a normal life in a new country, he needed to get a job.

Needed to get back to normality.

As the drizzle rattled against the metal of a nearby car, Sam sat in the seat of his forklift truck and looked out over the yard. Despite the constant clunking of machinery, it was a peaceful place to work, and in the few months with which he'd been employed, he'd found what he assumed was happiness. It wasn't something that came easily to him, but he had finally made peace with the death of his son.

Jamie would always be with him, the innocent and beautiful smile tattooed on his heart. The pain of his loss still ebbed away at it, trying to stop it from beating, but Sam knew he had channelled that pain into doing something good.

He hadn't been able to save his boy, but he had saved so many others.

Jasmine Hill.

Alex Stone and her family.

Jack and Mandy Townsend.

Good people who he had been able to help.

The time for drowning in his own misery had passed, and although he had thought his fight would continue, he looked out over the vast scrap yard and the multitude of broken or ruined items and refused to be one of them. The lads he worked with, of varying ages and backgrounds, had all welcomed him. They knew who he was, but in their eyes, they thought the things he'd done had made him a stand-up guy. Even the owner of the scrap yard, Martin McGinn, who Mel had contacted to get him the job, had told him he'd look the other way as long as he kept his head down.

Good people looked after good people, and Sam was coming round to the idea that he was one of them.

As he pulled the forklift truck into gear, it rumbled to life, and he headed across the scrapyard to move some of the old, broken fridges as Martin had requested. The rain didn't bother him, and after a few more hours, he'd be able to clock off, head home for some food and then make his way round to Mel's bar to spend time with her.

As the drizzle picked up, Sam broke into a smile, knowing he had found more than just peace in Glasgow.

He'd found happiness.

CHAPTER TWO

Tuesday mornings always felt like a slog. As Lynsey Beckett swiped her ID to get through the security gates of the BBC building, she offered a fake smile to the large security guard who watched her. She felt bad that she'd never remembered his name, but then, he'd been rather forward with his attraction to her and wasn't the most humble when she turned him down.

It happened a lot, and of all people, she was the last person to do it to.

Her rise in the journalistic world had been meteoric, her exposé on the damage being done by Lonoxidil, pushed out to the market by Prime Pharmaceuticals, had seen her become the BBC's golden child. Exposing the charitable enterprise, Head Space, a not-for-profit tackling mental illness, as a key stakeholder in the production of the drug, Lynsey had shown that the new 'Reach Out' programme, headed up by Head Space CEO, Nicola Weaver, was nothing more than a front to maximise profits. It had been a startling revelation and one that over six months later, she was still riding to more prominent places. Her editor, Tom Alderson, had probed her about the input of Sam Pope, wanting to be the one to be on the cusp of the story of his return, but Lynsey had refused.

Her snooping around Head Space had put her in the crosshairs of Daniel Bowker, the vilest man she'd ever met. After failing to intimidate her, he set his men upon her new boyfriend, Sean. After beating him into a coma, it was only then that the story exploded.

Sean was a good friend of Sam Pope.

A man the world thought dead, but the one man who could stop a criminal enterprise on his own. Not only did he bully the information out of Weaver's associate, he also saved her life when Bowker had taken her hostage. The least she felt she owed him was to say he'd never been there.

Her editor also had a few gripes with her running with the story, because he knew what would happen next. It didn't harm her chances that she was an attractive woman, with sharp cheekbones and mousey brown hair. Or that her Northern Irish accent added a sense of calm to every story they set her on.

And the opportunities and stories came raining down on her as the higher-ups saw an excellent opportunity to birth a new "star" in the journalism world, as well as be seen as promoting equality in their organisation. Tom didn't believe in check box exercises, but even he couldn't deny that she'd earned her shot at success.

Several stories crossed her desk, and Lynsey found herself in front of the camera almost daily. Her social media profiles grew exponentially, so much so that she handed control over to the BBC who employed an intern to delete any vulgar messages or pictures that would drop into her personal inbox on a daily basis. When it came to being recognised on the streets, especially on the streets between the BBC building and the large Westfield Shopping Centre in White City, she just shrugged, smiled and was as polite as possible.

While her life as a journalist had gone from strength to strength, so had her relationship with Sean. Their connection had been immediate, and while he had been open and honest about the rough past he'd walked through, she was even more attracted to the sweet, compassionate man he had become.

The injuries he had sustained at the hands of Bowker and his crew, just for being associated with her, would be life altering, but the fight he had shown had been incredible. Lynsey had watched with pride as he fought through his bouts of surgery and physiotherapy, and while it was a long road to recovery, she found herself holding his hand every step of the way. They had fallen in love with each other, and she focused on the thought of coming home to him that night as she trudged past Tom's office, towards her usual desk in the bullpen.

'Morning.' Tom's voice echoed from the room. Lynsey stopped, took two steps back and stepped into the doorway.

'Morning, Tom.' She sipped her coffee. 'How you doing today?'

'Oh, you know. Kate's got the arse with me for missing parent's evening last night, the kids are pissed at me for apparently "not getting TikTok", and I've got my boss breathing down my neck for the latest figures from the polls.' Tom sighed. 'Same shit, different day.'

'It's not all shit.' Lynsey smiled.

'How's Sean?' Tom asked solemnly, as if realising his problems weren't the worst that could happen.

'He's good. Walked two kilometres yesterday, so the damage to his spine is healing. He's still a little here one minute, gone the next. But it's a marathon.'

'You okay?' Tom stood; his arms folded as he leant

against the wall. While he'd been envious of her sudden rise, he had always made sure to look out for her.

'I'm getting there.' Lynsey shrugged. 'I'm not the one going through it, so—'

'But you are. Just in a different way. If you need anything—'

'I know, you're here.' Lynsey smirked.

'Big day today, right?' Tom said, not wanting to get bogged down in sentimentality. 'The Munroe case?'

'Yup.' Lynsey took a frustrated sip of her coffee. 'It'll get thrown out again.'

Despite trying to be a neutral journalist, the Munroe case had got under her skin. As the son of a billionaire tech mogul, Jasper Munroe had built himself up as a social media celebrity, using his unlimited wealth to promote the high life and cultivate a following of people who aspired to live the life he did. For a man who hadn't earned a penny of his fortune, Jasper had ensured he looked like a million bucks, and his social media profiles were filled with pictures of him with his chiselled body out, surrounded by palm trees, scantily clad women and expensive champagne. The man was a cretin and trawling through his profiles had made her skin crawl.

But this was the fifth time in two years that he'd been arrested and charged with sexual assault, and despite her growing list of connections, she still wasn't privy to the number of NDAs or other settlements he'd been involved with. That afternoon, there was going to be a decision to see whether Jasper would face any actual charges for the alleged assault of an eighteen-year-old called Hayley Baker.

Her account had been horrific, yet Lynsey knew what would happen. There either wouldn't be sufficient evidence to convict the man, or someone who claimed to have seen what happened would now decide they couldn't be too sure.

Either way, Munroe's limitless piggy bank would grease the palms of those he needed it to, and it would all go away.

The young girl wouldn't get justice, and a creep like Jasper Munroe, who had every opportunity the world has to offer, will get away with breaking the law because of who he is.

As she finished her coffee, Lynsey felt her fingers tighten and crush the coffee cup, causing the plastic lid to pop and a little of the remnants to splash over the top.

'Shit, sorry,' Lynsey said, looking for a tissue.

'Don't worry about it.' Tom chuckled as he ushered her to the door. 'Just go do your job.'

Lynsey squinted with suspicion.

'Do you want me to do my job how the BBC wants me to do my job? Or how I should do it?'

Tom smiled, placed a friendly hand on her back as he guided her through the door and then gently pushed her towards the desks.

'Come on, Lynsey. Like you'll do it any other way than your own.'

Lynsey nodded her appreciation, knowing Tom had basically just confirmed that he would go to bat for her if she ruffled a few feathers.

That's what she did best.

There was likely a number of very rich, very well paid executives within the BBC who made sure that the likes of Jasper Munroe weren't tarnished through their media outlets, given the extensive fortune and power wielded by the man's father. Dale Munroe was as infamous for his temper as he was famous for his fortune.

He would be a powerful enemy to make.

Lynsey sat down at her desk, cracked her knuckles, slid

her earbuds into her ears and began drafting the piece that would condemn not only Jasper Munroe, but the entire justice system that assigns punishment based more on the person's class, than the apparent crime they had committed. She had pretty strong evidence of witness tampering, and enough of an inkling about the NDAs to know that it would certainly stir up a complaint or two.

Having been face to face with Daniel Bowker, Lynsey wasn't scared of making enemies.

She had a commitment to this young woman, and unluckily for Jasper Munroe, Lynsey had a voice that she was more than happy to use to keep that commitment.

Tuesday nights were always quiet at Carnival, and Sam sat at the far end of the modest bar, a Diet Coke in his glass and his eyes on the screen. A Champions League fixture was being played out by two elite football teams, with commentators over-egging the importance of the result with every passing minute. Unfortunately for the locals, their team had already been eliminated in an earlier round, otherwise, the atmosphere would have been a little more rousing.

Sam didn't mind.

Apart from the usual locals who wandered in for a few drinks and a game of cards, he had been able to spend the evening talking with Mel, who stood seductively behind the bar and offered Sam the odd grin. She was as smitten as he was, and it showed on her face whenever they locked eyes. Not one for putting on airs and graces, Mel didn't wear much make-up, nor was she a slave to the latest fashion trends.

Her hair, tied up in a loose ponytail, was a shimmering brown, and it suited her dark eyes. Her face was strikingly pretty, and she wore a baggy check shirt and tight jeans, which, while offered comfort, still showed off her athletic body. Feeling she needed to compete with the muscular man she was dating, Mel had boasted about how, after her divorce from David was finalised, she'd decided to get into the best shape of her life, and she committed to two yoga sessions and three long-distance runs a week.

Sam had been impressed.

Despite his military upbringing and elite training, he still struggled with a long-distance run. The bullet wounds that had scarred his body didn't help, but when she'd invited him for one of the runs, he'd been surprised how much energy she still had after he stopped at ten kilometres.

Mel often spoke about the end of her marriage being a new beginning, and that David had grown tired of the adult lifestyle they'd been forced into by becoming parents at the ages of twenty and twenty-two, respectively. Eventually, his wandering eye had led him to another woman's bed, and Mel had kicked him out.

They sold the family home, and she moved into the flat above the abandoned store below with her pride and joy.

Cassie.

As smart a fifteen-year-old that Sam had ever met. The young lady was the brightest person he had ever come across, and her grasp on the world and the way it worked had caught him by surprise. Sam knew there was no point in lying to her about who he was, as she would see through it like she did most of the lies that came out of any politician's mouth. Cassie was more clued up on politics than Sam had ever been, and while he knew that most of them were bottom-feeding egotists, she would comprehensively pick apart their pledges of support to the nation and would then be able to discuss the ramifications.

It had baffled Sam, much to Mel's amusement, but

Cassie was headstrong enough to know that her mother was happy, and she made Sam feel welcome. There had been the odd grilling where the teenager had confronted Sam about the reports of the things he'd done. Sam had treated her with the respect she deserved, and he admitted to the deaths he'd caused and told her why.

Not once did she call him a monster. She highlighted there were other ways to resolution, but she understood.

David rarely visited, and when he did, he would shower her with gifts as a substitution for genuine affection, and Sam was wary of about becoming a father figure to her. There was a hole in him that he'd never filled, and although he had moved on from the guilt of Jamie's death, he wasn't ready to plug the gap he'd left behind.

She was a good kid, and like Mel, Sam enjoyed her company. When Sam arrived at the bar that evening, Cassie had even popped down to say hello, but now, as the clocked ticked a few minutes away from closing time, she would have been asleep, probably with an open novel lying carelessly on her duvet. Sam stood, did a lap of the bar, and collected the empty glasses, as the last of the usual patrons grunted their goodbyes and headed to the exit. As he returned to his seat, he placed the glasses on the bar, which Mel quickly collected.

'Thanks, love,' Mel said with a smile.

'Easy one tonight, eh?'

'Yeah, Tuesdays aren't that busy. To be honest, I keep the place open for the guys to have their card game. Make a little money, but it's more routine than anything.'

'Can I help with anything?'

Before Mel could answer, the door to the bar flew open, followed immediately by the loud, obnoxious voice of a young man, clearly intoxicated, as he bragged brazenly to his two mates about his sexual conquests. Decked out in smart suits and expensive shoes, they clearly had money and no problem in flaunting it. As they staggered in towards the bar, one of the accompanying friends stumbled into one of the tables.

Sam glanced at Mel, who rolled her eyes.

'Sorry, lads. We've closed.'

'Fuck off, darling,' the ringleader said. 'It's five to.'

'First off, don't tell me to fuck off.' Mel stepped forward, showing little fear. 'Second, I've already cashed up so I can't serve you tonight.'

'Look, lady, I can give you all the cash you want. Me and my pals here, we're celebrating. So why don't you be a good little girl and just get us some fucking drinks?'

'She said she's closed.'

Sam's voice cut through the tension like a warm knife through butter, drawing the twisted snarl of the drunkard and his two friends. Without even looking at the men, Sam calmly sipped his Diet Coke before placing the glass down firmly. Then, he turned, locked his eyes on the loudmouth and held his stare.

'No one's talking to you, dickhead.' The man turned to his friends, clearly for support. 'Who does this guy think he is?'

'Sam, don't—'

Sam held up his hand, and then stood, his imposing frame more evident and drawing a few anxious looks from the group.

'It's fine. These lads were just going to apologise, then they're going to leave. Isn't that right?'

The two friends exchanged a worried look, while the aggressive leader stepped forward towards Sam. Judging by the dilation of his pupils, Sam knew it wasn't just alcohol that the young man was tanked up on. Considering cocaine was rife in the banking industry, and the man walked with the arrogance and attire to match, Sam quickly ascertained the man's profession. Judging by the fury on the man's face, he didn't take too kindly to being told what to do.

'You ain't from round here, are you lad?' He tried to add menace to his words and emphasised cracking his knuckles.

'Very observant.'

'I'd hold back on the jokes if I were you.'

The man took another step towards Sam, who stood calmly. Sam looked at Mel, who shook her head slowly, then Sam turned back to the young man, knowing the fist was coming any second.

'Last chance. Apologise and leave.'

'Or what?' The man stopped and chuckled, throwing his arm out as if to display his friends. 'There's three of us.'

'That's good. It means you've got two people to pick you up off the floor.'

The fury flashed in the man's eyes, as Sam's threat clearly ignited the drug-fuelled rage within. Shooting forward with a confidence way beyond his ability, the young man threw a pathetic right hook at Sam. Without even flinching, Sam lifted his arm up, hooked the man's arm under his own, and then wrenched it back. The man yelped as his tendons twisted, and in one swift motion, Sam swung the man forward, slamming his face onto the thick oak bar before allowing him to flop to the floor. The splatter of blood on the wood told him the man's nose was broken, and as his friends rushed to his aid, they confirmed it. Lifting him to his feet, blood gushed from the obliterated nose that was now crushed against his face, and his lips were also split.

The young man could hardly stand, and luckily for him, his two friends shuffled him towards the door before they disappeared into the night. There was no chance of repercussion. They had done too many drugs for them to go to the police.

Sam stood casually, hands on his hips, watching until the trio hobbled completely out of sight of the bar window. Before he turned to Mel, he could feel her glare burning through him.

'You said you were done hitting people,' Mel stated with a wry smile on her face. She slowly walked around the bar towards Sam, her face telling him he wasn't really in any bother.

'Technically, I didn't hit him…'

Mel reached up, placed her hands on Sam's face, and then planted her lips on his. He hungrily reciprocated, and the two of them continued their embrace as they headed towards the stairway that led to her flat, ready to allow their attraction to take control. Halfway up the stairs, in the process of lifting Sam's T-shirt from his body, Mel quickly scurried back down to lock the front door, and the two of them hurried to her bedroom, giggling like teenagers as they fell onto the bed, ready for another night of passion.

CHAPTER THREE

'Despite the evidence put forward by the accuser, whose name has been kept hidden for their own protection, the case was dismissed on the grounds that there was no corroborating evidence to back up her claims. The prosecutor had been hopeful of a few more witness testimonies, yet these were not forthcoming and therefore, the case against Jasper Munroe was dismissed by the judge with the understanding that the name of the accuser will never come to light. As for Mr Munroe, he has already posted on his social media profiles to his millions of followers, claiming another victory for the justice system has been achieved and that he is, in fact, the victim in all of this. With multiple accusations levelled at the son of billionaire tech tycoon, Dale Munroe, one has to imagine that their sizable fortune might just be the reason why Jasper Munroe is walking away today as a free man.

'Lynsey Beckett, BBC News.'

'I can't send this out, Lyns. You know I can't.'

Tom dropped back in his seat, clapping his hands to his head in astonishment. On the other side of his desk, with her arms folded tightly across her petite frame, Lynsey stared back at him.

'Why? It's the truth.'

'It's speculation.'

'What? You think this arrogant rich kid isn't doing whatever the fuck he wants and using his trust fund to tidy up after himself?' Lynsey shook her head. 'Come on, Tom.'

With a desperate sigh, Tom lifted his coffee, took a swig, and wished it was something stronger.

'Be that as it may, there is no way I can pass this on to production.'

'Why? Because big bad Dale Munroe will give us a nasty phone call?'

'No, because he'll slap us with a fucking lawsuit.' Tom slammed his hand down on the table, trying to wrestle back his authority. 'Look, the world is a shit place filled with shit people. You, especially, know this. But there is still a very fine line with what we can put out there as truth to the public.'

'This is the truth. We've got evidence of NDAs, out of court settlements—'

'All of them legally binding, meaning they cannot be used to fuel your speculation that Jasper Munroe raped this girl.'

'So, she's a liar?'

'I'm not saying that, and that's unfair to even accuse me of it.'

'Sorry.' Lynsey held up her hand. Tom nodded his acceptance, and the two let the silence sit between them as she dropped into the chair opposite her editor. As the temperature cooled, Lynsey shook her head. 'Do you know how many rapes don't get reported to the police?'

'I couldn't even hazard a guess.'

'Too many. And the ones that do, there usually isn't enough "evidence" to convict, meaning the women get labelled liars and the piece of shit walks free as a bird. Yet, we celebrate our justice system like it keeps us all in check.'

Lynsey took a deep breath, knowing she was on the verge of breaking, and Tom stood. He walked to the cabinet that lined one of the walls of the room and he lifted the water jug and poured her a glass. She accepted with a thanks, and he leant against the desk, just in front of her.

'It's shit. I know that. You know that. Do I honestly believe that this Jasper Munroe raped this girl? Yeah, probably. He seems to have previous, he shows little remorse, and he has the money behind him to make this stuff go away.'

'Then why aren't we fighting it?'

'Because that's not our job,' Tom responded firmly. 'We are reporters, Lynsey. Not lawyers. If you want to seek justice in the court of law, then as admirable as it is, you're in the wrong profession. Our job is to report on the outcome, not to speculate about the shady dealings and the half truths. I'd love nothing more than to have a rich, vile rapist pulled from the streets and thrown in a cell, but we can't incite outrage with speculation. I know that you know that, and although you might hate me for it, I can't put that forward to go out today. It's not just your credibility that would be shot to pieces.'

Lynsey held her tongue. Despite the noble efforts to placate her, Tom had essentially admitted he didn't want to tarnish his reputation along with her own. She knew when recording the report that it would cause a stir, and likely lead to the very conversation that she was engaged in.

But someone had to speak up.

Someone had to do the right thing.

She had tried, but now, it would be swept under the carpet, and while a young girl has to deal with the devastation of being raped and getting no justice for it, a billionaire playboy was already celebrating a 'victory' and would likely be in the arms of another woman that evening.

It made her sick to her stomach.

She had wanted to make a difference, but she knew, despite his own selfish motive, Tom was right.

After a few more minutes of silence, Tom stepped forward, patted her reassuringly on her shoulder, before he walked back round the desk to his chair.

'So what do you want me to do?'

'Look, most of it is fine. It's factual, it's well written and your delivery conveys the right tone of disdain for the decision. But you need to re-record the ending.'

'So, take out all the evidence that points towards a miscarriage of justice?'

Tom sighed.

'The part where you go beyond the verdict and deliver your own.' Tom pinched the bridge of his nose in frustration. 'Lynsey, you're on the gravy train here. You're being fast-tracked to becoming one of the faces of this whole damn company. You've got the world at your feet, essentially, so don't wipe dog shit on it. You understand?'

With a deep, defeated sigh, Lynsey nodded and then stood, straightening her pencil skirt and her white blouse.

'Yup. Loud and clear.'

Before Tom could clarify her response, she stomped out of the office and headed back to her desk in the open-plan office. A few other journalists turned their head to her, but she ignored them, knowing her fiery temper preceded her and she'd be left alone. She found her way to her chair, opened her laptop and began to formulate ways she could edit her report, so it ticked the right boxes.

So it conformed to what was expected by the BBC.

So it hid away from the truth.

After half an hour, and not one effort being made to even change the report, Lynsey slammed her laptop shut, stood, and marched out of the office, knowing she needed to calm down and make peace with the fact that not everyone could do the right thing.

As always, Sam had woken before the alarm on his or Mel's phone went off, and he quietly slid from the sheets and headed to the bathroom. A quick shower was necessary after the night he'd enjoyed with his girlfriend, and after a quick blast under the water, he stepped out, wrapped a towel around himself, and began to brush his teeth. As he scrubbed them, he caught a glimpse of himself in the mirror.

His body, while meticulously sculpted through a strict diet and regular exercise, was littered with scars and burns, existing as a tapestry of his one-man war on organised crime. He remembered the pain of every single one.

The first time he'd taken his shirt off in front of Mel, he expected a gasp. Instead, Mel had tenderly traced her fingers over each one and had asked him what had happened.

She encouraged him to let his guard down, and he had.

It's what forged their connection, and it had been a long time since he had trusted someone in that way, and it was why he had spent every day since counting down the hours before he could see her again.

When he returned from the bathroom, Mel was gone, and he could hear her clattering in the kitchen. Quickly, Sam dressed and followed the smell of eggs and the sound of *Radio One* that grew louder as he stepped into the kitchen.

'Morning, Cass,' Sam said with a smile, as he walked towards Mel and gave her a gentle kiss on the back of her head.

Sitting at the table, with a myriad of open textbooks

and a half-eaten bowl of cereal, was Cassie. Already dressed in her school uniform, she raised her head from her textbook and smiled.

'Good morning.' Her smile grew mischievously. 'Should I start charging you rent?'

'Cass!' Mel interrupted, not turning from the eggs that were starting to poach on the stove.

'I'm just saying, if he's going to live here, he needs to pay his way.' She offered Sam another cheeky smile. Sam returned it in kind, pulled out another chair at the table, and sat down.

'What are you reading?'

'Biology.' Cassie turned to her mother. 'Which reminds me, although you might not be too old to have another child, I am too old to become an older sister.'

'Cass!' Mel chuckled again.

'I'm just saying, if you kids are going to be getting up to stuff, just make sure you use protection.'

All three of them laughed, and Mel plonked a warm cup of coffee in front of Sam, gently squeezed his shoulder, and then returned to the stove. Sam took a sip and wondered whether the warmness was from the coffee or the feeling of happiness.

'When's your exam?' Sam asked.

'Monday,' Cassie replied grumpily. 'I know these are just mocks, but I need to get this stuff to stick.'

'You'll be fine, my love,' Mel said as she began to dish up the eggs. 'You're the brightest kid I think I've ever known.'

'How many kids do you know?' Cassie retorted quickly.

'Shush.' Mel chuckled as she handed Sam his plate of eggs. Sam readily tucked into them, blown away by how Mel had perfected the poached egg, and he let out a groan of pleasure as he split the egg and watched the orange yolk ooze out.

'Worked up an appetite, did ya?' Cass offered at the opportune moment, causing Sam to almost choke on his breakfast.

'Cassandra!' Mel's faux distress caused all three of them to laugh, and after a few moments, the kitchen quietened down. As Sam finished off his eggs and Cassie stared angrily at the page, the news report on the radio cut through the pleasant silence.

Sam instantly recognised Lynsey Beckett's voice.

'*With not enough evidence to substantiate the claims, the case against Jasper Munroe was thrown out. The social media star was in a celebratory mood, claiming justice had been done and that people were just after the money and fame he could offer. As for the accuser, her name has been held back to protect her identity…*'

'What a fucking surprise.'

'Language, miss.' Mel cut in, chastising her teenage daughter.

'What's this?' Sam jutted a thumb towards the Amazon Alexa on the windowsill, where the news report was emanating from.

'You don't listen to the news much, huh?' Cass sighed. 'This guy, Jasper Munroe. He's some billionaire rich kid. He's all over *Instagram* showing off his wealth, but he's earned none of it.'

'Munroe?' Sam said to himself. 'I know that name.'

'Yeah, Dale Munroe. He's like one of the UK's richest men. It's his son. Fancies himself as a celebrity, but like, five women have accused him of sexual assault over the past year or so. Every single one has either been settled out of court or been thrown out. The guy is an absolute scumbag, and these women have no chance against a guy with that much money and a dad with that much power.'

'It's the way of the world, Cass,' Mel said solemnly, sipping her coffee. 'There are some people who are untouchable. Some people who are just out of reach.'

Sam frowned, and he knew Mel noticed. It triggered an urgent response from the doting mother, who turned to Cass and encouraged her to pack up her books and get ready to catch the bus. As Cassie started stacking her textbooks, Sam looked up at her.

'How many women have accused this guy?'

'I think about five or six. But I guarantee you there're loads more…' Cassie raised her eyebrows. 'Why?'

'No reason. When's your exam again?'

'Monday.'

'Well, I'll tell you what. Next Monday morning, I'll sit right here with you and go over some questions. Make sure you're prepared.'

'I'll hold you to that.' Cassie smiled, kissed her mum on the cheek and then headed to the door. As it slammed, Sam stood, collected his and Mel's dirty plates, and headed to the sink. As he ran them under the hot water, he felt Mel's hands slide around his waist and lock against his stomach. She buried her head into his back and sighed.

'I can't stop you from doing what you're about to do, can I?'

Sam put the plates on the rack beside the sink, dried his hands on his jeans and then turned, sliding his hands over Mel's shoulders and then kissed her on the forehead.

'I'm just going to see for myself.'

CHAPTER FOUR

As the limo pulled through the busy streets of Kensington, Jasper peered through the tinted window, just as the head office of Sure Fire Inc came into view. A giant in the tech world, the CEO and founder, Dale Munroe, had monopolised the network industry, swallowing up every competitor that specialised in building secure, office-based networks and essentially owned the rights to every major platform that was housed within organisations. While they all "owned" their in-house networks and secure channels of communication and file sharing, it was all built upon software that was owned by Sure Fire, and the business model had made Munroe one of the richest men in the country and was knocking on the door of the top ten richest in the world.

Jasper knew his father cast a long shadow, and while he was unlikely to ever escape the shade, he had decided that his own worth was in front of the public eye. His father was ferociously private, and while he didn't approve of Jasper's need for attention and adoration, it at least meant Jasper was never expected to inherit the family business. When Dale died, it was already agreed that the board would appoint a successor, and Jasper would receive an eye-watering annual salary in the nine-figure region. He was happy with that, especially as the only relationship he had with his father was one built on fear.

It was why, as the limo pulled into the private car park underneath the luxurious head office, his hands were shaking. As ever, Jasper opened the small vial that hung from a thin chain around his neck, patted out a bit of cocaine onto the inside of his index finger, and then quickly inhaled it. The sudden rush collided with his brain, sending it smashing into his own skull, and Jasper instantly felt more alive.

Ready to face the fury of his father.

It was a well-trodden path they had both walked over the past couple of years, with Jasper's increasingly worrying behaviour threatening to bring the family name and business into a scandal. They had enough money to make most problems disappear, but Dale had warned Jasper countless times of the consequences if he threatened the company with his actions.

As the limo came to a stop and the driver exited the car, Jasper took a few deep breaths. The door opened, and he stepped out, ignoring the driver as he stomped into the lift, his expensive Italian leather shoes echoing with each step. He pressed the button for the top floor and waited as the lift began its ten-storey ascent. The plush lift included a wall-to-wall mirror, and Jasper, still buzzing from the latest hit of cocaine, took a moment to admire himself in the mirror.

He was exquisitely put together. His hair was styled in a slicked back, skin fade and his strong jaw was freshly shaven. He used most of his spare time to sculpt a body that would cultivate likes and follows on Instagram, and he wrapped it in a wardrobe that cost tens of thousands of pounds. He'd put on his sharpest suit for the sit down with his father, who was pedantically stubborn when it came to office attire. The bespoke three-piece suit he wore cost over ten thousand pounds and fit perfectly to his toned frame.

From what he saw in the mirror, Jasper knew he was a good-looking man. It was no surprise that women threw themselves at him, and for the first decade or so, that was enough. But now, as he approached his thirtieth birthday, it was the ones who said no that were the most appealing.

There was nothing he couldn't have in this world, and he'd make sure that those women knew that.

As the lift came to a stop, the doors opened, and Jasper's attention was pulled from his own reflection by the thunderous voice of his disapproving father.

'Follow me.'

Dale Munroe was an imposing figure. Standing over six feet tall, the man felt taller. He commanded himself with such an air of authority that many crumbled beneath him. His white hair was cut neatly into a side parting, and his designer glasses sat on a thin, sharp nose. His dark eyes radiated tension, and he usually held people with an unblinking stare until they looked away. Every trick to consume power from people may as well have been written by the man, and as he marched powerfully down the carpeted hallway and past his personal assistant's desk, she could only offer him a feeble smile, and then a look of contempt at the son who meekly followed behind.

Although Dale Munroe sent fear through his workforce, he also commanded fierce loyalty and respect.

Jasper, who commanded neither, was seen as a smudge against the name, and those who relied on Dale Munroe for a salary saw him as a potential hinderance. He didn't really care; he had millions of followers who lapped up his every move and that was all the validation he needed.

The grand door to Dale's office was already open, and the elder Munroe marched through, immediately rounding the plush oak desk and sat in the hardbacked leather chair. The sleeves of his shirt were rolled up, and for a man in his early sixties, he was in great shape, owing to his frequent games of squash and golf, along with a live-in personal chef. Jasper sauntered in behind, trying his best to seem confident, and he bypassed the desk and looked out of the floor to ceiling window at the tremendous view of London.

'Not a bad view, is it?'

'It gets tedious,' Dale said, clicking the mousepad on his laptop before slamming it shut. 'As is your behaviour.'

Jasper turned, trying to purvey a sense of intimidation, but it immediately fell at the piercing glare of his father.

'Look, it was some dumb bitch who wanted fifteen seconds of fame.' Jasper shrugged as he approached the desk. 'So I fucked her, then she claimed rape and suddenly, it's big news.'

Jasper dropped into the seat.

'Don't you dare sit down,' Dale said through gritted teeth. His son instantly obliged. 'Let me make this clear to you. You are a disgrace to this family. I'm actually glad your mother died so she wouldn't have to see what a failure you are.'

'Ummm, excuse me?' Jasper held his hand up. 'I'm one of the most influential people on Instagram—'

'What does that mean, exactly?' Dale said mockingly. 'That a bunch of idiots think you're special? What have you ever actually achieved, son? Apart from potentially damaging the reputation of this company. The company that *I* built!'

The red mist descended, and Dale swung a powerful arm, slapping the glass of water clean off the desk and sending it careening across the room until it exploded against the wall. Jasper sat rigid in his seat. He'd seen the man's fury before, but rarely was it directed at him.

'I've done too much for you, Jasper. Maybe that's a

failure on my part. I've paid off every settlement, I've pushed for every NDA. Your behaviour is sickening, but if you went to prison, it would damage the share prices and I can't have people wanting to dig too deep into the company. It's too much of a risk.'

'Dad, I'm sorry. I—'

'Shut your fucking mouth and listen to me. And listen good.' Dale glared at his son in disgust. 'This is the last time. If you step one foot wrong again, I will make it my personal mission to extract every remnant of you from this business, I will ensure you are put in a deep, dark hole and that you will regret your inability to do as your told. Are we clear?'

Jasper nodded feebly.

'I said are we clear?'

'Yes, Dad.'

'Good. Now get the fuck out of my office. I'm sure you have some pathetic picture to post online.' Without even looking at his son, Dale lifted his laptop and returned to work, as if threatening his own son was as simple as ordering his lunch. With a meek nod, Jasper pushed himself from his chair and made his way to the door, doing his best to piece back his shattered ego. 'Oh, and, son. I will protect you this last time. You are my son. But I will not tolerate you anymore.'

'Thank you, Dad.'

Dale gave him a firm nod and then dropped his head back to his screen.

'Now fuck off.'

Jasper was more than happy to oblige, and he scurried from the office and back towards the lift, ignoring the sneer from his father's assistant. As he descended in the lift, he couldn't help but smile at his own reflection.

He didn't need his dad's approval.

Just his money and his protection, both of which he still had.

Before the lift doors opened, Jasper helped himself to another snort of cocaine, before he bounded to his limo, feeling the need to organise another celebration of his life.

'Thank you.'

Sam offered the young lady a smile as she placed the black Americano next to his mouse. She returned in kind and then headed back towards the front of the internet café. It was a family run business, with the owner a retired software engineer who knew enough about computers to run a simple business where he charged a modest fee for an hour's worth of internet for those who needed it. His eldest daughter, on a gap year from university, had been very chatty with Sam as he'd entered, probably due to him being the only customer so far that morning. Business was slow, and as she took Sam's order, she had already offered up her name, what she was intending to study and where she was off travelling in the new year. Sam offered her a few polite retorts before he settled down at the computer in the furthest corner, hoping that the distance between them would result in silence.

It worked.

The young lady returned to the till and to her phone, carelessly flicking her finger across the screen as she looked for anything to hold her attention. The café had only been open for five minutes, and Sam wondered if her enthusiasm would be maintained as the day dragged on. Sipping his coffee, he pulled up the search engine and typed in a name.

Jasper Munroe.

A library of articles flooded the screen, all of them

with the same sensationalised headlines, the majority of them from the previous day. All of them were basically regurgitating the same story, of how his latest court case was thrown out, how there had been previous instances of it happening, and some offered a little opinion as to why. It took Sam only five minutes to get the gist of it.

Jasper Munroe was a bad man.

He returned to the search engine, and, realising that there were hundreds of pages to shift through, Sam added the words 'sexual assault' to the search. The change in request reduced the number of pages, but not by loads, and that was the first red flag.

Cassie had been right.

This had happened a number of times.

Sam began to sift through the articles, scribbling down notes on a notepad that Mel had generously given him, and before he knew it, the young girl from the counter approached.

'Would you like another coffee?'

Sam looked up, realising that the café was full of customers, and the clock was fast approaching eleven. He'd been staring at the screen for a couple of hours and had gone through seven sheets of his pad. With a surprised sigh, he nodded.

'Yes, please.'

She flashed him another smile and then went to it, and Sam sat back in his chair. He rubbed at his eyes. The glare of the screen wasn't something he was used to. His back ached, and he tried to stretch his way through the discomfort. It had been four months since he had been blasted from the first floor of a building by a grenade and his plummet had been broken by the unforgiving metal of a train roof.

Still, it could have been worse. He could have ended up with his face ripped to shreds like Elias Defoe's had been.

For the first few weeks after he left Derbyshire, Sam had approached every corner with caution, half expecting the maniacal American to be waiting. Despite the disfigurement of his face, Defoe had been a brutal adversary, and Sam knew that a man like that didn't let go of a grudge.

The only saving grace was that it wasn't Sam who had mutilated the previously handsome Defoe, but Jacob Nash, the man's former partner and one of the deadliest men in the world. Sam knew that at some point down the road, there was every chance his path would cross 'The Foundation' once again, but Defoe's revenge was reserved for Nash.

Nash could handle himself, Sam was sure of it, but it had been a few months since he'd thought about either of them.

Months since he had thought about any of it.

All he could think about was Mel.

The way her pretty face exploded into a smile whenever he walked through the door. The low chuckle that escaped her when he made a dry remark.

Without realising it, thinking about Mel had brought a smile to Sam's face, and the young girl approached with his second coffee.

'Find what you're after, then?'

'Excuse me?' Sam was wrestled back to reality.

'You were smiling. I figured you found what you're after.'

'Oh, no. I was thinking about…you know what? It doesn't matter. Thanks for the coffee.'

The girl nodded, taking her cue to leave, but then her eyes fell on his screen.

'Jasper Munroe. He's a gobshite, isn't he?'

'You know him?'

'Of him. He's got a pretty big following on Instagram.'

The girl shrugged. 'Not my cup of tea. Too much of a daddy's boy.'

Sam chuckled and thanked her, and she walked back to the till. The internet café was busier than he would have expected, and he sipped the fresh drink, enjoyed the warmth in his throat and then decided to change tack. Sam had scribbled the name 'Dale Munroe' into his pad after the first few articles, but then got lost in a labyrinth of egotistical show-boating and clear miscarriages of justice. Having spent nearly two hours coming to the conclusion that Jasper Munroe was a dangerous man, it hadn't been until the young waitress had mentioned the parent that he found himself changing the name in the search bar.

After another hour of scanning through multiple articles and accusations, Sam clicked onto a train website and booked a ticket to London. He was a fifteen-minute walk from the station, and there was a train to London Euston leaving in twenty. Quickly, he logged out of his session, paid his bill, and headed off into the bitter cold of a December morning in Glasgow. The shop fronts were all adorned with Christmas decorations, and the streets were surprisingly busy with a number of people clearly trying to get ahead of their festive shopping.

With every step, Sam felt a surge of adrenaline course through his body.

There was too much smoke around Jasper Munroe for there to be no fire. Especially with a man like Dale Munroe hiding in the shadows.

A man who had too much money and power, and a clear, unwavering commitment to his son.

The two of them were a shining example of how unfair the world was, one which Cassie had expressed her doubts about.

Sam marched towards the station, heading for the Big Smoke, with the sole intention of putting the fire out.

CHAPTER FIVE

It was a sign of a bad day when Lynsey found herself looking at the clock, but today was one of them. After being undercut by Tom the day before, the idea of having the truth blurred so as not to upset the rich and powerful was a hard one to stomach. She had fallen in line, begrudgingly, and had voiced a more neutral summary of her report on the Munroe case.

Every word of it had felt like acid in her mouth, and she had spat them with such disdain it had driven her to buying a bottle of wine on the way home, which she shared with Sean over a Chinese takeaway and the latest episode of a crime documentary they had invested in.

Thinking about Sean, she smiled, as the man was facing very real problems and hardships, but never let his smile drop. Compared to what he'd been through, Lynsey's problems felt insignificant, but Sean had lived up to his surname with some sage advice.

'Comparing problems does no good for anyone. Your problem is relevant to you, so don't downplay it because you think someone else's is worse.'

They'd fallen asleep in each other's arms, and in the morning, he had left early for another intense bout of physiotherapy, and then he was off to spend the day with his mum. Lynsey had been thrilled at the rebuilding of their relationship, but she wished it hadn't been under such difficult circumstances. With her family in Northern Ireland, Lynsey had felt her relationship with her folks fading, which saddened her.

Maybe she should book a trip back for a week? She could even take Sean.

The day had been a blur, and although Tom had tried to instigate a conversation with her, the anger from the day before was still fresh. Lynsey shut him down and told him to leave her alone, something which had happened a few times over their working relationship. He was a smart enough man to give her some space, and Lynsey spent the rest of the afternoon angrily typing out a feature which put a microscope over the corruption of the justice system when it was the rich and powerful who were being put through it.

It was unlikely that Tom would pass it through to be published, and even if he did, she was certain that some of the higher-ups would quickly find a fault with it to ensure it never became available for public consumption. As the clock reached quarter to five, a few of the early birds in the office began to pack up their stuff, offering half-hearted goodbyes before they headed off into the brightly lit streets of White City. Lynsey lifted her phone, shifting through her podcast app to try to find something to fill the boredom, when she saw Tom's head appear from his doorway.

He locked eyes on her and approached, his mouth moving. Lynsey sighed and removed her earbuds.

'Everything okay, Tom?'

'Are you trying to piss me off?' Tom said angrily,

lowering his voice so as not to cause a scene. 'I mean, I thought you understood the position we're in?'

'The position *you're* in, you mean?' Lynsey said, refusing to back down. A few other journalists turned to see the commotion, and Tom lifted a hand to assure them nothing was wrong.

'My office,' Tom spat through gritted teeth. 'Now.'

As her editor turned and stormed back to his office, Lynsey rolled her eyes and followed, ignoring the other gazes that were transfixed on the escalating situation. She stepped through the door and closed it just as Tom twisted the control of the shutters, excluding everyone from watching them.

'I'm not going to back down on this, Tom,' Lynsey said, as she placed her hands on her hips.

'I know. I know.' Tom rubbed his temples. 'But you know what's going to happen here, right? If I pass this up the flagpole, someone is going to come down hard on my arse and question how the fuck I thought this should ever have been approved.'

'Because it's the truth.' Lynsey felt her voice raising with anger.

'It's a version of the truth.'

'A version? Jesus Christ, Tom. What happened to you? You used to be the most honourable journalist I knew.'

'How dare you?' Tom slammed his hand on the table. 'I've gone to bat for you time after time. Earlier this year, when they were pressing hard for your involvement with Sam Pope, I kept them from your door. Do you know the police wanted you, too? They thought you were hiding something, and they wanted to bring you in. I risked my entire reputation on telling them you had no connection to him. So don't you dare question my honour.'

The tension beat between them for a few moments, like a heart slowly breaking, and as Tom shook his head and sighed, Lynsey stepped forward and put a hand on his shoulder.

'I'm sorry, Tom. I know you're a good man.'

'I'm trying to save your career here, Lynsey,' he said sadly. 'They want you on TV more, they want you on adverts and billboards. But if you keep pushing things like this under their nose, they will put a stop to that.'

'I don't care.' Lynsey exclaimed defiantly. 'Tom, this is the BBC. It's paid for by the British public and they deserve the truth. It's why people want to work here, because they aren't controlled by some fat millionaire who only agrees to share news that fits with his political agenda. Not here. That's what we were told, and that's what we should be doing.'

Tom sighed, shrugged off Lynsey's hand and then shuffled to his chair. He collapsed into it, his hands over his face. He had worked with Lynsey for nearly four years, and their relationship was solid. A great friendship had blossomed, along with a working relationship that had been born out of respect and honesty.

He couldn't lie to her.

He wouldn't.

'We received a legal document from Dale Munroe's legal team yesterday, even after you made the changes to your report.' Tom shrugged as Lynsey's jaw dropped. 'There's a very real threat to you, me and the BBC if we keep his son in the headlines, so the decision has been made to drop it.'

'Sorry, "drop it"?'

'As in, the story is done.' Tom held his hands up. 'I'm sorry, mate. But we can't run the piece you wrote earlier, and top brass have said you are on very thin ice.'

'Well, they can go fuck themselves if they think I'm—'

'Lynsey. Please. Just take a step back. Take a day or two off.'

'You want me gone?' Lynsey could feel the heat growing inside her.

'Not at all. I think you just need to take a step back from all this. Take a little time, recalibrate and then get back here. You're too good to mess this up. So don't.'

Lynsey pushed her tongue into her bottom lip as she contemplated what was being said, and then, without a word, turned and stomped out of the office. Tom feebly called after her, but she ignored him as she marched back to her desk and slammed her laptop closed. Doing little to calm her rage, she furiously crammed her work equipment into her bag, lifted her coat from the back of the chair, and then headed to the exit. People were watching, but she didn't care. As soon as she stepped out of the building, she felt herself take in a deep breath. The cold air was a welcome slap to the face, and she could feel tears of anger threatening to creep over her eyelids. She shook the anger away and then walked casually through the mini town that was ensconced within the BBC grounds, where a number of shops, eateries and bars were open and experiencing a pretty heavy footfall. The usual artwork that adorned the pathways had been replaced with a more festive theme, and Lynsey walked halfway towards the main high street that led to Shepherd's Bush Underground Station, when she decided to lower herself onto a brick wall that surrounded what would have been a beautiful flower display in bloom.

In early December, it was just protecting the hard, cold soil.

Tom's reasoning, while well intentioned, had got under her skin, and she felt a tinge of regret for storming out. He'd understand.

He knew her well enough to know she needed to calm down.

To help do just that, she rummaged in her handbag

until she found her box of cigarettes. It was an infrequent habit, but one that she knew she could rely on to at least set her world straight, especially when the red mist descended.

As she placed one into her lips and cupped her hands to protect the flame from the cold, whipping wind, a voice interrupted her.

'You know those things are bad for you.'

Lynsey looked up at the owner of the familiar voice, and the cigarette dropped from her lip in shock.

Sam Pope offered her a smile in return.

'How's Sean?'

Sam's questioned was laced with concern, and Lynsey offered a reassuring smile as she sat down, placing the coffees in front of them. One of the independent coffee shops within the BBC grounds had a rather discreet seating area down the side of the premises, and Sam had agreed it was hidden away enough for him to sit for a few minutes. Lynsey admired the courage of the man, knowing he was one of the most wanted men in the country. He still waited for her outside its biggest news network.

'He's doing good.' Lynsey sat and took a sip of her coffee. 'I mean, he's got a long way to go. But he's a fighter.'

'That's good to hear.' Sam nodded to himself before sipping his own drink. 'And you?'

'Oh, I'm okay. Usual shit at work, but nothing I can't handle.' She fished inside her bag for her cigarettes and then held them up. 'Do you mind?'

'You go ahead.' Sam shrugged. He waited for Lynsey to finish lighting her cigarette before continuing. 'So…'

‘So…’ Lynsey mirrored. ‘I’m taking it this isn’t a social call.’

‘I wish it was. I really do.’

‘But…’

‘I need your help. But I’ll say right now, if you don’t want to do it, I completely understand.’

‘Sam. You saved my life. You saved Adrian’s life, and because of you, the people who did what they did to my Sean can’t hurt anyone else. You might not want to say that I owe you one, but I owe you one.’

‘I never did it for a favour.’

‘I know.’ Lynsey took another drag of her cigarette and made an effort to blow the smoke away from them both. ‘That’s not who you are. So…what do you need?’

‘I saw your report on Jasper Munroe–’

‘That prick.’ Lynsey couldn’t hide her disdain. ‘Don’t worry, they made me edit out all the good bits. Apparently, relaying the facts about a rich rapist is seen as a no-no by the BBC big wigs.’

‘The elite looking after the elite?’

‘Bingo.’ Lynsey shook her head. ‘Seriously, I showed them all the evidence that points to an extreme miscarriage of justice, and apparently, it wasn’t “neutral” enough for the BBC. Can you believe that?’

‘Rich people throwing their weight around to make sure the truth doesn’t come out? Yeah, I can.’

‘It’s a sad world, huh?’

‘Well…it doesn’t have to be.’ Sam pulled his notepad out of his pocket and placed it on the table.

‘What’s that?’

‘I did a little digging of my own. Just what I could find online. Seems like you weren’t far off with labelling the guy a serial rapist, and judging by the allegations against his father’s business, playing by the rules isn’t really a trait that comes naturally to the Munroe family.’

'Oh, I agree.' Lynsey stubbed out her cigarette. 'So what do you want?'

Sam's face was cold and emotionless.

'I want to do something about it.'

'What? Munroe?' Lynsey blinked her surprise. 'Why?'

'Let's just say I saw someone who was let down by the decision and that got me thinking. Then, my thinking got me digging, and that's brought me to you. You can help me get what I need next.'

'Look, Sam. I want to help you, but my hands are tied. My editor, who is being a real dick at the moment, has basically threatened my job if I keep sniffing around. Whoever I've pissed off, they're keeping tabs on what I'm reporting on, and I have strict instructions to stay away from Munroe from now on.'

'That's fine. I don't need anything from you but a name.'

'A name?' Lynsey sat back in her chair, perplexed.

'I need the name of the girl who accused Munroe of assaulting her. The one that got thrown out yesterday.'

'Why?'

'Because if I'm going to do what I'm going to do, I need to be one hundred per cent sure.' Sam's eyes carried the same threat as his words. 'I want to hear from her exactly what happened, so when the time comes for Jasper Munroe to answer for his crimes, he knows exactly which ones he's answering to.'

Lynsey looked down at her coffee. A feeling of guilt filtered through her stomach, causing it to tighten. Everything about Sean's anguish and recovery hung heavy around her neck, as it was only due to her investigation that he ever became a target. If she handed over the name, then she would be bringing another innocent person, this time, an eighteen-year-old girl, even further into this murky world. Her life had already been shattered by the actions of a selfish person.

Did she want to put her at even more risk?

'She's telling the truth—'Lynsey began.

'I don't doubt that. But you have to understand, Lynsey. I can't intervene based on hearsay. There's too much at risk. Her safety, your safety—'

'Your safety.' Lynsey interjected. Sam shrugged.

'I can look after myself. But she couldn't. Judging from what I've read, this guy preys on women who turn him down, because he knows he can get away with it. You've done things your way, the right way, and it's been knocked back. People don't want to press on the powerful, because they know they hit harder than anyone. So maybe, let's do this my way, because I'll hit them just as hard.'

Lynsey took a deep breath, tossing the idea over in her mind, and could only think about the tears the young girl cried as Lynsey interviewed her.

'What are you going to do?' Lynsey asked sternly, as if the validation was needed to satisfy her guilt.

'I'm going to give Jasper Munroe the opportunity to do the right thing.'

'And if he doesn't?'

'Then he'll find out how persuasive I can be.'

Lynsey sighed. It wasn't legal, but that avenue had already let her and the young girl down. What Sam was offering was justice.

'Hayley Baker,' Lynsey said quietly, and Sam quickly scribbled it down, along with the following address.

'Thank you, Lynsey.'

'I don't owe you one anymore, by the way.'

Sam stood and smiled.

'You never did to begin with.'

'Then why did I just give you her name and address?'

Lynsey stood as she asked her question, and to Sam's surprise, she wrapped her arms around him and squeezed. Sam hugged her back, knowing she was struggling with the decision she'd just made. Before he left and headed out to the address she'd given him, he decided to clear her conscience.

He pulled back, looked her dead in the eye, and smiled.

'Because it was the right thing to do.'

CHAPTER SIX

The bitter chill of the evening had led to an inevitable downpour of rain, with Sam once again grumbling to himself about the British weather. With only a few weeks until Christmas, companies were pushing out jovial advertisements of happy families and young kids playing in the snow. The reality of the situation was beyond the biting cold that chewed at the tips of his fingers. The likelihood of a wet Christmas far outweighed the possibility of a white one.

The rain didn't bother him too much, however, shortly after leaving Lynsey at the coffee shop in White City, Sam had made his way back towards the high street and within minutes, he was on the Hammersmith & City Line, heading back towards Baker Street. It had just turned six o'clock, and Sam noticed the increasing number of red football shirts that were filling the stations, as the away supporters for Middlesbrough FC were showing their loyalty by travelling down to London for a midweek game. Queen's Park Rangers Football Club was a stone's throw from where he'd just been, and Sam recalled venturing to the odd game during his youth. Although football wasn't a passion he harboured, he did enjoy the camaraderie and loyalty it fostered. Once he got off the train at Baker Street, he rushed up to the other set of platforms, fortunate enough to find a train heading to Watford within the next few minutes. Hayley Baker lived in a little village called Harefield, not too far from Rickmansworth Station where the train stopped. As it was in the midst of rush hour, Sam rejoiced when his train was designated a fast service, skipping out a large number of stops in between. It didn't take long for them to be bypassing Wembley Stadium, its magnificent arch lit up against the night sky. Once the train reached Harrow on the Hill and then Moor Park, the passengers thinned out and Sam managed to find a seat for the next few minutes until he disembarked at Rickmansworth. The large station was on the curve of a roundabout, with the exits offering quick passage to either the M25, a journey back towards Croxley Green, or a road towards the high street itself. Outside, the front of the station was dominated by a taxi rank, and Sam hopped into the first available one and gave the man the address.

The village of Harefield was surprisingly quaint, with a small high street dominated by the usual must-have shops that kept the residents happy and the local economy above water. A few nice pubs were littered among the back streets, with one in particular overlooking a gorgeous canal and surrounded by a picturesque housing estate. Eventually, the taxi pulled up in front of a well-kept garden, which separated the house from the street. Sam paid the driver and stepped out, double checking the door number against the address Lynsey had given him. He opened the gate and made his way to the front door, admiring the detached house and appreciating the peace and quiet that had obviously cost a pretty penny. A family who lived in a place like this wouldn't be expecting a random caller on a Wednesday evening.

Taking a deep breath, Sam reached up and pressed the doorbell.

Footsteps slammed behind the door and then it swung open, and a chubby, middle-aged man with thinning brown hair and a spiky beard frowned at Sam.

'Hello?' He seemed more sceptical than anything else.

'Hi, I'm sorry to bother you this evening, but I was wondering—'

'Who is it, dear?' A woman's voice echoed from somewhere behind the man, who turned in frustration.

'I don't know. Some guy.' He turned back to Sam. 'What do you want?'

'I'm here to help your daughter with—'

The man angrily shot out of the doorway and latched his hands to the lapels of Sam's jacket, trying to intimidate him. Sam sighed, allowing the man to push him back a few steps before he exerted his superior strength and stopped them.

'You stay the fuck away from my daughter, you hear me? God damn press, you make me sick. She's been through enough as it is.'

'Henry—' his wife called from the door.

'Not now, Ange!'

With a heavy sigh, Sam reached up, grasped Henry's wrists and pulled them off him. It was a small display of his superior strength, and one that didn't go unnoticed judging by the worry in Henry's eyes. As he took a step back, his wife, Angela, rushed to his side, both of them staring at Sam with concern.

'We told the press we wanted to be left alone,' Angela cried.

'I'm not with the press.'

'Then who the fuck are you?' Henry spat, trying to maintain a level of authority. Sam lifted his hands to appease them.

'Look, Mr and Mrs Baker, my name is Sam Pope.' Both of them froze. 'I'm just here because I want to help your daughter. That's all.'

'He does look like him,' Angela said through the side of her mouth.

'How the fuck would you know?' Henry turned to her, his hands up in confusion.

'I follow the news, dear.' Angela turned to Sam. 'Forgive me, but that's quite a bold claim to make. How can we trust you?'

'You have no reason to, really. As you can imagine, I don't carry any ID. But I can tell you that the reporter your daughter spoke to, Lynsey Beckett, gave me this address and like me, she believes that your daughter was let down by the justice system. Believe me, I know what that feels like.'

Sam didn't want to guilt them into accepting him, but it couldn't hurt. The papers had splashed his entire private life across them when he was arrested a few years prior, with the death of his son used as the main incentive for his murderous rampage.

'Look, legally, we've been told to keep away from the Munroes and not to talk to anyone,' Henry said quietly, worried about any nosy neighbours.

'Well, legally isn't how I go about things.' Sam offered a warm grin. He could see the two of them weighing up the situation. Although a little defensive, the Bakers were clearly good people, and the very thought of going against the law was causing them a moral quandary. Before either of them could answer, the front door was wrenched open once more and there stood Hayley.

Strikingly beautiful, even without her make-up and the dark circles under her eyes, she coughed loudly to wrestle the conversation her way.

'I'll talk to you.'

'Hayley, go back inside...' Henry began, trying his best to be protective. Sam understood.

'No. He came here to see me. I'm eighteen years old and I can decide how I want to handle this.' Hayley turned her gaze back to Sam. 'Come with me.'

Hayley turned and disappeared back into the house, as the three of them watched. Her parents turned back to Sam, who politely awaited permission. After a deep sigh, Henry stood to the side and Sam stepped by, accompanied by Angela, as they headed to the house. As soon as they stepped in, Angela nodded to the stairway, which Sam followed up, admiring the tasteful décor of the house. He didn't know what the Bakers did for a living, but it was certainly fruitful. As soon as Sam stepped onto the landing, Hayley called him from the open doorway of her room. Sam obliged, stepping inside, which was as tastefully decorated as the small portion of the house he had seen. She offered him a forced smile as she welcomed him in, before she sat on the edge of the king-size bed, which was adorned with cushions. Sam left the door open, wanting to ensure that Hayley felt as safe as possible. He'd have happily had the discussion in the front room, but he could understand why she might not want to discuss her ordeal in front of her parents.

Sam looked around at the neatly kept room, his military background approving of the tidiness. He pulled the chair from her desk where a closed laptop sat, turned it to face Hayley, and then took a seat. Sam sat as openly as he could, aware that he could be an intimidating presence. After a few moments of silence, Hayley eventually broke it with a tentative question.

'So what do you want?'

'I want justice,' Sam replied firmly. 'Do you know who I am?'

'Yeah.' Hayley nodded. 'I know you've done some

pretty bad things to some pretty bad people, and if the police knew you were here, they'd be here in a heartbeat.'

'So, you know that I don't mess around? That I take things seriously?' Hayley nodded again. This time, her lip quivered as a tear formed in the corner of her eye. 'I need to know what happened to you.'

'Why?' Her voice cracked.

'Because if I'm going to do something about it, then I need to know what crimes I'm holding Jasper accountable for.' Just the mention of the name caused Hayley to shudder. 'I'm not trying to upset you, Hayley.'

'I know,' Hayley said, taking a deep breath to compose herself. 'It's just, so many people have called me a liar. The police did what they had to do, but when it's my word against his, there was only ever going to be one winner. I can't prove he raped me, but he did. I swear.'

'I believe you.'

'It feels like you're the only one,' Hayley said quietly. 'I've had to shut down every social media account I had. Some people were just saying the most awful things.'

'I don't care about them. I care about you and what that man did to you.' Sam stepped forward and dropped down to one knee. He reached out and held Hayley's hand, offering her a warm smile. It was enough to set her at ease and then she recounted the night it happened. How she and her friends were clubbing in some of the celebrity hot spots, thinking it would be fun to try to spot a few reality TV stars. When Jasper Munroe invited them to his VIP section, they couldn't believe it and the billionaire made his interest very clear. An after party saw them back at one of his London penthouses, and after a bit of fondling, Jasper forced her to perform oral sex on him. Too scared to say no, she had obliged, but when she said she wanted to go home, he demanded she stay the night. Her refusal saw him not only strike her across the cheek, so she fell on the bed, but it unleashed a rage that he'd kept hidden from the public profile he kept.

He held her down on the bed by the back of her neck, threatened to choke her to death if she screamed, and then proceeded to rape her.

Sam felt his fists clench with fury.

Hayley wept as she recounted the horrible ordeal, and when she slunk, broken and shameful from his apartment, she was quickly whisked away by one of Jasper's entourage to a prestige cab that took her home. Once she'd gone to the police, his lawyers got in touch, offering her a sizable chunk of money to sign an NDA.

'But you refused?' Sam said, showing his respect with a nod.

'I didn't want his money. If I had taken it, then I'd have remembered that night every time I spent a single penny of it. I just wanted him to admit what he did and to pay the price of his actions.'

'He will.' Sam stood. 'He will.'

Hayley wiped away her final tear and then looked up at Sam.

'What are you going to do?'

'I'm going to give him the chance to do the right thing. If he doesn't, then I'll do the right thing and make him.'

Hayley stood and wrapped her arms around Sam, burying her face into his muscular frame.

'Thank you.'

'You don't need to thank me.' Sam stepped back, holding her by the shoulders. 'I'm sorry that this happened to you.'

Sam turned to leave, but Hayley called out to him. He turned back, just as she took her seat back to the desk and lifted up her laptop.

'I don't know if this helps, but he posted on Instagram

saying that he was celebrating 'justice being served' tonight, at Visage.'

'Is that a nightclub?'

'It's *the* night club.'

Sam patted her on the shoulder.

'Thank you. I'll be in touch.'

With that, Sam headed out of the room and back down the stairs, offering a raised hand as a goodbye to Angela, who watched from the hallway. The front door was still open, and as Sam stepped out, he was greeted by a plume of cigarette smoke and a broken Henry.

'I'm sorry, Sam.' Henry shook his head. 'It's been a rough few weeks.'

'I can imagine.' Sam patted Henry on the arm. 'You've got a brave daughter up there. You should be proud.'

'I'm ashamed.'

'Ashamed?'

'Of myself.' Henry stared at the ground as he spoke, tears rolling down his cheeks as his smoke filtered into the cold sky. 'She's been so brave through it all. So strong. But me, I've been smoking. I've been drinking. Anything to get the thought of that sick bastard hurting my girl out of my head.'

Sam regarded the man carefully. Henry Baker was an average man, one who would be hard to pick out of a crowd. But he'd worked hard his whole life to provide for the family he loved, and Sam knew that took strength.

It took character.

'It's not your fault, Henry,' Sam said calmly. 'Trust me, there are bad people in this world, and they only get that way by stepping on the good ones.'

'I couldn't protect my own daughter. Do you have any idea what that's like?'

Instantly, Henry regretted the question, and as the

drizzle began to fall, Sam ran a hand through his wet, dark hair and sighed.

'I know exactly what it's like. You feel helpless. Powerless. Like a failure. But I never got the chance to hold my Jamie again. He was taken from me. Jasper Munroe might have taken something from your daughter, but she is still here. She's upstairs, trying to get through this. It wasn't your job to protect her then, but it's your job to be there for her now. So go be there for her.'

Sam's words collided with Henry like a high-speed train and seemed to knock the pity out of him. He stood tall, straightened his shoulders and flicked his cigarette. It was as if a light switch had been flicked on, and the man realised that the pain and suffering he was feeling wasn't his to feel. There was a dad that his daughter needed right then and there, and he wasn't fulfilling the role.

He would now.

'Thank you, Sam.' Henry extended his hand. 'You're a good man.'

Sam took it, shook it firmly and then nodded his promise to the heart-broken father.

'We'll see about that.'

CHAPTER SEVEN

As the DJ mixed the music into a flawless transition, Jasper Munroe let out a cheer, stood up from the leather sofa with a bottle of champagne in his hand and began to dance. It had just gone past ten o'clock and Visage was starting to fill up nicely, with the richest clientele in London making their way through the doors of the exclusive club, knowing they were part of the city's elite. Jasper, as was customary, had the largest VIP area, with the thick, black ropes cordoning off his entourage from the less rich, a symbolic show of power and wealth that he revelled in.

Three of his friends, all of them rivalling him for arrogance, were dressed to the nines, adhering to the strict dress code by wearing tight fitted suits, only they had butchered the smart look by insisting on wearing shoes with no socks. As had become customary on nights such as this, Jasper had cast his eye over the rest of the nightclub and then hand selected the women he would like to invite to his private area, as if he was picking out a pet at a shelter home. The bouncers rolled their eyes but seeing as how they were paid and tipped handsomely, they would approach the women and then guide them back to the group of insufferable young men. Jasper was a good-looking guy, but his known wealth and supposed 'celebrity' status made him an attractive proposition, and a number of the young women who had been lucky enough to catch his eye were already cosying up to him. As he stood and danced, one of the girls seized her chance, turned her back to him and then rubbed herself against his groin.

'Oi oi!' Jasper hollered to his pals, who all whooped and cheered as the young lady gyrated against his crotch. The other girls all laughed and sipped champagne, revelling in the attention and luxury afforded by Jasper and his crew.

'He's got a stiffy!' one of Jasper's friends called out, and they all laughed once more. Jasper collapsed onto the sofa laughing, while the girl pulled out her phone, turned the camera to take a selfie alongside him. It went straight on Instagram, and she turned away from Jasper, more concerned with the immediate likes the image gained.

'I can give you some tips if you like.' Jasper leant over and spoke into her ear. 'Well, I can give you a tip…'

The girl giggled, and then returned to her screen, radiating in the instant gratification of seeing the number of likes increase by the second. Jasper shrugged, looked around at the rest of the club, and nodded his head to the music. The DJ was spinning through the usual repertoire of dance songs that dominated the charts, and gaggles of young people danced across the dance floor.

This was his domain.

Here, he was untouchable.

Every girl in the nightclub wanted to sit with him, and every guy wished they were him. His earlier dressing down from his father had become a distant memory, as had the inconvenience of the rape charge. Once again, it paid to be rich, as his father's legal team had batted away every obstacle and pretty much destroyed the case. There had likely been payments or threats sent the way of anyone who could have been called as a witness, but Jasper didn't care. It wasn't his job to keep the wolves from the door. That was why his father had such a diligent legal team, and while Jasper didn't know the specifics, he was aware that his father's company had been through more than enough legal battles.

'To the justice system.' One of his friends yelled, lifting a glass of champagne into the air.

'To Hayley Baker,' another one said jokingly.

'Fuck Hayley Baker,' Jasper spat, as if the name disgusted him. A few of the girls sheepishly looked at their drinks. They all took a swig, and then Jasper pulled his vial from his chair, tapped a line of cocaine onto his finger, and inhaled it enthusiastically. Immediately, the bouncer motioned to the bar manager, who stepped over the rope.

'Can we help you, buddy?' Jasper's friend asked.

'Apologies.' The man turned to Jasper. 'Mr Munroe, we have a strict no drugs policy…'

'I have a strict no dickheads policy,' Jasper said aggressively. 'So why don't you go back to work?'

'I'm afraid if you are going to be partaking in drugs, we will ask you to leave.'

The effects of the cocaine kicked in and Jasper's pupils dilated, and his aggression rocketed. He stood angrily, noticing the bouncer readying himself.

'Do you know who the fuck I am?' Jasper barked. 'How about I buy this shit hole of a club and fire you? Or better still, I could take one video, telling people not to come here anymore and like that' – Jasper snapped his fingers – 'this place would be forgotten about.'

'Sir, I must insist—'

'Fuck off,' Jasper said, waving the man away. Before the manager could react, the attention of everyone in the night club turned towards the dance floor, where a scuffle broke out. Jasper and his friends cheered in excitement, but very quickly, that excitement soon faded to a very real sense of fear.

After leaving the Baker residence, Sam had walked back up towards the small, picturesque high street in Harefield and hailed a cab from one of the local cab ranks. Under the advice of the driver, he took the taxi through Rickmansworth towards Watford, where the driver has recommended the fastest train back to London. After paying the driver, Sam walked into Watford Junction Station, purchased a ticket from the self-service machine, and hopped onto the first fast train to London Euston. It took a little over twenty minutes, and Sam was impressed with how quickly he was able to get back into the centre if the city. It was no surprise to him that many people were looking to move further away from London for more affordable housing, especially when the time it took to return was minimal. Checking his watch, Sam decided it was unlikely Jasper would be in the club yet, so decided to venture out from the station and he headed down the road opposite the grand Euston Station, walking past the greenery that had since died in the winter months. London was awash with Christmas lights, and the evening footfall, even for a Wednesday, was heavy. As he made his way through Tavistock Square, he took a moment to read the plaque, commemorating the lives that were lost in the horrific bombings. It was a sombre feeling to read the names of people whose lives were snatched away in an unprovoked act of cowardice.

The world was a scary place.

Continuing on, he saw a sign for the Brunswick Shopping Centre, which he followed, passing a few pubs that were packed to the walls with after-work drinkers, all of them merrily putting the world to rights and cash in the pub owners' tills. Sam hadn't had a beer in a long time, and while he had fond memories of drinking with Theo, he didn't miss the lack of control that alcohol promised.

The Brunswick Shopping Centre was an arcade of bars and shops, tucked between Russell Square Train Station and a housing estate, but it provided Sam with what he needed. The clothes shop was a run of the mill high street brand, one that was a staple of most high streets, and Sam headed straight to the men's section and began perusing the suits. The young lady who worked there offered her help with an eager smile, smitten with the hunky customer. The shop was a few minutes from closing, and he was the only customer there. Helpfully, she found a navy suit in his size, along with a crisp white shirt and a smart pair of brown brogues. Sam felt like an alien when he put it together, as formal attire wasn't something he was accustomed to.

It wasn't a patch on the camos he wore when he served in the armed forces.

Judging by the approving nod of the shop assistant, Sam looked the part, and he paid by card at the till, having taken the tags out so he could wear it out. He stuffed his old clothes in a bag and handed them to the first homeless person he could find, and then he sat in one of the uninteresting restaurants and ordered some dinner. He didn't often dip into the money Etheridge had left him, preferring to survive on the basics his own could afford, but he needed the suit to gain access to Jasper.

It was a worthy cause.

By the time he'd finished his meal and enjoyed a coffee, it was almost ten o'clock, and Sam made his way towards Leicester Square, where the exclusive Visage was located on a remote backstreet. The brisk walk did him the world of good, allowing him to walk off the adequate meal and also get his mind focused.

Visage was a nondescript building with nothing more than a small, metal sign on the wall next to the black door. A burly man stood in front of it, his hands clasped at his front and his eyes firmly on the queue of people who were itching to get in. A membership was needed for immediate access, but they often opened the door to a select few, usually attractive women, which meant those selected felt an unearned sense of importance.

Sam didn't have the time to stand on ceremony, and he knew he was unlikely to be picked from the crowd. Instead, he just headed towards the door, where the hulking bouncer held his hand up.

'No chance, mate.' The bouncer chuckled and shoved Sam in the chest.

'I'm here to see Jasper Munroe.'

'The fuck you are.' The bouncer took a step towards Sam. 'I'll give you three seconds to fuck off.'

'Or what?' Sam shrugged. 'Will you make me?'

The onlookers in the queue watched in excitement as the bouncer's eyes bulged with rage. Instinctively, he threw a hand towards Sam to grab him by the shoulder, but Sam saw it coming from a mile off. Quick as a flash, Sam threw his left arm up to deflect it, and with his right, he swung a vicious fist into the centre of the man's throat. With his air supply cut off, the bouncer stumbled back, clutching at his throat and gasping for air. Sam grabbed the man's shoulder to hold him in place, kicked the back of his legs to bring him to his knees, and then drilled a solid elbow into the man's skull. The bouncer fell forward, his lights firmly shut out, and the queue of wannabe entrants froze in fear.

Sam straightened his blazer, adjusted the cuffs of his shirt, and then wrenched open the door and stepped over the threshold and into the club. The music was surprisingly cheesy and loud for such a revered establishment, but Sam marched past the cloak-room attendant, who called after him, and headed up the dark stairwell to the main dance floor. Flashing lights beckoned him from the top of the stairs, and as he entered, he was greeted by the sight of a few hundred expensively dressed, attractive people either dancing in groups on the dance floor, or gathered in their private booths, washing away their inhibitions with alcohol. It was a place that Theo would have thrived in, with his late friend's ability to chat with women something that Sam had envied.

The place also reminded him of where he met Lucy all those years ago, when they discussed their dislike for the forced nature of night clubs.

A lifetime ago.

News of Sam's assault of the bouncer had obviously filtered through the security headset, as two more muscle-bound men in dark suits stomped their way across the dancefloor in his direction and Sam met them head on. The first one threw a reckless left hook, which Sam dodged, and followed up with a wicked uppercut that sent the bouncer stumbling back into the dancers. Panic spread across the dancefloor, and the second bouncer drew his fists up, looking decidedly calmer than the first. He and Sam sized each other up for a few moments, and then the bouncer threw a punch. Sam absorbed it with his own arm, then threw a knee into the man's ribs. It caught the man off guard, lowering his stance, and Sam obliterated his nose with a sickening right hook.

These men were paid to keep things in order.

Not to fight one of the most dangerous men in the country.

As the bouncer collapsed to the ground with blood gushing out of his nose, the previous bouncer returned, still swaying from the devastating blow Sam had given him.

Sam's fight wasn't with them, so as the bouncer threw another laboured punch, Sam easily deflected it, drilled the man with a vicious right to the gut and left him on his knees, coughing and spluttering.

He stepped over the rope of the VIP section, his eyes burrowing into the now terrified looking young man who slowly slumped into his seat. A few of his associates were clearly hyped up on drugs, with one of them shaking on the spot, like a coiled spring ready to bounce.

'Hello, Jasper,' Sam said calmly, staring down at the man. 'May I take a seat?'

'Who the fuck are you?'

Sam took the seat opposite, anyway, pulling it closer to the table of drinks that was filled with empty bottles and cocaine residue. The women, who had been enjoying an exciting evening, now watched on with terror, and Jasper looked around for any help he could find.

The music died down and all eyes turned to the VIP area, and the club manager who was racing in a panic to them.

'I'm calling the police,' the manager cried out. Sam held up a hand.

'Apologies for assaulting your staff, although they did start it,' Sam said. 'Give me two minutes and I'll be out of your hair.'

'Get this man out of here,' Jasper demanded. The manager, shaking with fear, tried to unlock his phone.

'Put the phone down,' Sam demanded. 'Like I said, I just need two minutes to talk to Mr Munroe here and then I will leave. Or I will kill him on your premises. Your choice.'

The threat stopped everyone in their tracks, and Sam turned back to Jasper, knowing he had everyone's full attention.

CHAPTER EIGHT

FIVE YEARS EARLIER…

'Where is he?'

Sam asked as soon as he stepped into the kitchen. Lucy was sitting at the breakfast bar in their modest, three-bedroom home, her hands cupping a warm mug of coffee. Her usual positivity had been replaced by a look of disappointment.

'He's in his room.' She sighed. Sam nodded and then approached her, resting a hand on her shoulder. He had been at the military base in Tidworth for the past few days, prepping for a new mission which General Ervin Wallace had specified was a matter of national security. Lucy understood the secrecy that came with Sam's role within Project Hailstorm, but it had begun to drive a small wedge between them. The money was great, but the exacting toll of Sam's work and his absence was beginning to take.

'Did they say why he did it?' Sam asked, his eyes drifting towards the staircase.

'Nope. Just that he's been acting up more and more.' Lucy shook her head. 'He misses you.'

'Don't blame this on me,' Sam said curtly. 'Sorry, but I can't be blamed for having a job.'

'I'm not blaming you, babe. It's just the reality of the situation. You know how much he loves you, and when you go away, it affects him. You grew up with a military dad. You know what he's going through.'

Sam conceded and apologised, before leaning down and kissing his wife on the top of her hair. She leant back, burying her head into his solid chest.

'So, what did he do, then?'

'He snatched a toy from another kid and when they tried to get it back, Jamie pushed them over.' Lucy sounded ashamed.

'I'll speak to him.'

Sam kissed her again and then headed up the stairs. Lucy had been upset when she had called him, explaining how their usually polite son had behaved badly. The nursery, which Jamie had adored since his first day, was usually glowing with praise for the boy. But Sam knew Lucy was right, and that his continued absence was beginning to impact his son's behaviour. While he had grown up following his dad from military base to military base, Sam had just adapted to his childhood like it was perfectly natural. The fact that his own mother had left them at such a young age might have accelerated his bond with his father wasn't lost on him.

One thing was clear: Jamie was more like Lucy than he was Sam.

He was a quiet, sensitive boy.

Sam reached the top of the stairs and as he stepped across the landing, he wrapped his knuckles on the door, emblazoned with a rocket ship with his son's name on it. Slowly, Sam pushed the door open and as always, his son was lying on the floor, gazing his eyes over a book. The Gruffalo *was a firm favourite and Sam knew it off by heart due to the number of times he'd sent his son to sleep with it.*

'Jamie. You okay, buddy?' Sam stepped in. Jamie didn't look up and didn't respond. 'Are you ignoring me?'

'I made Mummy sad.'

Sam felt his heart melt, and he lowered himself to his knees and squeezed his son's foot.

'You did.' He agreed. 'But she will be fine. You'll just have to say sorry. Do you know why you made her sad?'

'Because I wasn't a good boy at nursery.'

'And why weren't you a good boy at nursery, eh? You know how to be a good boy. So, what happened?'

Jamie shut the book and stood up, so he was eye level with his dad. Unlike Sam's dark eyes, Jamie's were bright blue like his mother's, and he had also inherited her blonde hair.

'Harry was playing with the race cars, and he wouldn't share with me—'

'Did you ask nicely?'

'I did. Katie asked him to share, too.'

Katie was Jamie's key carer at the nursery, and on the few occasions that Sam had met her, she had always been nothing but full of praise for their son.

'So, if he wasn't behaving well, why didn't you behave well?'

'Because I took them.'

'But that's not good sharing, is it?'

'But he didn't share with me—'

'That's not okay, though. You can't do bad behaviour just because someone else does. That's not how to behave, is it?'

'But if I can just take it, why can't I?'

Sam sighed. His son was an exceptionally intelligent child, especially for one so young. But as with all kids, their own innocence clouded the reality of the world. Jamie wasn't being a bad kid because he wanted to. He just didn't understand the repercussions and impact of his actions. Sam reached out and held his son's hand.

'Because it's better to be good than to be strong.'

'But I am stronger than Harry. So I can take it from him.'

Sam hugged his son and then looked him in his beautiful eyes.

'Being a good person makes you stronger than anyone else. So whenever you can, always choose to be good.'

Jamie nodded and then hugged Sam, catching him off guard and taking his breath away. A wave of guilt flooded over him, and Sam wondered if maybe Lucy was right. Maybe it would be best if he walked away and found something closer to home.

'Are you always good, Daddy?' Jamie asked, looking up at his dad with adoration. A smile spread across Sam's stubbled jaw.

'I try to be.' Sam nodded. 'If I can do the right thing, then that's what I always try to do.'

Jamie nodded, and moments later, the two of them were headed, hand in hand, down the stairs to see Lucy, and to embark on another loving afternoon as a happy family.

The fear and tension spreading through Visage was palpable, and the manager pleaded with everyone to stay calm. A few people were scurrying to their phones to call for the police, but Sam's threat of killing a known celebrity would ruin the reputation of the club, and the manager was keen to preserve it. Sam found it repugnant, but he knew that threatening the wealth and status of the elite was the best weapon he had.

He would be given the time he had requested, and that was all he needed. As the manager demanded a few moments of cooperation from his rich clientele, Sam kept his eyes locked firmly on the arrogant socialite before him. Jasper was trying his best to look non-fussed, slouching in his chair and looking to his friends for support and validation. Sam had already clocked their clear abuse of cocaine, and they sat on the edge, weighing up whether to intervene or not.

He hoped they didn't.

This would be a lot smoother if they sat still.

After a few more moments of staring a hole through Jasper, the agitated rich kid frowned and stood up.

'This is fucking bullshit.'

'Sit down.'

'You've made a big fucking mistake, pal.' Jasper scoffed, fishing his phone from his pocket. 'In two seconds, this will be all over the internet. Do you know who I am?'

'Yes. You're Jasper Munroe. Do you know who I am?' Sam posed the question like a threat.

'I don't care.'

'My name is Sam Pope.' The mention of his name caught Jasper's attention. 'Now I suggest you sit down, and you listen carefully to what I say next.'

Wanting to save face, Jasper sighed, rolled his eyes and then sat as if he was humouring a child. He waved his hand.

'Get on with it, then.'

'A few months ago, you raped a young lady.'

'Fuck off—'

'Her name was Hayley Baker,' Sam continued.

'Hey, dickhead. The case was thrown out—' One of Jasper's friends interjected.

'Interrupt me again and I will break your jaw. Do you understand?' Sam cut his stare from Jasper and glared at the friend, who quickly shrunk in his seat. 'Now, the case was thrown out, but that doesn't make you innocent.'

Jasper smirked, revelling in his clear escape from justice. He shrugged his shoulders.

'What can you do, huh? I didn't create the British justice system.'

'No. But you did cheat it.'

'If you say so…' Jasper leant forward. 'See, the thing is, Sam, was it? The thing is, I don't give a shit. If people were really so mad about what I did, then they wouldn't throw themselves at me. People would drink my spit for a slice of my attention. Just like everyone in this place would pull you apart if I clicked my fingers.'

Sam raised his eyebrows and then turned and looked around at a few of the surrounding watchers. A look of worry spread throughout them like a plague, and Sam nodded.

'Go on then.'

'Go on, what?' Jasper frowned.

'Click your fingers.'

Jasper huffed in anger, furious that the man before him showed little fear or respect. Obliging Sam, Jasper snapped his fingers and Sam didn't flinch.

Nobody moved.

Everyone was well aware of who was sitting at Jasper's table. Sam raised an eyebrow in surprise, and irate, Jasper leapt to his feet.

'Someone fucking do something then.'

Whether he was just clumsy or the drugs that were coursing through his veins were causing him to lose coordination, one of Jasper's friends tried to leap from his seat, but in the process, he dropped his flick knife. A few of the women in the VIP area squealed with terror as the man scrambled for it. Sam listened, fully aware of the commotion a few feet to his right, but he kept his eyes trained on the increasingly scared Jasper. The friend eventually scooped the knife in his hand, flicked open the blade and then foolishly lunged at Sam. Swiftly, Sam shot to his feet, twisting his body out of the way of the clumsy lunge and he drilled his elbow down into the top of the man's spine, driving him down onto the drink and drug-covered table below. As the man hit the wooden surface and sent drinks splattering, Sam easily pulled the knife from his hand, expertly spun it, and then drove it down as hard as he could.

The entire club gasped.

The man screamed in agony.

Jasper went white with fear.

Sam stood, straightened his blazer, and then glanced down at his handiwork. The man was lying across the table, whimpering, as blood pumped from the knife that had been pushed through the back of his hand and embedded in the wood beneath. A rising panic was filling the establishment, and Sam returned his gaze to the rich kid who had suddenly lost his confidence.

'You have three days, Jasper,' Sam said calmly. 'Three days to admit the truth and to do the right thing.'

'You're playing a dangerous game, buddy,' Jasper said, trying not to look at his wounded friend. 'Do you have any idea who you're dealing with?'

Sam ignored the threat and continued.

'If you don't, then you and your dad will be hearing from me again. Do you understand?'

The mention of the senior Munroe caught Jasper's attention, with Sam underlining he had done his research. The name Dale Munroe usually elicited fear among anyone who had ever crossed Jasper's path, and despite knowing he would never have his father's respect, Jasper knew he could usually rely on his father's legacy to keep people away.

Not this time.

Jasper muttered something under his breath, so Sam took a step closer to him, causing him to flinch.

'Do you understand?' Sam repeated, amping up his intimidation. Jasper fell back into his seat and nodded.

'Good. Clock's ticking.'

Sam turned and headed back across the dance floor towards the exit, knowing that the police would soon be trawling the area with every available resource they had. Jasper Munroe was a big name on the internet, meaning this interaction would likely go viral.

Which meant Sam was effectively telling Commissioner Bruce McEwen of the Metropolitan Police that he was on his doorstep. He'd have to move quickly, and as he stepped across the dance floor; he appreciated the fact that the bouncers he'd taken apart were in no shape for another round. The manager yelled at him to leave, acting tough after the fact, but Sam ignored him. A few of the patrons stepped out of his path, clearly worried about the danger that Sam promised, and without looking back at Jasper, Sam descended the dark staircase, with the only sound he could hear being the anguished screams of Jasper's ambitious friend.

Sam knew it was a dangerous game he was playing.

But it was one he was willing to play until the final move.

Sam stepped out into the downpour that had enveloped London, threw his hand in the air and a black cab immediately swerved to him. Sam threw open the back door and dropped into the seat, the driver welcoming him with a cheeky Cockney accent.

'Euston Station,' Sam said politely. 'I'm in a rush.'

'No problem, fella.' The driver revved the engine, and they pulled away. 'I'll have you there in no time.'

Sam sat back on the leather seat and felt the exhaustion of the day begin to flood through him like a broken water pipe. He just wanted to see Mel.

He wanted to go home.

CHAPTER NINE

Jasper sat anxiously on the sofa in his father's penthouse suite, the floor to ceiling window offering an incredible view of London, the bright lights sparkling off the River Thames. Cheyne Walk was known for its affluence, and the famous road sat in the middle of the luxurious Chelsea, one of the richest parts of the city. A hugely popular "reality" television series had been filmed within those streets, and Jasper had regularly turned down invitations to appear.

In his mind, he was a bigger star than the TV series itself, and he didn't want them leeching off his name. The irony of doing the same thing to his father was apparently lost on him.

But not Dale Munroe.

From the seething look in his eyes as he poured himself a glass of expensive scotch, that anger had bubbled to the surface, and as he took a calming sip of the warm liquor, he sighed. It was just past midnight when Jasper had called, panicked, saying he needed his dad's help. Dale had been in bed for over an hour and his wife, Beatrice, his third attempt at a successful marriage, had moaned about the time. Dale had left her asleep in their king-sized bed between their Egyptian cotton sheets. Once he'd let Jasper in, he'd admonished his son for waking his stepmother, and then ushered him into a home office that was bigger than most houses. Jasper had collapsed onto the sofa, his hands shaking, while Dale stomped to his drinks cabinet and helped himself to a drink.

He didn't offer Jasper one.

As the anger began to settle in the room like a gentle dusting of snow, Dale finally marched to his desk, placed his drink on a coaster and then turned to his son, resting the small of his back against the varnished oak.

'What did I say to you earlier?' Dale spoke as if he was telling off a child. 'I told you this would be the last time.'

'Dad, I didn't do anything—'

'Really?' Dale shook his head. 'So, you've turned up here, pissing your pants like a little kid and begging for my help for no reason, then?'

'We were assaulted.'

'You look fine to me.' He swigged his drink again. 'Actually, that's a shame. A good slap might actually sort you out.'

'He just burst into the club...' Jasper began, ignoring his father's threat. 'We were in our usual spot, me and the boys, and then we heard this noise, right? Like, a fight or something. Anyways, we look up, and this guy is just taking apart the bouncers. Then, he sits himself down in front of me and tells the owner he wants a two-minute chat or...get this...he would kill me then and there.'

'He threatened to kill you?'

'Yup.' Jasper shrugged. 'He knew Hayley Baker's name...said I had up to three days to confess to what I did, otherwise he'd be back for me and you.'

That threat pricked Dale's attention, and he went from arms folded to bolt upright in a millisecond.

'He said he was coming for me?' Dale's mouth twisted into a violent sneer. He was not a man who got threatened. 'Who the hell is this guy?'

'I asked him if he had any clue who he was dealing with, but he just ignored me.'

'What did he say exactly?' Dale could feel his fist clenching.

'He just said he'd be back for both of us. And then Marco tried to play the hero and lunged at the guy with a knife. Ended up face down on the table with the knife through his hand. He's in A&E now, but yeah, pretty messed up.'

'I don't give a shit about Marco.' Dale waved it away. 'What did this man look like?'

'Errr, was pretty big. Definitely worked out. Late thirties, early forties.' Jasper shrugged. 'He gave me a name if that helps?'

'Yes, it helps, you dozy little prick.' Dale spat angrily at his son.

'He said his name was Sam Pope.'

Dale Munroe froze on the spot. The icy feel of an ice cube sliding down his spine twinged through his body, and an explosion of anger rushed from his brain, shot through his powerful right arm and with a rage filled roar, Dale swung his fist at his son. It connected brutally with his son's perfectly tweezed eyebrow, sending him sprawling back on the sofa, whimpering in terror. Dale didn't offer any words, he simply turned and headed back to his drinks table. He lifted the decanter and poured out two glasses of Scotch into thick crystal tumblers. Without a word, he walked back to the sofa and slammed the drink down on the pristine table. It was his way of apologising, and Jasper simply held his hand to his eyebrow, trying to stop the blood that was now flowing from a small gash. Dale reached across his desk, lifted a box of tissues, and then hurled them at his son. Deflecting the blow, Jasper then took a tissue and held it to his brow, shaking with fear from his father's uncontrollable rage.

'Dad? What's wrong?'

Dale placed his drink back on his desk, held the edge of the wood with both hands and bowed his head, taking deep breaths to control himself. Eventually, he stood up straight but didn't turn to his son.

'Do you have any idea what you have done?'

'I didn't do anything.' Jasper pleaded. 'The court threw the case out, remember?'

'You fucking idiot. Do you have any idea who this man is? Or are you so consumed with your own worthless existence?'

Jasper bit his lip. His father's belittling of his achievements hurt, despite how hard he tried to ignore them. He wasn't his father, he never would be, but he still wanted just a crumb of respect from him.

A sliver of love.

'Who is he?' Jasper eventually conceded.

'Sam Pope is a fucking boy scout, that's who he is.' Dale knocked back the rest of his Scotch and then grimaced at the after burn. 'The man has singlehandedly taken down criminal empires and terrorist units. He's the most wanted man in the country.'

'So why is he after me?'

'Because you raped that girl. You can make all the claims you want, Jasper, but the only reason you aren't rotting in a prison cell is because of me. The power I hold and the money I have. Do you know how much I've spent on paying people off? Or to intimidate a witness? All so my son didn't end up being passed around a prison cell like an old sock?'

'Well, can't you just pay him off?'

'Not this one.'

'Everyone has a price—'

'Not Sam Pope. Do you understand the damage it could do if he comes after me? If he comes after Sure Fire?' Dale shook his head and walked back to his drink's cabinet. The severity of the situation was making the scotch a very desirable solution. Jasper, with his hand still clasped to his eyebrow, stood.

'Dad?'

'There are things you don't understand, son. Things you will never understand. The deals we had to make. The things we had to do,' Dale said, almost to himself. 'We took over the industry, but if someone was to peel back too many layers, turn over one too many stones, then it all comes crashing down. Do you understand me?'

'I…I…don't follow.'

'That's because you've always been too naïve and too much of an embarrassment to fully understand what it is we do. What we have done.' Dale spoke through gritted teeth. 'To you, this company is nothing more than a trust fund that allows you to run around, fuck whoever you want and then rely on daddy to pick up the bill. I have a right mind to hand you over to Sam Pope myself.'

'Dad, please.' Jasper dropped to his knees. 'I'm begging you—'

'Get the fuck up,' Dale said with disgust, pouring another drink.

'I can't go to prison. It will ruin me.'

Dale knocked back the entire drink in one go and then wiped his lips with the back of his hand. The fuzz of the alcohol was beginning to leak into his brain, and he knew another drink would mean he wouldn't make a clear decision. He needed to act now, and while his pathetic excuse of a son was weeping, he himself needed to take an extreme step.

This had to be controlled.

Sam Pope needed to go away.

After a few more moments of reflection, Dale slammed his glass tumbler down on the drink table and turned back to his son.

'Get up and get out of my sight.' He beckoned Jasper to his feet. 'I will handle this.'

'What are you going to do?' Jasper asked as he got to his feet. Dale grabbed him by the scruff of his collar and ushered him to the door of the office. He yanked it open and then shoved Jasper through.

'What's necessary.'

With that, Dale slammed the door, leaving his bleeding and terrified son to make his own way out. He rested his head against the door for a matter of seconds, trying his best to contain his rage. Threats to his business were commonplace, whether it be a nosy reporter or an overly ambitious hacker. Whenever they reared their head, Dale had been swift in his response, usually ensuring a conflict free resolution or the complete destruction of the individual's life. Either way, with the means at his disposal, Dale had ensured the safety of Sure Fire Inc for years.

But sometimes, just sometimes, a threat came along that couldn't be bought. Couldn't be reasoned with.

Couldn't be intimidated.

Slowly, he ambled back to his drinks table, poured out a final glass of scotch, and then stepped behind his impressive desk and dropped into the leather chair. He slid open the drawer and pulled out the discreet mobile phone, plugged in the charger and waited a few minutes for enough power to boot up the home screen. The phone had only one number in it, and as he clicked the call button, he swallowed his entire drink.

The call connected.

Dale took a deep breath.

'We have a problem.'

In his line of work, there were no set hours.

Many of the jobs that had been sent his way over the years had come through at the strangest of times, and he wondered if the elite knew they were an exacting bunch of people. The rich and powerful were never used to the word no, which is not something he ever offered.

There was no job he wouldn't undertake.

That was the nature of his work and what had set him apart from any other 'fixer'. When people operate in the billion-pound bracket, their problems are usually very real and very urgent. It allowed him to command such an extortionate fee, and also meant he could never complain when a call interrupted his sleep.

As was his guarantee, he answered on the third ring, with his mobile phone bursting to life on his bed-side table. The phone was placed exactly in line with the edge of the table and was placed equidistant between his glass of water and his bedside lamp.

As he sat up to answer the call, he folded his duvet to the side, and swung his legs over the side of the bed, planting both feet on the wooden floor. Despite being in his mid-forties, he was in the best physical shape of his life. Not overly muscular, he preferred to maintain a trim body through callisthenics, focusing on his mobility and strength as opposed to power. His short, dark hair was tinged with grey, which stood out against his black skin.

With perfectly manicured fingers, he lifted the phone and answered.

'We have a problem.'

It was Dale Munroe. The two of them had formed a fruitful relationship over the past decade or so, with the billionaire reaching out whenever someone needed to either change their mind or be stricken off of the earth itself. Either way, he could oblige, and both outcomes were charged at a seven-figure rate.

'Hudson. Are you there?'

'Describe we…' he eventually said. His well-spoken voice was clear and concise. Hudson had made it his mission when dealing with the elite to hold the mirror up to them.

They did not share problems.

He was there to solve them.

'Okay, I have a problem. Well, my son does.'

'What has he done this time?' Hudson sighed, standing from his bed and walking through the immaculately clean bedroom of his expensive, four-bedroom home. Every piece of furniture or artwork was placed with such care and attention, and he found that home décor had worked wonders with his OCD.

'The usual. Only this time, he's found himself an admirer.'

Hudson stepped into his pristine bathroom, pulled the light chord and the white tiles were immediately illuminated. The ceramic sink was embedded into the immaculate tile work, and he looked at himself in the sink to ceiling mirror that ran the length of the wall.

'Your son often has admirers,' Hudson said calmly. 'You don't usually require my services for such a small job.'

'This one is Sam Pope.'

The mention of the name would have caught most men off guard, but Hudson continued with his routine as if he was just shifting through junk mail.

'Has he made contact?' Hudson asked, as he squeezed some toothpaste onto his toothbrush and then set it on the side of the sink, ensuring it was dead straight.

'Not with me. With Jasper. He's given Jasper three days to hand himself in, otherwise he'll be coming for him.'

'Surely the police can protect him,' Hudson suggested, as he pulled his razor and shaving foam from the organised cabinet. 'You have considerable sway, I recall.'

'He's threatened to come for me, too.' Dale sounded more worked up than usual. *'Anyone else, and I'd turn the other cheek. But I can't have Sam Pope snooping around my business. If he gets a sniff of what we've done to keep on top—'*

'What *you've* done,' Hudson corrected.

'Yes, what I've *done to ensure the dominance of my company, then he will keep digging and—'*

'I understand. When was he last seen?'

'He left Visage, the nightclub, a few hours ago. What time is it now?'

'It's one thirty-four.'

'I'm sorry for calling so late.'

'No, you're not, and I don't expect you to be.' Hudson took a couple of bottles of moisturiser from the cabinet and lined them up in an orderly fashion next to the razor. 'My flat fee is the same. Non-negotiable. I will require access to your police contacts immediately, and then I'll be in touch. Hopefully, this can be resolved without violence.'

'Hopefully.'

'And if it cannot be, then so be it. I'll be in touch.'

Hudson disconnected the phone and placed it on the shelf that ran the length of the mirror. He then lifted his toothbrush and began scrubbing his teeth, the first of a number of steps to his usual morning routine. He was a man of strict habits, and it didn't matter that he was awoken four hours earlier than usual. He provided the best service he could, which was why every billionaire or high-profile socialite had his number. It was an eclectic but carefully considered customer base he held, and Dale Munroe had been one of his most consistent employers.

Over the past decade, he'd paid Hudson over ten million pounds for his services, and Hudson had always delivered. This one would be no different, despite the extra challenge of the target being Sam Pope. The man's reputation was that of legend, but as with all problems, there was a solution.

And that's all Sam Pope was.

A problem.

As he spat the toothpaste into the sink and then slathered shaving foam onto his neck, Hudson was already formulating his solution.

He always found one.

Without fail.

CHAPTER TEN

Even in the cold dark of the early morning, Lambeth Metropolitan Police Station was a depressing sight. A three-storey structure of grey stone and dull windows, it had long been underfunded and fallen way behind on the upkeep. At four o'clock in the morning, a skeleton crew of officers were working the night shift, with the Contact Centre working tirelessly to answer the incoming calls from the public, despatch an officer from a rapidly thinning police service and then continue through the night. A few other officers were at their desks, swigging as much coffee as possible as they tried to work their way through an avalanche of paperwork and red tape. It was the side of the job they didn't show on television, nor put on their recruitment drives.

The dull, repetitive strain of protocol.

Situated underneath the station itself, through a series of ID secured doors, was the Operation Command Centre, nicknamed the 'Nerve Centre'. Those who were granted access to this room were treated to a floor to ceiling and wall to wall display of CCTV cameras, all of them scanning their local districts and recording the blissfully unaware city. The analysts manning the cameras were meticulously trained, with their competence on the computer systems only beaten by their sharp eye.

They needed to be alert and quick.

Two of the analysts were working tirelessly to support an ongoing call when Inspector Gough walked in, a mug of coffee in his hand and a tired look across his chubby face. Approaching the last few years of his service, retirement was beckoning him with both hands. An injury in a traffic collision had almost forced an early retirement, but the cushy job of supervising the Nerve Centre meant he could see out the remainder of his thirty years' service and head off into the sunset with a full pension.

Usually, he greeted his employees with a nod or a smile, but today, he just grimaced.

He didn't feel comfortable.

Not after the phone call he'd just received about an incoming visitor. Moments later, there was a call made to his personal phone, and with his team distracted by their work, he hurried to the secure emergency exit that was hidden at the end of the corridor. As he reached up to open the door, he sighed, wondering why on earth an order like this would come through.

But orders were orders.

He pushed open the door to be greeted by an immaculately dressed man, who stepped through without even offering so much as a thank you. Gough estimated the man was in his early to mid-forties, about five ten and, judging by his trim physique, in great physical condition. Gough gave a shameful glance down to the gut that hung over his belt, and then quickly followed the gentleman as he strode towards the contact centre.

'I'm Inspector Gough. Who are you exactly?'

'You can call me Mr Hudson,' Hudson replied, his eyes searching the corridor. 'I believe you were expecting me.'

'I am, but I must say, I'm not too comfortable about this—'

'I didn't ask if you were comfortable with my being here. I stated that you should have been expecting me.'

The man's attitude caught Gough by surprise, and his brow furrowed. Before the two of them could step out into the main control room, where the team would witness this stranger among their highly secure midst, Gough opened a door to a private control room, where three high-spec monitors were displaying a variety of streets and buildings all under the watchful eye of the CCTV cameras. Hudson stepped in, removed his wet trench coat to reveal an expensive three-piece suit. Gough closed the door behind them.

'Listen here, this is my command, and I am a senior officer here in the Met. So how about a little respect?'

Hudson calmly looked over the screens before turning back to Gough. The inspector was clearly a drinker given the condition of his skin, and his pale, washed-out face couldn't have been more in contrast to the smooth, dark skin of Hudson. There was likely less than a decade between them, but it looked plenty more than that.

Hudson pulled his lips together in a forced smile.

'You are a senior officer. Inspector Simon Gough. Twenty-eight years of service. Married to Julia. Father to Beth and Mitchell. Currently residing in Mitcham. Shall I go on?'

A mixture of fury and fear spread through Gough, as he regarded the puzzling man before him. A man who had clearly just made a thinly veiled threat.

'Look, I don't know who you are, but—'

'I've already taken the time to introduce myself, and I'm afraid I do not have the time to do it again.' Hudson held his hand out to guide Gough to the seat. 'You know why I am here. You've been given your orders and I trust, given the knowledge I have just demonstrated, we won't have any more interruptions. And as for showing some respect, that is something you earn. Not demand.'

Gough went to respond, opened his mouth, then just slumped into the seat. There was an off-putting quality about Hudson that told him to play along. His superiors had cleared the man for access to the command centre, as long as it was kept out of sight. The only way someone like Hudson would be granted such access in short notice was either through fear or money, and both possibilities filled Gough with dread. It meant Hudson was a criminal, working outside the defined parameters of the law, yet Gough's own superiors had allowed it to happen. As he began to draw up the cameras from the night before, he quickly realised who Hudson was looking for.

Sam Pope.

Tracking the CCTV footage from outside Visage at the time of an alleged attack by Pope, Gough's eyes widened as he saw the known vigilante step out of the club, hail a taxi and then disappear into the back seat.

'Follow it,' Hudson demanded, his unblinking eyes locked on the screens. Gough did as he was told, following the black cab from camera to camera, the car entering and exiting the screen from different angles. Once it stopped at London Euston Station, Hudson demanded he bring up the footage from within the station. That sort of request usually required a warrant or written consent by the owner of the business, but Gough doubted this would be heading to a court of law, so he obliged his unnerving guest.

Sam Pope strode through the station, his suit wet and his steps powerful. He boarded a train, and Hudson held up his hand for Gough to wait. As soon as the train began to depart, Hudson spoke.

'Stop it there,' he demanded. 'Now, bring up a manifest of any train that left Euston Station last night at eleven fifty.'

Gough huffed audibly, clattered his fingers across the keys and manipulated the necessary databases. Within minutes, he was proud to have an answer, as if he needed to prove his worth.

'Just the one. Glasgow.'

Hudson nodded, peered one more time at the still image of Sam Pope stepping out of the nightclub on one of the monitors and then lifted his coat from the back of the chair.

'Thank you for your assistance,' Hudson said coldly, as he slid his arms into the coat. 'Now, if you could see me out. I have some calls to make.'

'Hold up,' Gough said, stepping between Hudson and the door, irritated by the lack of information. 'I want to know what the fuck is going on here.'

'A weak man has to swear to get his point across.'

'Weak? I'll knock ten shades of shite out of you right now if I have to.'

Hudson smiled. That alone told Gough he was stepping beyond a line.

'There is a hierarchy in this world that very few people know about. I suggest you forget you ever saw me. If you don't, and any information about my being here gets out, then that wonderful family of yours will die. Do you understand me?'

Gough's mouth opened in shock and then his eyes narrowed with fury.

'Who the fuck do you think you are?'

Hudson didn't flinch.

'I already told you, you can call me Mr Hudson. Now, please see me out, before you make me do something you will most certainly regret.'

Without another word said, Gough hurried Mr Hudson back down the corridor and through the security door, slamming it shut behind him with hands that were shaking with fear. Hudson didn't care.

He had what he wanted.

He knew where Sam Pope was going.

'We will shortly be approaching Glasgow Central Station. All change, please.'

The automated voice crackled over the speakers, and Sam slowly blinked himself awake. His head was pressed against the window, and as the blurriness subsided, he saw the rain covered streets of Glasgow through the droplets that were pelting the window. His neck ached, as did his shoulders, but he was just happy to have gotten some sleep.

The cab driver had probably violated a number of traffic laws to get him from Visage to London Euston as swiftly as he did, but Sam was grateful. It meant he was able to get the overnight train back to Scotland, finding himself and just a few passengers condemning themselves to the journey. As it was overnight, the journey was seven and half hours, and as the train slowed to a stop, he checked his watch.

It was nearly seven thirty.

He'd drifted off to sleep a little after two o'clock, the adrenaline from his assault on Visage keeping him awake and alert until they were sweeping through the Midlands. He'd made a swift exit from the club and arrived at Euston less than ten minutes before boarding, meaning there wasn't much time to hang around. The fact that the train hadn't been called to a stop told him he'd escaped detection and that comfort, plus the exhaustion of the day, soon allowed him to drift off into a deep, yet clearly uncomfortable sleep.

The doors to the train opened, and he exited, following

the few other passengers as they stretched and walked towards the barriers, and Sam stepped through and glanced around wearily. There wasn't a cavalcade of police officers ready to greet him, and it drew a smile to his face. He stuffed his hands into the pockets of his blazer, dipped his head, and stepped out into the rain. As he walked through the wet streets, he wondered about the aftermath of his actions.

Although he had left a little mess behind, Sam knew he'd made his point loud and clear. There was no doubt in his mind that Jasper Munroe knew the severity of his crime, the fact that he would hold him accountable for it and what the conditions of his proposal were.

Jasper Munroe had three days to make a full confession to the police, otherwise, Sam would be back.

The threat to not only Jasper but also to his dad, had been subtle but deliberate. The research Sam had done had indicated that whenever he hit a legal snag or a problem, Jasper went running to his father. Dale Munroe, the feared businessman, clearly had some skeletons in his closet, and Sam had unearthed enough legal complaints against the man to know that threatening to expose him would push Dale to make a big decision.

Would Dale, one of the most ruthless businessmen in the country, really let his son's behaviour jeopardise his company? Sam didn't often lean on the kindness of billionaires, but he could most certainly lean on the potential damage to their business. If anyone was likely to push Jasper towards making the confession, it would be the man whose billion-pound empire was at stake.

Jasper's idle threats had been quashed when Sam had injured his friend, and given the heartbreak of Hayley Baker and her father, Sam had been happy to shed whatever blood was necessary.

Jasper Munroe was evil, and he belonged behind bars.

If putting one of his friends in hospital and scaring his super rich dad was enough to make him do the right thing, then Sam was satisfied with his actions.

After another few minutes, Sam rounded the corner onto Mel's road and he felt his heart pound with happiness. He could have headed back to his dingy flat across town, but he had allowed himself to be drawn to Mel. It was a magnetic pull, one which told him he was falling in love with the woman, and he realised, as he walked the final few steps through the pouring rain, that all he wanted was to see her face. The bar was closed, with the lights off and the chairs turned over on top of the tables, but Sam pressed the buzzer to the door beside it. Mel responded with a buzz of her own, unlocking the door to the stairwell, and Sam pushed it open and climbed the stairs towards her flat. She greeted him at the top with a large smile and a kiss. She then pulled back and looked at his soaking wet suit.

'You scrub up well.' She chuckled. 'Drowned rat what you were going for?'

'It's a look, isn't it?'

'Come on, kettle's on.'

Mel led Sam by the hand through the narrow hallway of her flat, past the bathroom and Cassie's room, where the door was open, and the bed was made. As a military man, Sam appreciated that. He stepped into the heart of the home, the kitchen, where *Radio One* was playing in the background and Cassie was sitting at the table, shovelling spoonfuls of cereal into her mouth while looking over some more textbooks.

'Morning, Cass.' He offered. She looked up and started laughing.

'I don't know what's sillier. Your suit or the fact you look like you took a dip in the Clyde.'

'You two are very kind.' Sam joked, and Mel chuckled

as she made him a cup of tea. A few seconds later, she passed him the piping hot mug, which he accepted with a thankful smile. Mel nodded towards Cassie, as if to say to Sam to keep quiet.

'Was your trip okay?' she eventually asked, and Sam nodded his understanding.

'Yeah, fine. I just had to take care of a few things.'

'What, like beating up some people in a nightclub and then threatening Jasper Munroe?' Cassie interrupted, looking at both of their confused expressions in irritation. 'It's all over the internet.'

'What is?' Sam asked, sipping his tea.

'Someone who looks a lot like you, and who the police are certain is you, fighting in a nightclub and then threatening Munroe.' Cassie shrugged. 'So, how was your trip to London?'

Sam smiled. She was a smart kid, and Sam had warmed to her immensely. He looked at Mel, who beamed with pride, and he took a sip of tea.

'It was eventful.' He nodded at her books. 'You ready for your exam yet?'

'Nope.' She sighed. 'We still on for early morning revision?'

'You betcha.' He lifted his mug.

'Off to school, you.' Mel motioned and stepped forward to kiss Cassie on the head. Cassie leant in to accept it, and then, to the shock of both Sam and Mel, she wrapped her arms around Sam's wet body and squeezed him.

'Thank you,' she said quietly. 'That meant a lot.'

Sam looked at Mel in surprise, who, in turn, looked like she was welling up. Sam patted her on the back, awkwardly trying not to spill his tea. She let go and then scarpered out of the kitchen, clearly a little embarrassed at her display of affection. For a street-smart kid, she wasn't too keen on letting her guard down.

But it had meant the world to Sam.

As she rushed down the stairs and slammed the door behind her, Sam turned to Mel and shrugged.

'That was a surprise.'

'Well, she knows what you did. You didn't have to go to London, but you went. Because it meant something to her.'

'And it was the right thing to do,' Sam added, as Mel slid in for a cuddle and then immediately backtracked.

'You're a good man, Sam Pope.' Mel smiled. 'Do you think he'll listen?'

'I think I got through to him. If Cassie's right, there will be enough buzz to get people talking, and that might be enough to tip him over the edge.'

Sam shrugged and Mel stepped forward, ready to hug him, but retracted her hands as soon as they touched his drenched blazer.

'You need to get out of these clothes.' She raised her eyebrows suggestively. 'Shall we?'

Sam put down his cup of tea, and let Mel take him by the hand, leading him out of the kitchen and towards her bedroom. As he followed her, Sam tried to search his memories for the last time he had been this happy.

CHAPTER ELEVEN

'I understand.'

Commissioner Bruce McEwen squeezed the bridge of his slightly crooked nose and closed his eyes. He knew taking on the role as head of the Metropolitan Police Service would be stressful, but there were some things he couldn't account for.

The tumbling economy.

The rise in the cost of living.

Things that would turn good people desperate, and therefore, the likelihood of crime increased.

One of the things he didn't account for was the inexplicable return of Sam Pope. The vigilante had long been declared dead, his charred remains identified in an abandoned, burnt-out factory down some back-alley road in South Carolina. Whatever the events that had led him to that situation, McEwen would never know, but when he finally replaced the retiring Commissioner Stout, he didn't envy his predecessor for having to tackle such a problem.

But now Sam Pope was back, and the same problem remained.

Not that the man was a violent and dangerous individual whose targeting of criminals was making the Met look bad. As far as McEwen was concerned, he could always stand on the moral high ground of being on the right side of the law.

Something that Sam would never be able to do.

The real problem that had returned was that the British public didn't hold the former soldier in the same regard as the Met did.

To many, he was a hero.

To many more, he was a necessity.

Although he would never admit it, sometimes McEwen found himself following the same train of thought. The world wouldn't weep for the loss of people like Dana Kovalenko or Slaven Kovac, and the country was certainly a better and safer place without them. But that safety was always fragile, as the more support Sam Pope got, the more likely he'd either die a martyr or inspire other, lesser-trained people to take action.

Either way, without him knowing, Pope was putting lives in danger.

Also, as he awaited the next furious tirade to explode from his speaker phone, McEwen wondered if Sam knew that he was making some very powerful enemies.

'Do you understand me?'

Dale Munroe's voice was shaking with anger, and McEwen was tempted to disconnect the call.

'I just said I did, didn't I?' McEwen decided to wrestle back some authority and emphasised his thunderous Glaswegian accent. 'May I remind you, Mr Munroe, that ever since the incident in Suffolk five months ago, we have doubled our efforts to bring Sam Pope to justice.'

'Yet, he is able to basically walk up to your front doorstep and take a big, steamy piss on it.'

McEwen ignored the insult.

'Well, I'm sure the favour you called in earlier will go

some way to placate you.' McEwen shuffled uncomfortably. 'We will also be doing our own follow up on what your associate discovered this morning.'

'My associate will handle things from here, Bruce. Like I said, nobody threatens my son or my business.'

'With all due respect, Mr Munroe, it is not something we can just allow a member of the public to handle.'

'And with no due respect to you, Commissioner, *your resources are clearly not up to handling this situation. Give my associate twenty-four hours, and this whole Sam Pope problem will be gone for good.'* Dale's voice was laced with menace. *'Do we have an agreement?'*

McEwen sighed. The lavish office that was assigned to him upon his ascension to the top job suddenly felt smaller and more in keeping with the claustrophobic feel of the usual police offices. He looked up at the wall, at the litany of certificates and accolades that had been bestowed upon him over the years.

At that moment, he felt like a fraud.

Just another police officer at the beck and call of the untouchable elite. Dale Munroe had a lot of sway within political circles. His stranglehold over data protection and business networks had made him one of the most powerful men in the country.

People respected him. Feared him.

Many of those people could have some say in how long McEwen sat on his throne.

With a regrettable sigh, McEwen answered.

'Yes.'

'Good.'

Dale Munroe disconnected the call, and McEwen sat for the next twenty minutes, trying to figure out how he was going to get the Met to pull back from hunting Sam Pope, when after the surprise appearance the night before, he was all they could talk about. They were close, and they had information that could lead them to him.

But just like the powerful elite who had warned McEwen off, Sam Pope was out of reach.

In fact, judging by the threats of Dale Munroe, Sam Pope was rapidly running out of time.

As he disconnected the call and tossed the phone onto the desk of his study, Dale Munroe cursed under his breath. Beatrice was still asleep, and Dale looked at the gold Rolex wrapped around his wrist.

It was a little after eight o'clock, and Dale hadn't been to sleep since his son had woken him up, pleading pathetically for his help and dropping a potential business-ruining problem squarely on his lap. The threat of anyone looking into his company usually sent Dale into a paranoid rage, where he threw as much cash as possible at the most expensive lawyers to make it go away. He had even bought out the majority shares in companies that had so much as raised a grievance against his business practices for the sole purpose of shutting them down.

But this was different.

This was Sam Pope.

There was a small voice in his head telling him to concede to Sam and march his son into the police station himself. But a man of his stature wasn't used to being bullied, and now, in his early sixties, he refused to change. The issue that brought was he had read everything about Sam Pope over the years.

The man was essentially living out a lot of people's fantasies, appointing himself as the Sheriff of England and going after the bad guys. He'd taken down some of the biggest criminals in the country, as well as legitimate business heavyweights like Nicola Weaver. Perhaps it was his training as an elite sniper, as once Sam Pope had someone in his sights, he rarely missed.

Dale stroked his powerful jaw, grimacing at the grey stubble that he'd have to eradicate later, and turned to the man seated on the sofa across from his desk.

'Do you think he'll listen?' Dale asked, lifting the cup of coffee from his desk. Mirroring him, Mr Hudson lifted his own coffee mug and sipped.

'I believe so. Yes.'

Hudson was a fascinating man, and one that Dale truly appreciated. There were no complications when dealing with him. Usually, when shady deals were being made underneath dirty tables, there were many dominos to line up. Just one small hiccup and the whole thing would collapse.

But with Hudson, there was none of that.

He was as he advertised himself.

A problem solver.

He wasn't cheap, and Dale was fully aware that he had furnished the man's bank account in the tune of millions, usually under the façade of 'consultancy'.

But Hudson never failed.

He always delivered.

Finishing off his caffeine hit, Dale placed the mug down on his desk, interlocked his fingers behind his head, and leant back in his chair. While he was struggling to stay awake, Hudson looked like he had enjoyed a full ten hours of sleep. The reality was, Hudson had been awake as long as Dale had, yet he'd been hard at work in the hours since.

It just added to the mystery of the man. Dale had been interested at first, wondering if Hudson had a family or anyone he cared for. But the man shared nothing.

Dale didn't even know his first name.

He didn't know if Hudson was even his name.

'So, how are you going to handle it?' Dale asked, his eyes fixed on the down lights that had been built into his ceiling.

'As always, we will go with as little mess as possible.' Hudson spoke with precision, hitting every syllable. 'The less trace back to you, the better.'

'Do you need to be there?'

'I have contacts in Glasgow—'

'Of course you do,' Dale said with a chuckle. The man was a marvel. Hudson didn't look too impressed at the interruption.

'As I was saying, I have contacts in Glasgow. Not the best, but there are three of them. They've already confirmed they have eyes on Sam and have followed him to an establishment within the city centre. I've told them to hold back for now, scope the place and if he doesn't re-emerge then to go in and take him by force when the coast is clear.'

'Are they capable?'

Hudson lifted his mug, took an elegant sip, and then placed it down again.

'We shall find out.' He offered Dale a reassuring nod. 'As always, my dear friend, we will solve this problem. You have my guarantee.'

'Oh, I don't doubt you, Mr Hudson. You're the best at what you do.' Dale pushed himself out of his chair and headed to the door of the office. 'Help yourself to anything you need.'

Hudson nodded and watched as his employer left and disappeared into the rest of his abode. He looked around, admiring the fine ornaments that adorned the shelving units and the classy décor of the entire room.

Dale Munroe was a loyal customer. One who Mr Hudson had enjoyed working for over the years.

Sam Pope was certainly a problem.

But Mr Hudson hadn't found a problem he couldn't solve and there was nothing more important to him than his reputation.

A reputation he was willing to kill for.

As the lunchtime rush was beginning to end, Mel warmly smiled at the final customers as they settled their bill and thanked her for their meal. She didn't offer anything too fancy, but her health-conscious pasta dishes and sandwiches always went down a treat. The portions were generous, and the prices were agreeable, meaning not only were her customers satisfied, but they would also likely return. The local businesses usually piled into her shop from noon onwards, many looking to scurry back to their desks with a sandwich in tow, while a few would gather around one of the tables for a team lunch, and an hour or so of forced conversation.

She loved the buzz that lunch time brought and as she handed the receipt back to the final two customers and thanked them; she poured herself a drink and treated herself to one of the leftover sandwiches. The investment in Carnival was a risk, but after her divorce, she knew she needed a fresh start and thankfully, it was paying off. She wasn't raking in money, but she had enough for her and Cassie to get by and not having to answer to anyone but herself and the tax man was a liberating feeling.

Also, her blossoming relationship with Sam had added another layer of happiness, one she didn't account for and one she certainly didn't expect with the most dangerous man in the United Kingdom.

He was upstairs, catching up on some sleep after his long day, and she looked at the remaining lunch food to see what she could pull together for his lunch.

The door opened.

'Sorry,' she said, turning and covering her mouth as she ate. 'We're closed. I forgot to turn the sign around.'

As she turned back, her face dropped as three burly men stepped in, all of them scowling. Two of them had their heads shaved, and one of them had replaced his hair with a tacky tattoo of a spider's web that wrapped around his cranium. The apparent leader, who had shorter brown hair, stepped forward, flashing a crooked grin and exposing his yellow teeth.

'We're not here for the food.' He grunted. 'Where is he?'

'Like I said, we're closed.' Mel tried her best to stay calm. 'I'd like you to leave.'

The leader chuckled and turned and looked at his cronies for affirmation. He then motioned his thumb towards Mel.

'She's sweet, isn't she? Quite pretty as well.' The man's accent was thick with Glaswegian menace. 'Listen here, sweetie. We know he's here. So why don't you just tell us where and we'll make as little mess as possible.'

'Get out,' Mel demanded. 'Or I'll call the police.'

'The fuck you will,' the tattooed thug piped up from the back, covering the exit with his stocky frame. The leader held his hand out to quiet him.

'Let me handle this.' He turned back to a clearly worried Mel. 'Tommy over there. He has a bit of a temper. And also, a bit of a thing for pretty ladies. So, why don't you just tell us where Sam Pope is, and maybe I'll keep him on his leash. Or I'll let him extract the information from you however he deems fit.'

Mel froze on the spot and shot a worried look beyond the leader to the tattooed Tommy, who blew her a terrifying kiss. During the first few weeks of her romance with Sam, she had wondered what would happen when someone came looking for him. It had seemed like an inevitability at the time, but as the months passed and nobody came looking, the idea of Sam's previous life catching up with him began to fade.

It was no coincidence that these men had appeared less than twenty-four hours after Sam had threatened Jasper Munroe, and as Tommy leered at her from across the room, Mel became very aware of just how dangerous a life with Sam could be.

Not just for her.

But for her daughter.

'So…' the leader said with a smug smile. 'Where is he?'

'I'm here.'

Sam's voice cut through the tension in the bar like razor wire, and he stepped out from the doorway behind the counter. His hair was still damp from the shower, and he'd thrown on his trousers and a black T-shirt that clung to his wet, muscular frame. While his voice exuded menace, his face was locked in a terrifying stare, one which Mel had never seen before.

'You're not as tall as I'd pictured.' The leader chuckled.

'Let's do this outside, shall we?' Sam didn't so much as ask but threaten. 'This lady has nothing to do with this.'

'Lead the way.'

Sam turned and headed back through the kitchen of Mel's bar, and instantly the leader began to follow. He signalled for the two others to leave through the front and meet him round in the alleyway behind. A small parade of shops and businesses ran the small stretch of road, meaning if they were quick, they could cut off both exits of the alleyway.

The leader would follow through the property, cutting off any option for Sam to try to retreat.

As his men rushed through the door and split into different directions, the leader smirked at Mel, whose eyes were watering with fear. Just to hammer home to the seriousness of the situation, the man pulled a knife from his pocket and stomped through the shop, watching as Sam pushed open the door that led to the alleyway behind.

The job had been to deliver Sam Pope.

It didn't say they had to deliver him alive and being the man to kill him was a temptation too strong to ignore.

CHAPTER TWELVE

Sam had just turned the water off when he heard the door to Carnival open on the floor below. Mel's apartment above her business was a modest home for her and her daughter, and during the quieter times of the day, it was possible to hear the business booming below. After his long trip to London and back the day before, Sam was tired, and after Mel had treated him to a morning between the sheets, he had fallen asleep.

Lovingly, she had left him to rest, going about the rest of her day and getting her business ready for the lunchtime rush.

He had awoken during the final half hour of the busy period, and after a few minutes of lying peacefully under the duvet, he left the bed and made a quick, naked dash to the bathroom where he freshened up and then hopped in the shower. The water crashed in a warm, welcoming downpour and it had given him time to reflect on the threat he'd made to Jasper Munroe.

He hoped it was enough to scare the family into making the right decision, as he didn't fancy another trip back to England. But he was a man of his word, and if

Jasper didn't confess to his crimes, then Sam would take action.

He'd step back into the life that Mel was unknowingly forcing him to leave behind.

As he stepped out of the shower, he pulled open the door to allow the steam to filter out and to hear the muffled voices below.

'Sorry. We're closed. I forgot to turn the sign around.'

Sam chuckled to himself, as Mel often found herself in a similar position and usually ended up salvaging a lunch for a hungry customer from what was left over. The gruff, threatening voice caused him to take notice.

'We're not here for the food. Where is he?'

Sam knew what was happening. Dale Munroe was reacting to the threat against his son in the way most powerful, rich people did and that was to try to snuff out the source of the problem. Instead of contemplating the reasons for Sam's intervention, Dale had gone directly into fight mode, and just as he did with any competitor or legal threat he came up against, he'd decided to try to squash it under his oppressive boot.

Sam quickly got dressed, keeping the doors open, so as to listen to the conversation. Walking as lightly as possible, he ventured out onto the landing, slipping on his boots and trying to visualise what was waiting downstairs.

There were at least two men, one of whom was most certainly the leader. Judging by their tone of voice, this was something they'd done before, meaning violence was certainly an avenue they were willing to venture down. The threats to Mel's safety and dignity were very clear, and Sam felt his fists clench until his knuckles turned white and his nails began to break the skin of his palms.

He stepped down the stairs as gently as he could and then turned into the supply cupboard that was beside the stairwell. He opened it slowly, avoiding any noise, and dipped inside. Mel's toolbox was on the floor, tucked underneath a shelf, and she'd taken advantage of Sam's previous life as a handyman. He had put right a few issues with her property and had taken pride in saving her money.

He flicked it open, removed the weighty steel hammer, and then tucked it into the back of his jeans, the handle pressed against his spine. He made sure his T-shirt concealed it from view, closed the door to the storage cupboard and then stepped into the kitchen.

'So…where is he?'

Sam could sense the impatience in the man's gruff voice and stepped through the doorway.

'Here I am.'

He looked to Mel, who looked dismayed at Sam. Clearly, she wanted to protect him, but he offered her a comforting smile.

'You're not as tall as I'd pictured,' the leader of the trio said, his crooked teeth revealing themselves in a horrible smirk.

Sam laid out his terms and then turned and walked back through the kitchen. Mel's bar was situated in the middle of the parade of shops, and the alleyway behind stretched a good thirty feet in either direction. He could hear the men scrambling out of the front of the shop, no doubt looking to cut off the exits and trap him in the narrow alley behind.

Sam had no intention of running.

He pushed open the back door and was greeted by a bitter chill and the dank, permanent smell of rubbish bins. His wet hair only heightened the cold, but Sam's adrenaline was kicking in, pumping a warmth through his body. He turned and backed himself against the wall, concealing the weapon further, and he waited.

The man with the tattooed head came into view first

on the right-hand side, puffing heavily after running as fast as he could. Sam ascertained that he was a smoker, as that level of running shouldn't have left him so out of breath.

The other man appeared on the left, his fists clenched and looking like he had a serious problem. Finally, the backdoor of the bar swung open, and the leader stepped out, his stained teeth offering a nasty grin.

'Well, well, well. The mighty Sam Pope.' The leader waited for his goons to creep closer. 'I'll be honest. I didn't think I'd find you in a shit heap like this place.'

'I'm assuming Dale Munroe sent you.'

The leader shrugged.

'Couldn't tell ya, and to be honest, I couldn't care. I got a call from a guy I know, told me you'd be on the train and to follow you. Then, I'm guessing this Munroe guy gave the order to bring you in.'

'Probably,' Sam agreed. The leader chuckled.

'Probably. Now, he didn't say what state you needed to be in.' The leader made a show of his knife by tossing it back and forth between his hands. 'Figured I'd get paid the same either way and let's face it, killing you will probably get me a lot more work.'

'How very forward thinking of you,' Sam replied dryly. He looked to the other two men, who were edging forward. 'Another option is for you to walk away.'

The leader chuckled loudly and shook his head in disbelief. The tattooed thug smirked, while the other just stared blankly at Sam.

'That's a good one,' the leader said through his laugh.

'Last chance,' Sam offered. 'Just remember, I did give you the option.'

The smile quickly evaporated, replaced with a furious growl.

'Get him!'

Like obedient lap dogs, the two thugs approached, with

the tattooed man getting overly confident and launching straight for Sam. Sam shifted his body weight back onto his left foot, evading the man's flailing arm. Sam snatched the man's wrist and tugged him towards him, using the man's momentum to drive him straight into a solid elbow. As his bone connected with the man's jaw, Sam turned the man's woozy body and pushed him into the other approaching thug. As they tumbled onto the wet concrete, Sam turned to the leader.

'Your move.'

The leader's eyes flashed with anger, enraged at the challenge, and he lunged forward with the knife, trying to gut Sam where he stood. Sam weaved to the side, his hand sliding to the hammer pressed against his spine, and he withdrew it without issue. He swung it forward, the metal head crunching the bones of the man's wrist, causing him to yelp in pain and drop the knife. Sam spun the hammer in his hand and then swung again, this time driving the flat, iron head of the hammer into the leader's ribs, before thrusting a vicious kick into the man's ankle, sending him to the ground, screaming over his broken bones.

As the rain began to lash down, Sam turned to the other two, both of whom had scrambled to their feet and were cautiously standing with their fists up. Sam placed his foot on the fallen knife and dragged it behind him, protecting it from their murderous gaze.

The tattooed man, with his lip split and blood pouring down his chin, roared with anger and lunged, swinging a few hard punches at Sam, which he absorbed with his lifted arms. He then caught the next fist flush with a swing of the hammer, obliterating the bones of the man's hand, before driving the hammer into the bridge of his nose. As the man stumbled backwards, his eyes blurred from the pain, Sam swung a brutal elbow into the side of his tattooed skull, shutting his lights off and sending him sprawling to the ground, unconscious.

Sam stopped for a moment, admiring his handiwork, before looking at the final thug. The man held his stance for a few seconds, weighing up whether he fancied the same fate. Then, without a word said, he dropped his hands, turned and ran as fast as he could back down the alleyway. Just as he was about to round the corner, the leader screamed out from his prone position on the ground.

'You fucking coward!'

Sam stood, waiting until the man had disappeared from sight, and then he turned and locked his eyes on the man on the ground. With his henchman unconscious, the colour drained from the man's face and as Sam took calm steps towards him, he threw up his one good hand in defence.

'Please…it wasn't personal.'

Sam stopped a few steps away, the hammer hanging lazily from his hand by his side and the rain crashing into his imposing frame.

'I'm guess that didn't go how you thought it would?'

'Look, I'm a professional. Okay? I was just doing my job.'

Sam lifted his foot and then brought it down slowly on the man's broken ankle, applying more pressure as slowly as he could. The man howled in agony.

'If Munroe didn't send you, who did?'

'Please. Ah. That fucking hurts!'

'Who sent you?'

'Hudson. His name's Hudson.'

The pathetic whimpering of the man trailed off as Sam took his foot off the busted ankle.

'How do I find him?'

'I don't know,' the man said wearily, the pain beginning

to overwhelm him. Sam stepped forward and pushed the man's chest with the bottom of his foot, sending him sprawling on his back. Sam then knelt on one knee and lifted the hammer. Slowly, he turned it so the claw was directed at the broken thug, and he raised it above his head.

'How. Do. I. Find. Him?'

'Jesus…look, look, look…I've never met the guy. Okay? He just contacts me when he needs things done in this city.'

'How does he contact you?' Sam reached down with his other hand and grabbed the man's shirt, holding him in position. By the fear in the man's eyes, Sam must have been terrifying.

'Phone. By phone.' Using his good hand, the man reached into his leather jacket and returned the phone in a shaking grip. 'Last number.'

He unlocked the phone and handed it to Sam, who pressed the *call* button and waited for the call to connect. Still wielding the hammer above his head, Sam kept his eyes fixed firmly on the grounded thug until a voice answered.

'Is it done?'

Sam held the phone out and then swung the hammer as hard as he could.

When Dale Munroe returned to the office, he looked like a different person. Gone was the weary, agitated old man who'd greeted Hudson in a panic hours before. Replacing him was the picture of power he always presented himself as. The expensive, three-piece suit was tailormade to fit his frame and the red tie was affixed to the crisp, white shirt with a gold tiepin. He had marched back into the office, accompanied by his long-suffering assistant, and immediately sent her on a coffee run for both him and Hudson. When she returned, Hudson thanked her politely, took the coffee and then awaited further instruction.

Dale didn't converse for a full two hours, going about his business from his home laptop and berating a few of his directors on an hour-long call about the impact his son's behaviour could have on their share prices.

After that call had ended, Hudson's phone, which was lying perfectly straight on the table, began to vibrate. Dale sat up instantly, clicked his fingers, and pointed.

'Is that him?'

Hudson checked the screen.

'Yes.'

'Put it on speaker,' Dale demanded, as he stood and stomped around the desk. He turned the chair around to face Hudson and sat on the edge of it, the rage and excitement both shaking through his body. Hudson waited for his employer to settle himself and then answered.

'Is it done?'

What followed was the sickening sound of metal hitting flesh, and a harrowing scream of pain. Dale flashed a confused look at Hudson, who kept his emotions in check. Eventually, a voice came through, but it wasn't thick with the expected Glaswegian accent.

'Is this Hudson?'

Instantly, Hudson knew he was speaking to Sam Pope. There was a clinical, almost calming tone in the man's voice. A tone that told both him and Dale that Sam was in complete control. It was admirable.

'You can call me *Mr* Hudson.'

'Whatever. Why did you send these men after me?'

'That is my business, Mr Pope.'

'First, you can call me Sam. There's no need for formalities the way this is going, is there?'

'Oh, I don't know. I believe respect and a little decorum should be a mandatory requirement. Don't you?'

'Respect isn't sending these men to threaten an innocent woman to find me. Now, seeing as they pulled a knife on me and tried to kill me, I'd say this is very much my business. So, I'll ask you again. What do you want?'

Hudson tried to raise his hand to stop Dale, but it was in vain.

'Because I told him to.' Dale was seething, his eyes bulging, and a little saliva hung from the side of his mouth. 'You had the nerve to threaten my son and my business, and you thought you could just walk away. Do you have any idea who you're messing with?'

There was a slight pause.

'Dale Munroe. CEO and Founder of Sure Fire Inc. Three times married. One child. Eighteen previous lawsuits pertaining to illegal activity and malpractice. Enjoys sushi. Member of the prestige Halloway Golf Club. Should I go on?'

Hudson nodded. Sam was certainly impressive.

The colour had drained from Dale's face, as the very real threat of Sam Pope had made it very clear he had done his research. The man wasn't used to being threatened. He had enough money and enough sway to ensure every problem that ever reared its head was eradicated quickly. He'd tried to do the same with Sam, but it had backfired spectacularly.

Instead of squashing the problem by sending those men after him, he had just made it worse.

After allowing Sam to hold control over the conversation for a few more moments, Dale took a breath and tried to wrestle back control.

'You're in a very dangerous place right now, Sam. Do you understand me?'

'Loud and clear.'

'It's one thing to threaten my son, but to try to threaten

my business, everything I've worked for, then you will make a very powerful enemy.'

'You can tell a lot about a man by his values. The fact that your business means more to you than your son is a pretty sad indictment of the man you are. But you have the chance to do the right thing, Dale. I'm giving you the chance to do the right thing.'

Across the table, Hudson looked up at Dale, whose emotions were clearly driving his thought process. Hudson didn't appreciate it. Everything should be meticulously planned, and emotion should never be the dominant force within a decision.

'The "right thing"?' Dale chuckled. 'Tell me, Sam, father to father, what's it like to not be able to protect your son? What's it like to fail him?'

Dale flashed a grin at Hudson, who refused to react. The silence on the other end of the call told them both that the cheap shot had hit Sam, and he was containing his fury. After a few audible deep breaths, he responded.

'Your son has three days to do the right thing.' Sam's words were cold. Hate-filled. *'If you want to protect your son, Dale, then I suggest you help him get there.'*

'I will send people after you, Sam, I swear…'

Sam hung up the phone. In a fit of anger, Dale picked up Hudson's phone and hurled it across the grand office, watching it shatter as it clattered into the brick. Hudson sighed and then turned back to his employer, waiting for the man to clear his mind of his anger and offer the next instruction. It took a few minutes, and a large glass of Scotch, but eventually, Dale Munroe took his seat behind his desk and looked to his problem solver.

'I need you to take Sam Pope out of the picture.'

'It might require a little more finesse than I first thought.'

'I don't give a fuck if you drop a nuke on the bastard. I

just want this problem done. Okay? I want Sam Pope taken care of.'

'With all due respect, sir. If we keep sending men after him and he keeps stacking them up, the police will soon see a pattern. The video of him threatening your son, followed immediately by a number of fallen criminals won't be too hard to piece together. The police will soon follow that trail to your door.'

Dale frowned, placed his elbows on the desk, and dropped his head into his hands.

'What do you suggest?'

Hudson stood and buttoned his blazer.

'We give them what they're looking for.'

Intrigued, Dale looked up and after a few more minutes of explanation by his trusted employee, Dale had offered the man his private jet and any resources he needed.

Moments later, Hudson was already out of the door and heading to Glasgow.

CHAPTER THIRTEEN

'Respect is not demanded. It is commanded.'

The voice of Hudson's father always rang loudly around the stone walls of their cellar, echoing off the stone walls and leaping back from the shadows. As a former member of the Nigerian military, his father had been exiled in disgrace after a series of war crimes that should have led to the death penalty. Luckily for his father, but unfortunately for Hudson himself, he managed to flee the country and arrived in England, where a former ally and criminal had given him refuge.

But his father struggled to adapt, having gone from a world of strict tradition, where his word was gospel, to a multi-cultural country where he was treated like an outsider, caused his father to break.

And quickly.

For years, he'd helped his regiment hold the small village of Kuyello almost hostage, and he had risen up the ranks until he'd effectively lived like a king. Hudson would never know his mother, as he was born out of wedlock, and his father kept him close by, as a trophy and potential successor. But at the age of five, they had to leave, leading them both to the small, rundown flat in Croydon, where the world ignored their every move.

From king to pauper. That's how his father had described it, and when his efforts to make in-roads into the local community were dismissed by sceptical locals, it was Hudson himself who was the focus of his attention.

Of the rage.

Strapped up in the cold, stone cellar of their derelict building, his father would lash Hudson with his belt, decrying the tears of the young boy as weakness and telling him stories of how men braver than he would be forced to go through such torment. How his ancestors were stolen from their homelands and put through a brutal life, just so those who had money could make more.

Hudson would never forget the lessons, and as he grew older and blossomed into a powerful man himself, he became increasingly numb to his father's abuse.

Once a week, he would voluntarily slip into the bonds that his father had placed in there, and he would drop to one knee. With his head high, he would accept lashing after lashing, the skin on his back scarred and bleeding, but he would not break.

He would not give his father the respect he demanded.

In refusing to even wince at the pain his father imposed on him, he knew that he was doing what his father never could: command the respect of another man. For years in Nigeria, he had led by fear, and when he hit eighteen years of age, Hudson knew that the time would come when he would need to exert his own dominance if he wanted a life for himself.

For thirteen years, he was neglected. Scraps from his father's plate, followed by the verbal abuse of never amounting to anything. Accusations of reliance on his father, who had taken what he wanted, when he wanted it. On the rare occasion he had spoken up or questioned why his father would run from his fate, he would receive a monumental beating that his father ensured would go unreported, and therefore untreated.

The moment came, a few weeks after he turned eighteen, when Hudson refused to get into his bonds. Enraged, his father demanded his son drop to his knee and take his lashings, to which Hudson questioned who administered his father's. Realising the power balance shifting, his father made the foolish decision to try to lash Hudson without restraining him, allowing the young man to overpower him and send him crashing to the floor.

Hudson didn't hold back.

After kicking his father until he couldn't get up, Hudson stripped him naked, and then he lifted the belt, ensuring the buckle was out, and whipped his father until he couldn't lift his arm. Lying as a flayed and bloodied mess, his father spat in his direction, and then feebly offered a heartfelt apology.

'I just wanted to make you a man I could respect.'

With no love in his eyes, Hudson dropped to his knees and cradled his bloodied father in his arms, his head resting on his knee. Tenderly, he lowered his mouth to the man's ears.

'Respect is not demanded. It is commanded.'

As his father's eyes bulged with fear, Hudson wrapped the belt around the man's neck and then pulled it as tight as he could, staring into the eyes of his creator as the blood vessels burst. As the life choked from his father, so did the man's control, and Hudson left the flat that evening and never went back.

Never checked to see if the body had been discovered and if it had, what state it was in.

He adopted the name Mr Hudson, just so it would open doors for him, and as he had spent the majority of his life in South London, he also wouldn't face any potential prejudice for having a strong Nigerian accent. He trained himself to speak eloquently, spending as much time as he possibly could watching how the rich and powerful acted.

How they dressed.

How they cared for no one but themselves.

Killing his father had been easy, and it didn't take Hudson long to find a rich person with a serious problem, and once he eliminated it in cold blood, his name spread. He became a solution to the elite, with his lack of ethics or questions making him a frightening yet sensible investment.

He quickly amassed a fortune, and with it, he was able to polish his reputation further with expensive clothes and elocution lessons.

From an uneducated boy from a war-torn village in Nigeria, to a well-spoken, well-groomed assassin, Mr Hudson knew the life he lived was one he had earned.

He hadn't demanded it.

He had commanded it.

The Munroe private jet was an expensive monument to their extensive fortune, and Mr Hudson appreciated every bit of it. From the gold trimming to the leather seats, it was a luxurious aircraft, with the journey overseen by an attractive air crew, all of whom were paid handsomely to turn a blind eye to what was being transported. While Jasper Munroe had a penchant for wild trips that no doubt involved class A drugs and lurid behaviour, Hudson was very aware that this trip was considerably more dangerous. He could tell by the looks on the faces of the private cabin crew, who were trying their level best to smile through the fear.

Hudson was not alone on the plane.

He was accompanied by three mercenaries, all of whom had extensive armed forces training and a greater appreciation for wealth than the law itself.

The three men were as nondescript as they came, with Hudson not even bothering to remember their names. To him, they were foot soldiers, the ones who would carry out the necessary deeds if required. Hudson himself had killed many people, but such was his reputation now he barely needed to lift a finger.

As dangerous as he was, he was just as clever, and having other people pull the trigger was a power play that his years of deliverance had afforded him.

These men knew who he was. They knew that the problems passed his way were always solved, which meant they would be paid handsomely and were unlikely to face too much resistance. Even when they were briefed that Sam Pope was the target, the only response he got was a disgusted grunt from a former soldier who thought Sam was a pathetic socialist.

To them, Sam was wasting his time trying to save the world, especially when he could put his considerable skills to the market.

Hudson, however, found Sam fascinating. It hadn't been hard for him to research the man and knowing the number of criminals the man had brought down, seemingly for no other reason than the good of the world, it made him a dangerous opponent.

People who did things for the cold, hard cash had a limit. Although he himself had endured enough of a painful past to push him further, there was still a price Hudson required to put someone in the ground.

But not Sam.

He did it because he thought it was for the greater good.

The right thing to do.

The man stood for more than himself, which meant he would fall for it, too.

If a man was willing to die for his convictions, it meant he would fight for them with everything he had.

The uncomfortable truth of it all was that Jasper Munroe was a rapist. It was apparent, with the sheer number of accusations and dropped charges over the years, that the man had no remorse for his actions. Protected by a powerful father and a limitless budget, the man made himself out to be the victim of it all, especially as he had been targeted by the most dangerous in the country.

But he wasn't a victim.

Not yet.

As Hudson sat, with one leg draped over the other, he turned his head to the window and looked out at the clouds in contemplation. The rain was rattling against the side of the jet, ruining his view, but he didn't mind. It was a short flight, and although Hudson knew he swam in some undesirable circles, it didn't mean he needed to enjoy the company he kept.

Nor the people he worked for.

If he had it his way, he'd hand Jasper Munroe over to the police himself.

But he wasn't paid for his morals.

He was paid for his ability to fix problems before they got out of hand.

Jasper Munroe had been out of hand for as long as Hudson had known his father, yet it wasn't his business to intervene. Having grown up with a silver spoon hanging out of every orifice, Jasper existed in a world where nothing was out of reach, and everything was his, if he so wished it. It was a world away from the trauma that Hudson had been through, and it was why Hudson had little respect for the man. While Jasper's childhood moulded him into the spoilt rich kid he was today, Hudson's had carefully sculpted him into one of the most dangerous and efficient men in the country. Jasper's body was coated in trashy tattoos that he showed off to his bizarre followers, whereas Hudson would only ever remove his shirt in private.

His back was a tapestry of abuse, an ugly reminder of the evil he has been subjected to and the violence he was forged in.

A violence that made him sick to his stomach when he imagined the opportunity afforded to someone like Jasper, and the arrogance of the man to throw it away.

Jasper Munroe was not worth killing for.

However, the eye-watering seven-figure sum his father would pay Hudson for the protection was.

To most, they would see it as a father doing his best to protect his son. Proof that there was no price on life.

But Hudson knew the truth.

Dale Munroe wasn't paying him to keep his son out of prison. He was paying him to keep someone like Sam out of his affairs, to keep the wolves from the door and to ensure the future and prosperity of the man's unimaginable fortune.

Hudson knew it.

Dale knew it.

Even Jasper himself, deep down, knew it.

As the wheels of the plane squealed loudly upon touching the tarmac, the pilot's soothing voice crackled over the intercom, announcing their arrival. Hudson looked over at his crew, all of whom were puffing their chests, ready to lock and load. The cabin crew nervously prepared the jet for its eventual stop, and Hudson offered them a polite smile to settle their nerves.

They knew they were transporting some very dangerous people.

Well, one at least.

Hudson only required the backup in case things went south.

But they rarely did.

As the door to the jet finally opened, Hudson unbuckled his belt and stood, stretching his legs in his expensive suit as he buttoned his jacket. Thanking the crew, he followed the rest of them down the steps and into the private hangar at Glasgow Airport. It was set back a good distance from the hub of activity that was the main terminal, and he was happy to see the luxurious Range Rover already waiting for them in the hangar. Dale Munroe had ensured him the journey would be as seamless as possible and had been true to his word. The other three men looked at Hudson, who walked with his shoulders straight, heading to the vehicle. The keys were resting on the driver's seat, and he reached in and tossed them to one of his crew. Just as he pulled open the door to the back of the SUV, the designated driver spoke.

'So, when do we kill this man?'

Hudson flashed him a disappointed look.

'We're not here to kill anyone.' Hudson pulled the cuff of his shirt just past the end of his jacket sleeve and adjusted the cufflinks. 'Not if we don't have to.'

The three men looked confused. The driver, seemingly appointed as the spokesman of the trio, stepped forward again.

'We were told—'

'I told you we had a problem to solve.' Hudson regarded the man with no fear, which clearly made him uneasy. 'Now kindly, all three of you, get in the car and do as I say.'

'Or what?'

One of the other men spoke up, braving the cold in a T-shirt and flexing his muscles. Hudson had little time for the empty display of intimidation.

As cold as the wind that whipped around them, Hudson turned to the man, with the fury of his violent past burning in his eyes.

'I'll kill you. All three of you.' Hudson's face dropped, and he offered a smile. 'Now…shall we?'

He gestured to the car and then clambered in himself. The three men slowly followed, each strapping their seat belts in silence as the very real threat of violence was trapped in the car with them.

They knew about Hudson's reputation.

Soon, so would Sam Pope.

CHAPTER FOURTEEN

The evening had given the city of Glasgow a night off, the constant downpour dwindling as the sun set and faded into a dry, winter's night. It was a few hours before Mel would need to open the bar, and as she walked through the gates of the Necropolis, she pulled her puffer jacket tightly around her body and shivered. In the early days of her business, she had tried to cater to the after-work crowd, but found the stress wasn't worth the income it generated. Having worked so hard to cultivate a happier life, it wasn't something she would sacrifice for a little extra cash every month.

The temperature was brutally low, and the chill in the air was exacerbated by the eerie sensation she felt whenever she stepped foot in the famous cemetery. Although a calming destination, the surrounding feeling of death and finality shrouded the entire grounds in a macabre atmosphere, and as she could see every breath that filtered from her mouth, it felt like the dead reaching out to snatch her soul. The Necropolis was a beautiful creation, with its rows of tombstones, regardless of size, all laid out in imperfect rows, winding their way up the hill to the chapel that rested neatly on top like the cherry of a very morbid cake. Some of the tombstones jutted out of the ground and up towards the night sky. Thick, concrete pillars that were a tribute to the deceased and at some point, loved by people who wanted to honour them. She often found herself reading them in fascination, with some of them stretching back over a hundred years, while others were a memorial to a life lost way too soon.

As the wind whipped through the cemetery and snaked its way among the stones, Mel pulled her woolly hat down further over her ears, and then clasped her gloved hands together. She wouldn't feel warm for the next few minutes, until she saw Sam, sitting on a wooden bench at the top of the hill, casting his eyes over the eternal rest. As she approached the bench, he turned, smiled, and stood.

'This is romantic,' Mel said dryly, and wrapped her arms around him.

'You know me,' Sam replied with a smile, squeezing her as hard as he could. They both knew why they were there but didn't want to admit it. 'How did you get on?'

'Oh, it was fine. The police came in, asked a few questions. Took a few notes. But luckily, I can't afford CCTV, so they had to take my word and their own assumptions.'

'What did they think?'

'Considering one of them is a known drug addict in the area, they believe that he jumped the guy in the alleyway, they had a fight and both beat the piss out of each other.' Mel shrugged. 'Just another standard Thursday afternoon in Glasgow.'

Sam forced a smile, but his brow furrowed. The fact that Mel had to cover for him was bad enough, but he had also put her in danger.

'I'm sorry.'

'Hey, look at me.' Mel reached up with her gloved hand and turned his face to her. 'You're a good man, Sam

Pope. I know you give yourself a hard time for the things you've done, but if you didn't do them, the world would be a worse place.'

Sam reached up, resting his own palm on the back of her hand.

'No matter how hard I try to walk away from it, I can't. No matter how good things could be, I just can't let that side of me go.'

Mel watched Sam and felt her heart breaking. Pushing up onto her tiptoes, she planted a kiss on his icy lips.

'Never change, Sam.' She smiled. 'The world needs men like you. Men who are willing to do the right thing, no matter the cost.'

'But there is a cost…'

Mel felt a tear forming in the corner of her eye, and she pulled away from Sam and wiped it. She cursed herself under her breath. For years as a single parent, she had prided herself on her toughness.

'I know,' she finally admitted. 'But my daughter lives in a world where rich men can rape women and get away with it. Unless…well…'

She looked up at Sam, her eyes watering but filled with love.

'Unless someone does something about it.' Sam finished her sentence with a sigh, and then reached out and grabbed her hand, clutching it as hard as he could. 'If I can make Cassie feel like this world is a little bit better than she thought—'

'Then you've done more than enough.' Mel squeezed Sam's hand, the tears now flowing without control. 'Like I said, you're a good man.'

The heartbreak finally kicked in and Mel stepped forward and buried herself in Sam's chest. He wrapped his powerful arms around her, shielding her from the cold, and he held her as tightly as he could.

‘I can’t stay,’ Sam said, his voice cracking ever so slightly. ‘Not now—’

‘I know,’ Mel said, pulling away. She reached up and wiped the tear that was threatening to fall over Sam’s eyelid. ‘I know.’

‘This Jasper Munroe. He’s done some terrible things.’ Sam shook his head. ‘The women he’s hurt. The lives he’s destroyed. The law doesn’t apply to them, and it means he gets to do it again and again—’

‘Unless someone fights back,’ Mel said, her face melting into a proud smile. ‘Unless you fight back, Sam.’

‘I can’t change the things he’s done. Those girls will have to carry that injustice for their whole lives. But I can stop him from hurting others, and I can make him face the consequences of his actions.’ Sam grit his teeth. ‘But I can’t put you and Cass in the firing line.’

Mel stepped forward again, pushed up on her toes and planted her lips on Sam. She kissed him firmly, and he reciprocated immediately, the two of them clutching each other with no intention of letting go. The freezing wind whistled past and eventually, Mel stepped back, her cheeks wet with sadness, and she held Sam’s hand intensely.

‘Go do what you do,’ she said with heart-breaking approval.

Sam nodded and refused to let go of Mel’s hand. After a few more tender moments, he eventually did, and his chest felt heavy. Mel took a few steps away from him and then turned back, smiling at him one more time. Sam watched her, memorising her face and cursing himself for the situation he was in.

For the path he walked.

The life he chose.

Just as Mel was nearly out of earshot, Sam called out to her.

‘What time is Cass’s exam on Monday?’

Mel turned, wiping her tears with the back of her sleeve.

'First thing. But I understand...'

'I'm a man of my word, Mel.' Sam smiled. 'Save me a plate, eh?'

Mel chuckled through her tears.

'I'll hold you to that, Sam.'

The two of them held each other's gaze for one last moment, before Mel turned and strode back down the hill, battling the cold and the floods of tears. Sam watched on, his heart cracking as a painful reminder of what he was sacrificing.

Jasper Munroe needed to be brought to justice.

Otherwise, he had broken both his and Mel's hearts for nothing.

The bar was quiet that evening, besides the usual locals who came in and enjoyed a quiet moment to themselves, and Mel was thankful for it. After the meeting with Sam, she had been inconsolable, but as soon as she had returned home, Mel had done what she had always done.

Put on a brave face and cracked on.

Cassie had known something was wrong, pushing her mother for answers as she prepared dinner, but Mel kept it together enough to avoid alarming her daughter. Cassie had grown fond of Sam over the past few months, and the last thing Mel wanted to do was distract her daughter this close to her exams. Although her father, David, saw her from time to time, Cassie had consigned him to the same place that Mel had.

Just another man that had let them down.

Mel was adamant that she wouldn't allow Cassie to tarnish Sam with the same brush, and so when she told her daughter she was going to open the bar, she did so with a smile on her face.

Luckily, she didn't need to keep it up for long, as the regulars showed her the same enthusiasm as usual, before slinking off to their tables and drowning themselves in the alcohol. Usually, she would try to brighten their day with a quip or an anecdote, but as her heart was still busy disintegrating, she quietly prepared their drinks, took their money, and then left them to it. She put the sports channel on the big screen and let it hum away in the background, not caring what was on show.

It would at least draw their attention even further away from any potential conversation.

The evening drew on, and Cassie popped down to say goodnight. Mel knew she was a bright kid so giving her an extra tight squeeze did little to help her daughter's theory that something was wrong. As she thundered back up the stairs to their flat to head to bed, Mel began gathering the few empties that had been left on the tables. The final customer was sitting miserably in the corner, his face buried in his phone and over half a pint still to drink.

Mel checked her watch.

Technically, she was still open for another twenty minutes, but given the chance, she'd close early. But then the idea of not heading upstairs with Sam sunk in and she sighed, meandering back towards the counter when the door opened. In walked a resplendently dressed man with dark skin and short, greying hair. His clean-shaven face was set in a pleasant smile, showing two rows of perfectly white, straight teeth.

'Cutting it a bit fine,' Mel stated and then forced a smile. 'Nice suit.'

'Thank you, my dear,' Hudson said sincerely, taking a few steps towards the first chair to hand and sat down with authority. He draped one leg over the other and then regarded Mel with a cold stare. Mel shuffled uncomfortably.

'Can I get you a drink?'

'A coffee,' Hudson said politely. 'I've been up since the middle of last night and it's been a long day.'

'Tell me about it,' Mel replied, and then began navigating the barista machine. 'Americano?'

'Delicious.' Hudson smiled as he looked around the property. He took in the carnival themed décor, which didn't entirely mesh with the sport that was being shown on the screen. He accepted the need to attract customers, but he found the obsession with marrying sport with alcohol tiresome.

'You're not from around here,' Mel said, not looking up from the machine.

'I am not, no.'

'Business or tourist?' Mel asked, rolling her eyes at the mundane conversation she found herself in. The other customer had finished his drink, and he stood, shuffled to the door and grunted his goodbye as he left. The door closed and her new customer answered.

'Business.' The man's voice sounded colder. More threatening. 'Perhaps you can help me.'

Mel turned to the man, and she dropped the coffee in shock. On the table, the man had placed a handgun.

'Look, mister. Take what you want—'

'Oh, come on. Look at my suit. Do you truly believe I need your money?' Hudson tutted and wagged his finger. 'No offence, my dear, but it doesn't look like business is booming.'

'Then what do you want?' Mel held her hand up. 'Please, I have a daughter upstairs.'

'I'm looking for your friend,' Hudson said calmly, interlocking his fingers and resting his hands on his raised knee. 'Sam Pope.'

Mel knew her reaction gave the game away immediately, and her eyes darted to her phone on the side. Hudson followed her gaze.

'Don't be silly now, Mel, is it?' Hudson stood, and he fastened the button on his jacket. 'I looked up your business on the journey here.'

Hudson waved to the door, and Mel's eyes bulged with horror as three more men stormed in. Unlike the three thugs Sam had ably dispatched earlier that day, these men were terrifying. Their muscular arms were covered in tattoos that wormed their way from the cuff of the sleeves onto their hands, and under their coats, she could see the guns that were tucked into their waistbands.

'I don't know where he is.'

Hudson sighed. The designated driver of his crew stepped forward menacingly.

'The bitch is lying.'

'Language, please,' Hudson said sternly, holding up his hand. 'Mel, these men and I are being paid a rather large sum of money to find Sam Pope. Now, while I am trying my best to politely engage with you, these three men were not taught the same manners.'

'Fuck you,' the designated driver spat. Hudson turned, his eyes bulging with fury, and the man quickly lifted his hand up and stepped back. 'Sorry.'

Hudson's ferocious glare snapped into a smile.

'Apology accepted.' He turned back to Mel. 'Now, these men are trained to extract information out of prisoners and believe me, I'm pretty sure they enjoy it.'

Hudson stepped past Mel and behind the counter. He located the kettle and then headed to the sink. He topped it up with water, placed it back on its stand and switched it on, the water slowly beginning to boil.

'Honestly, I don't know where he is.' Mel's strong accent enhanced her defiance. 'I saw him earlier, and he said goodbye to me. Told me he was heading after that rich kid who I assume is paying you to find him?'

'Almost correct,' Hudson said calmly as he watched the kettle. 'A watched pot never boils, does it? But no, it's not him as such, but his father. A terrifying man in some respects, yet he can afford the best. And also, you do know how I can find him.'

'Honestly, I swear I don't know where he is.'

Hudson's smile dropped, and Mel felt true fear. Maybe for the first time in her life.

'You may not know where he is, but you know how to find him.' The kettle clicked off and steam filtered from the top. Hudson turned to one of his men. 'Get the daughter. She's upstairs.'

Mel screamed, but the other two men held her back, grasping her arms as the other stomped up the stairs to the flat above. After a few moments of commotion, footsteps pounded back down the stairs, and a terrified Cassie was dragged into the kitchen.

'Mum?' she asked in terror.

'It's okay, baby. It's okay.'

'Hello. You can call me Mr Hudson.' He smiled at Cassie and then turned to the man who was holding her arms painfully tight. 'Hold her down, please.'

Mel struggled and groaned again as the man pushed Cassie forward, pinning her head to the sideboard. Hudson lifted the kettle and turned to Mel.

'Now, I will give you one last chance to tell me where I can find Sam, otherwise I will disfigure this beautiful daughter of yours.' Hudson motioned tipping the kettle. 'Do you understand?'

Cassie was crying, the fear of the situation causing her to shake, much to the amusement of the man who had her held in place. Mel felt her world collapsing, and the thought of her daughter suffering made it hard for her to breathe.

The words were struggling to make themselves heard, and Hudson shrugged and turned to her daughter.

'The haulage yard,' Mel managed to scream, drawing Hudson's attention away. 'I don't know where he lives, I've never been.'

'Go on.' Hudson held his arm steady, the weight of the full kettle seemingly taking little effort.

'He works at the haulage yard, just outside of town.' Mel's voice was shaking with fear. 'It's closed now, but it opens early. They might be able to tell you where he lives. Just please, leave my daughter alone. Please.'

Hudson regarded the desperate mother for a few more moments, and then withdrew the kettle and placed it back on its holder. With a smile on his face, he stepped away from the bar counter and out towards where his henchman was restraining Mel.

'You're a good mother. I can see that.' Hudson's voice had returned to the soft, charming tones of before. 'Please understand that I took no pleasure in this. I am just doing my job.'

'Fuck you!' Mel spat, raising her chin as if inviting him to strike. Hudson sighed.

'I understand you're angry, so I will forgive the profanity. Fellas, please let them go.'

On his command, the men relinquished their grips and Mel pushed past them and rushed to Cassie, wrapping her arms around her, before putting herself between her daughter and the intruders. Hudson nodded with approval.

'Get out,' Mel demanded.

'I will, but lastly, I need your phones.' Hudson's voice went cold again. 'It's not optional.'

Without resistance, Mel handed her phone to him and then marched Cassie upstairs to find hers. Despite her feeble attempts to keep it, Cassie handed it over, the trauma of the past few minutes rendering her teenage rebellion moot.

Mel returned downstairs on her own, and she slammed Cassie's phone on the counter. Hudson lifted it and opened the back and removed the battery and SIM card. He placed the empty shell next to Mel's phone, which had also been stripped.

'Thank you, Mel,' Hudson said politely, pocketing the phone contents in the inside of his suit jacket. 'I am sorry that we had to meet under such circumstances.'

Hudson motioned for his men to leave, and like obedient dogs, they filtered out of the bar and into the bitter cold of the evening. As the last one to leave, Hudson turned back and offered Mel a nod goodbye, and her face was contorted into a hateful scowl.

'I hope you do find Sam.'

'Let's hope so.' Hudson smiled.

'So he can kill you.'

'Well, we shall see. Don't do anything stupid now, Mel. If I have to return, I will kill your daughter as slowly as possible and make you watch every second.'

With that terrifying threat looming over her, Mel watched as the well-presented man stepped out of her bar, and as soon as he disappeared from view, she fell to her knees and began to cry.

CHAPTER FIFTEEN

Jasper was struggling to sleep.

To his millions of followers on social media, he had shrugged off the supposed threat from Sam Pope and had basked in the support from his loyal fanbase. They were busy claiming his innocence, pointing out the court's decision a few days earlier, and Jasper had hoped that would satisfy his anxiety.

The world saw him as a playboy, living the life they all dreamt of. There were no rules that applied to him, nothing that was beyond his grasp and therefore, to them, he was the personification of success.

Yet, his ego could only keep the nerves at bay for so long.

He enjoyed the comments on his posts and savoured the women who declared their loved for him.

But he still couldn't sleep.

All he could see when he shut his eyes was the very real threat of Sam Pope sitting across the table from him in Visage and effectively turning over the hourglass that would tick down to the end of his life.

In his latest video, he had dismissed Sam as less than

an inconvenience, not wanting to boost the aura or ego of a man who clearly was insane.

But Sam Pope was a man who rarely missed.

The genuine fear in Jasper's mind was that his father wouldn't be able to stop him before the three-day deadline. The last thing he wanted was for Sam to humiliate him, or worse still, hurt him. The other alternative was to admit to his crime and go to prison.

His father's connections with the upper echelons of the police force would likely make his stay comfortable, but the thought of being locked away with other criminals terrified him. Stripped of his status, he'd be an easy target and he was certain there would be at least one inmate who'd be champing at the bit to take a billionaire's son down a peg or two.

The thought of either outcome had begun to dominate his mental space, and while he put on a brave face for his posts or when out in public, Jasper knew he was crumbling.

Alcohol wasn't helping.

Drugs were having little effect.

He just needed it to be over and he needed to sleep.

But just as he was beginning to doze off in the early hours of Friday morning, he was awoken by the buzzing of his phone and the terrifying voice of his father.

'My office. Now. Car's outside.'

With bleary eyes, Jasper had peeked through the curtains of his penthouse and saw the black Mercedes waiting in the middle of the road, the engine running and the lights on. Wearily, he dressed and soon found himself being whisked away to his father's office, a place where the only thing he felt was intimidation. There was no future for him at Sure Fire Inc, a fact he had long since accepted, but every time he stepped foot in the building, it reminded him of how little his father thought of him.

Of how little he meant to him.

As the car pulled into the private car park underneath the building, Jasper snorted a line of cocaine, knowing it wouldn't build the bridge between the two of them, but it would at least numb whatever was coming his way. The driver stepped out, opened the door and ushered Jasper to the lift, and he thought back to two days prior, when his father berated him for his behaviour.

His mind raced to the look of disgust on Dale Munroe's face, as Jasper had explained what had happened at Visage.

The disappointment.

The hatred.

Jasper took a deep breath and stepped into the lift, and let it carry him to the top floor, where no doubt, his father would be waiting, overflowing with the usual contempt for his son.

The doors opened to no one.

Surprised, Jasper poked his head out into the dark hallway, the usually brightly lit corridor hiding its expensive décor in darkness. At the far end of the corridor was his father's office door, which was slightly ajar, and offering the only existence of light with a thin sliver that ran across the carpet and up the wall. It was freezing cold, and the air blowing from his father's office sent a shiver down his spine. Jasper marched towards it, his fingers twitching, and he wished he were anyone else in the world.

His mind was a mess.

He wanted to run.

But defying his father wasn't an option, and after a few moments to settle himself, he pushed open the door to the office and stepped in with a smile.

'Dad.'

His father didn't respond. Instead, he was staring at his laptop as if engrossed in a film while his fingers clicked across the keys. Jasper looked around anxiously. The view of the city was obscured by the darkness of the early morning, and Jasper felt completely alone. One of the windows, which was split into two, was open, letting in the freezing temperature that didn't seem to register with Dale one iota.

Even with the one man who had sworn to protect him, Jasper had never felt so vulnerable.

After what felt like an eternity, his father spoke.

'I'm not used to being threatened. Well, not with any real intent, anyway.' Dale finished typing and then turned and looked at his son. 'I don't like it.'

'I'm sorry, I don't understand.'

'That's just the thing, son.' Dale stood, straightening his sports jacket. It was odd for Jasper to see him in casual wear, but it was a testament to how little they socialised as a family. 'You never understand, do you? You think, because of the life *I* built for you, there are no consequences to your actions. That you can run around like a sick little deviant, and I will always be there to pick up the pieces.'

Jasper shuffled anxiously.

'I don't think—'

'Precisely. You never think.' Dale cut him off, looming around the desk and making Jasper, despite his impressive physique, feel tiny. 'I guess that's my fault, really. You've never had to struggle for anything in your life, have you? Never really had to dig in and work hard. I always saw this, everything I've built, as your birth right, but the longer I live, and the more I see, the more I know that's not true. Because if it was, you would at least give a shit about this company, instead of treating it like a bank account.'

Jasper could feel himself shaking. The cocaine was coursing through his blood stream and playing havoc with his emotions.

'I'm sorry, Dad.'

'You're sorry, huh?' Dale nodded and then cracked Jasper with a thunderous backhand across the face, sending him stumbling towards the open window. Dale followed, instantly grabbing the scruff of Jasper's jacket and holding it tight, in complete control of the situation.

'Dad. What the fuck?'

'Do you know what I was writing when you walked in? I was writing the suicide note I would pass onto the police if I were to throw you out of this fucking window!'

'Please…Dad.'

'I spoke to Sam Pope yesterday. He started running down legal issues of the company and told me, unless I handed you over, he was coming for everything I had. Everything that actually matters.' Dale's eyes were wide with disdain. 'But I can't do that. You have my name. That name means something to the shareholders, and I can't let him, or you, drag it through the mud any longer. So, throwing you out of this window would solve all my problems, wouldn't it?'

Jasper squealed with terror, alarmed by how surprisingly strong his dad was.

'I can fix this—'

'No, *you* can't. But I've already sent someone who can.' Dale pushed Jasper away, relinquishing the hold and allowing his son to regain his composure. 'This whole thing will be over today, and then there are no more chances. No more bail outs. I will throw you out of this window and tell the world you couldn't cope anymore. Now, I'm sure you have some pointless shit to post on the internet, so get the fuck out of my sight.'

Without any attempt to disguise the hatred in his voice, Dale turned and marched back to his desk. Calmly, he pulled the laptop towards him and continued with his business. Jasper took a few deep breaths, fought the temptation to cry, and then rushed from the room and headed to the bathroom. As soon as he stumbled into the cubicle, the vomit exploded from his throat, and after a few moments, he was a whimpering mess on the tiled floor.

As the hideous stench of sick filtered through his nostrils and the burning sensation stung the back of his throat, Jasper tried to catch his breath.

Tried to grasp any sense of himself.

He was having a panic attack, and he knew, unless his father solved the problem, he was only a day away from losing both his life and mind.

———

As always, Martin McGinn was awake before his alarm, and his bedroom was pitch-black. His wife, Jane, was still fast asleep, and as it wasn't even five o'clock yet, he saw no reason to wake her. As an overworked nurse, Jane needed all the rest she could get when her shift pattern allowed it. Carefully, he cancelled the alarm, gently kissed his wife on the head, and slipped out of bed. As was habitual, he had laid out his clothes the night before, and he gathered them up in his arms and tip-toed out of the room and to the bathroom. Once inside, he quickly freshened up and dressed. Despite being in his mid-thirties, nearly two decades of hard labour had aged him significantly, and his thinning hair had been shaved off to avoid the inevitable island of hair at the front of his skull. His beard, which was thick and speckled with grey, hung from his jaw. He pulled the T-shirt over his portly stomach and then exited the bathroom. Before he headed down the stairs of his modest family home, he dipped his head into the two bedrooms, where his seven and four-year-old sons slept.

Jimmy and Drew.

His pride and joy.

As he stepped lightly down the staircase, he thought

about them and their futures. When he was at school, he was a terror, more interested in impressing the girls and his friends than studying. Luckily for him, he didn't lack work ethic, and so when he inherited his father's humble haulage business, he spent the next twenty years turning it into a profitable business.

It wasn't glamourous, but it filled him with pride to see his family name emblazoned on the signs of the gate. He also took great pride in hiring ex-convicts to help run the business, believing that people should be given the second chance society so often deemed unattainable. A few of the guys who would be on shift with him had done time, but he would never hold it against them.

All the guys were a good laugh, and they were all trying to turn over a new leaf.

Even Sam Pope.

When Mel Hendry had reached out to him, he hadn't expected the most wanted man in the UK to be the reason why. But Mel had been a good friend over the years, and once Martin had met Sam, he hired him on the spot. No matter what shift he was given, or the weather conditions, Sam would arrive to work before he was required and would leave long after he should have. Martin attributed it to the military training Sam had gone through, which had been extensively covered in the press over the past few years. Sam had a convincing fake identity, which checked out after Martin had done the required checks and meant Martin could play dumb if he needed to.

But he had no problems hiding Sam Pope from the world and giving him the chance to build a new life. Based on the things Martin had read, Sam was a hero, and instead of being vilified by most of the press and the national police service, he should have been commended.

After a quick breakfast, Martin slipped into his overalls, covered his bald head with his woolly hat and then made his way to his pickup truck, which was thick with frost. After scraping it away, Martin dropped into the driver's seat and brought the engine to life. It was only a fifteen-minute drive to the yard, and with the roads empty, he cruised along at the speed limit, tapping his fingers to the cheesy songs on the radio. The morning chill was evident across the tops of all the cars and their windscreens, waiting patiently to annoy anyone in a rush that morning.

Martin loved Glasgow.

The high buildings that lined the streets were rich with gothic aesthetic, and with the fog sagging over the roads like an ethereal haze, he found the town looked magical at that time of the morning. Almost to the second, he arrived at the gate of the McGinn Haulage Centre in fifteen minutes, and after fumbling with a freezing cold lock, he opened it up and pulled his truck onto the gravel-covered forecourt. Again, the winter chill had descended upon his business, and every piece of metal had a light dusting of frost, shimmering under the glow of the still-present moon. Across the forecourt was the office, which was a hut that he'd converted into a waiting area for his customers, along with his own private office. It wasn't anything fancy, but he didn't need it to be. Beyond the hut was the work garage, where some of his employees either worked on the vehicles that were dumped or took apart other appliances at the request of the paying customer.

It was hard work.

But it was fulfilling.

He flicked the lights on in the office and turned the coffee machine on, knowing it would take a few minutes to warm up sufficiently. It only offered store-bought instant coffee, but he and most of his customers liked it.

Martin popped into his office, hung his thick, waterproof jacket on the hook and powered on his laptop. He quickly cast his eyes over his emails and then headed back to the waiting area to grab his coffee.

As he stepped through the door, he started.

'Who the hell are you?' he asked, his Glaswegian accent in full bloom. The well-dressed man smiled and adjusted his cufflinks. He wasn't particularly big, but his mannerisms didn't sit quite right with Martin.

'Good morning, Martin, isn't it?' He extended his hand and flashed his perfectly white teeth. 'You can call me Mr Hudson. And let me just make it very clear right now that I don't want to hurt you if it can be avoided.'

CHAPTER SIXTEEN

Sam pulled the cord as he stepped into the bathroom and waited for the dim light to flicker alive. It was a small cupboard of a room, with a toilet and sink squashed against one wall and just enough space to squeeze past to the shower cubicle.

To call it an actual room would have been generous.

As the cheap bulb brought the beige tiles to life, Sam put his hands on either side of the sink and dipped his head. For the past four months, he had been sleeping better than he had in years. For too long, most nights were disturbed by recurring horrific dreams, where the many people he had lost along the way would visit him.

Whether it was the ones he had loved and lost, or the ones he had sent to the afterlife himself.

The ghosts of his past would visit him, reminding him the pain and tragedy he had suffered, and usually holding him to account for the same curse he had put on those he had killed. It never mattered that the people he killed were criminals.

Eventually, every life he took became a burden he would have to carry, and while he was steadfast in his belief that he was just fighting back, it was clear that doubt was lurking in his subconscious. For a long time, he had wondered if he had gone too far, losing himself in the legend he had built and was actually enjoying squeezing the trigger.

It wasn't the case, and he had managed to accept that.

Just as he had finally accepted the death of his son, Sam knew he couldn't let the doubt and the broken past hold him down and steer him off the course.

The nights had been easier since, and although he rarely dreamed, he hadn't awoken in a cold sweat in months.

Not since he finally said goodbye to his son.

And not since he had met Mel.

But that night, he awoke after just a few hours, grunted with fear as he startled awake and realising that his sheets were soaked with sweat. It was December in Glasgow, yet he was a dripping mess, and he couldn't recall which pale, sunken face was speaking to him, but he was certain it was one that he had cared for.

Had loved.

Sam peeled his T-shirt from his muscular, scarred body and blew out his cheeks. It was a little after five in the morning and he knew there was no chance of going back to sleep, so he decided to take a shower. Unlike the power shower that he and Mel had shared countless times, the water trickled out of the head with a depressing lack of effort, and the lukewarm water was barely enough to wake him. After a few minutes of uncomfortable washing, Sam stepped out and got dressed.

His movements were sluggish, and he knew it wasn't due to the sleep.

It was saying goodbye to Mel.

It was knowing that the path he had chosen meant that he wasn't afforded the luxury of the love of a good woman, or the opportunity to see where something could go. As much as he wanted to stay, he knew that Mel was in danger as long as Dale Munroe was hunting for him. Sam had made the first move, and with the clock ticking on Jasper's confession, Sam was certain that Dale Munroe and the mysterious Mr Hudson wouldn't just wait for the final grain of sand to tumble through the hourglass.

They would hunt Sam.

So he needed to leave.

He had packed his meagre belongings into his sports bag the night before, and they were sitting on the small coffee table alongside his passport, his wallet and his Glock 17. He didn't have many bullets left, but he hadn't had to use it once since he blasted one through Dana Kovalenko's forehead.

He hadn't needed to.

With his phone fully charged, Sam slid it into his back pocket, and then slipped into his parka jacket. Although the garment was a little faded in colour, it was in fine condition and had been an absolute bargain from the local charity shop. As much as he had loved his bomber jacket, it wasn't highly practical against the harsh Scottish winter. He'd also purchased a woollen hat and some thick leather gloves.

The streets outside were still bathed in darkness beyond the few working streetlamps, and Sam stuffed his belongings into the pockets of his coat, lifted his bag from the table and stepped out of the apartment.

The morning was remarkably fresh, with the frost that covered every vehicle a testament to the dropping temperatures. Sam could see his own breath, and he slung the sports bag over his shoulder and made his way down the side streets of Glasgow, heading towards the heart of the city.

There would be no trains running to London for at least

an hour, and in the freezing cold temperature, he figured the chill would wake him up enough to find an early-opening coffee shop. Once he had found one, he could take a seat, enjoy the caffeine and then make a plan of action. As he turned onto one of the major high streets, he saw the parade of shops, and headed towards them, hoping one of the many chain coffee shops would be opening at six.

He pulled his phone from his back pocket.

Five minutes to.

He was happy to wait.

As he was about to pocket it once more, it suddenly came alive, the phone buzzing wildly in his hand before the screen lit up.

It was Martin.

Sam sighed. He liked Martin. He was a good man and was exceptionally good to his staff. When Mel had reached out to him to get Sam a job, he'd been more than accommodating. He told Sam that he believed in second chances, but that Sam himself didn't need one.

As far as Martin was concerned, Sam was a necessity for the people that the police and the government didn't care about anymore.

Martin, like Sam, was an early riser, and Sam knew that his boss would have already arrived at his office, and was looking for someone to cover an early shift. Sam knew he had somewhere else to be, but Martin had been good to him.

Better than most.

Sam's father, Major William Pope, was widely respected throughout his tenure in the army, working off the basic principle of if you can help someone, then you should.

Sam lifted the phone and took the call.

'Morning, Martin.'

'Sam.' Martin sounded agitated. *'Sorry to call so early.'*

'You always call this early. Everything okay?'

Martin hesitated, and Sam registered the uncomfortable silence.

'One of the boys has let me down this morning. Any chance you can cover for an hour or so until the rest of the lads get in?'

Beyond the door of the Starbucks, one of the morning shift employees waved to Sam and then began to unlock the door. It was six o'clock, and Sam knew the main shift started at eight. Martin usually had one of his team start at six, in case any tradesmen needed to beat the morning rush. It was a pretty smart business move, and Sam knew an hour out of his day wouldn't hurt.

Martin had been good to him, and if this was the last time he'd see the man, he'd like to help one last time.

'Sure. I'm just grabbing a coffee and then I'll be in. See you in twenty minutes or so.'

Martin hung up the phone without a goodbye, drawing a frown from Sam as he stared at his phone. Everyone was allowed a bad morning from time to time, but Martin was always polite and positive.

Sam stepped into the coffee shop, wondering what had caused Martin to be so curt. Moments later, he stepped back onto the high street, coffee in one hand and his sports bag in the other, ready to find out.

The gate to the haulage yard was open, and Sam crossed the threshold, scanning the forecourt and the entrance to the scrapyard itself, in the hope of finding his manager. Martin was nowhere to be found, and Sam took the final sip from his coffee and then headed towards the entrance to the office, his boots crunching against the gravel beneath. Martin's truck was in its usual spot, and Sam checked his watch as he stepped towards the door.

Eighteen minutes past.

He didn't feel too bad, as if any customers had arrived, Martin would have been more than capable of dealing with them. In fact, the early morning shifts usually consisted of the two of them sitting in the manager's office, with Martin repeating his takes on the state of the management of his beloved Glasgow Rangers Football Club. Like the city itself, the club had once been a giant of Europe, but had found itself facing increasingly harder times as the years went by. As a born and bred Glaswegian, Martin usually spoke about his club and his city with a passion that Sam envied.

Sam pushed open the door and stepped in and the Glock 17 shot out from the side and the barrel pressed against the side of his head.

'Nice and easy, sweetheart.'

The Cockney accent belonged to a gruff, muscular man, with a thick beard and a disposition that screamed ex-military. Sam slowly lifted his hands in the air, and his eyes darted towards the door to Martin's office, where two more men, clad in black, emerged, their gloved hands holding similar weapons that were trained on Sam's chest and skull.

There was no doubt in his mind that all three of them were aching for a reason to pull the trigger.

Sam stayed calm, refusing to give them one.

'You guys here for a fridge?' Sam joked. 'We got a few new ones in and…'

'Keep talking,' the man said, pressing the gun as hard as he could against Sam's skull. He pushed Sam away slightly and then motioned to Martin's office. 'In there.'

Sam nodded and obliged, walking between the two other men in the cramped office, their guns held steady and their aim undoubtedly deadly. Sam held his hands up again, and then he placed the empty coffee cup on the reception desk. Martin's door was still open, and he stepped through.

'Sam.'

Martin called out to him, his voice trembling with fear, as a combination of fearful sweat and horrified tears streamed down his face. Sitting behind his desk, Martin had both hands flat on the table and he was sitting upright. Behind him stood an immaculately dressed man, whose grey pinstripe suit looked as crisp as his neat haircut.

In his hand was a Desert Eagle, the metallic weapon shimmering under the light. It rested neatly in his hand, and the man kept his eyes locked on Sam as he tentatively stepped in.

'You okay, Martin?' Sam kept his eyes on the armed man.

'He's fine.' The recognisable voice cut in. 'It's a pleasure to finally meet you, Sam. You can call me Mr Hudson.'

'You're the guy on the phone.' Sam confirmed. 'Tell me, how much do you charge to protect a rapist?'

'Oh, I charge quite the fee. However, I don't see myself as protecting a rapist,' Hudson said eloquently. 'I see myself as a problem solver. Now the problem that I have been given to solve is that you have threatened the son and the business empire of my client—'

'Dale Munroe.'

'My client,' Hudson stated, with clear irritation. 'Now, he would like that threat to go away.'

'Whatever you want with me, this man here has nothing to do with it. He's a good man. He's got kids. Let him go and you and I can thrash this out.'

Hudson began to chuckle, the reaction catching Sam off guard and instantly making him uneasy.

'Oh, Mr Pope. You are impressive.' Hudson re-emphasised his grip. 'You actually have no regard for your own life.'

'Like I said, let him go.'

From outside the hut, the distant sound of sirens began to wail, echoing off the tall buildings of the Glasgow streets like a banshee howling into the night. Hudson raised his eyebrows.

'You hear that?' He held his other hand to his ear. 'That's the sound of a solution. You see, Mr Pope, I am a professional. I am also the best at what I do. My client is a very well-known figure in this nation and many others, and you being blasted half to hell a few days after threatening his son wouldn't be a good look, would it? Instead, you being arrested and being thrown into a deep, dark hole… now that's a much cleaner solution isn't it?'

'I don't know.' Sam shrugged. 'Seems less fun.'

'Well, as fun as it would be to dance with you, Mr Pope, like I said, I am a professional. If you try anything, I will put a bullet through this man's skull, and they will most certainly hold you accountable for it.'

The sirens grew louder, and the three men at the front of the office removed their black jackets to reveal the McGinn emblazoned polo shirts, usually worn by the crew. The flashing lights became visible, bursting through the shuttered blinds of the office as the police cars crunched onto the gravel.

'I'm sorry, Sam,' Martin slurred, shaking his head. Sam offered him a smile.

'You've got nothing to be sorry for.' He turned back to Hudson. 'You on the other hand. You will.'

'We'll see,' Hudson said, and then yelled to his men. 'As we rehearsed, guys.'

All three men dropped to the floor, their hands behind their heads. They had concealed their weapons behind the stand that housed the coffee machine, and by the time the police discovered them, Hudson and his men would be long gone. The police burst through the door, with yells of Sam's name roaring from their mouths. Hudson tucked his gun away and held his hands up, as the police burst through and immediately piled onto Sam, the two eager officers pinning him to the desk where Martin had been held hostage. Sam gritted his teeth as they roughly pulled his arms behind his back, slapping the handcuffs on him and confiscating the Glock tucked in the back of his jeans. As they hauled him back up, the detective made a show of reading him his rights, acting the tough guy as two officers stood on guard, their metal truncheons in their hands.

Sam shot a glance at Hudson, who kept his eyes locked on the situation. The police were already talking into their radios, describing Hudson as a customer, and his crew as part of the staff.

By the time the police had done any further checks, Sam knew all four men would be long gone. Martin watched in horror, offering Sam an apologetic nod, as he was roughly led back through the office, an officer gripping an arm each and two more following. The detective stayed behind to begin taking statements, and piece together how the biggest slice of luck had landed on his desk.

Sam Pope.

Arrested in Glasgow by a local detective.

While the headlines wrote themselves, the detective began to fall for the pack of lies Hudson was ready to deliver, as Sam was stuffed into the back of a police car, and moments later, was being driven to what he presumed would be the most heavily guarded jail cell they had.

CHAPTER SEVENTEEN

It didn't take too long for the police to wrap up their initial questions, with the young detective clearly keen to get back to the station and progress with what would likely be the biggest moment of his career. He questioned Martin vigorously as the proprietor of the business, but under the pressure of a watching Hudson, Martin lied admirably.

The story was simple.

Sam had burst into the office, having watched Martin open the door to his first customer and demanded a working vehicle. After being told they didn't have any that were ready to go, Sam had held the men at gunpoint until Martin had called in his team of mechanics, who were played ably by the mercenaries wearing Martin's branded polo shirts.

He felt sick as he had told each lie.

Not only because he knew he was under the threat of death if he didn't, but because he had betrayed Sam. The man may have come from a world that Martin would never understand, but the one thing he did know was a good person when he met one. For all the bodies he'd piled up and crimes he had committed, Sam Pope may have been the best man he had ever met.

Now, because of Martin's fear, he would likely spend the rest of his life in a concrete box.

After interrogating Martin, the detective turned to Hudson and the rest of the "staff" for corroboration, which they all effortlessly provided. The detective nodded and scribbled down a few more notes.

'That's all I need for now.' He offered them a smile. 'Well done on calling this in, boys. The mandate to get this man off the streets is getting bigger by the day, so you've done the world a big service. I'll send a team of officers later today just to have a look around and get a few more details.'

'Thank you, officer,' Hudson said with a firm nod.

'Stay safe, guys.' The detective turned and left with a spring in his step, and he bounded across the gravel to his car and pulled out of the courtyard. Hudson watched through the blinds, letting them snap shut as he pulled his fingers back.

'Well, that went well, didn't it?'

Hudson flashed his perfect smile to the room and frowned at the response. His crew were looking glumly at the ground, clearly disappointed they didn't get to satisfy their itchy trigger fingers. Martin was staring at the desk in disbelief. As far as Hudson was concerned, he had thought beyond the obvious. Dale Munroe was a passionate man, who had allowed the very real threat cloud his judgement and thus, hired more mercenaries to put Sam Pope in the ground. Not only would it have solved the impending problem for his son, it would have also given Dale Munroe the title of the man who got rid of Sam Pope.

But it would leave too many questions.

Too many possible roads back to him.

That's what he and the mercenaries failed to realise.

The biggest victories were often achieved with the most minimal of moves, and while everyone was preparing to move their next pawn forward, Hudson had already arranged his pieces across the board.

Sam Pope was in the hands of the police, who would no doubt ensure he was locked away. There was no bloodshed and therefore, no reason to look further. When they did return later for the names and addresses of those involved, Martin could very well tell them the truth, but by then, they'd be long gone.

Sam Pope would be removed from the equation, and Hudson would be able to return to his decadent life with a heavier bank account.

He was the consummate professional and took pride in it. As the depressing atmosphere began to drag the entire moment down, Hudson made his way through the office to the door.

'Right, let's make our way, shall we?'

The mercenaries grunted and obliged, the three of them marching out of the door in a row, and one of them lit a cigarette the moment he stepped through. Hudson wafted away the smoke and smell and then turned back to Martin, who had ventured into the reception area.

'You've made a mistake,' he said glumly.

'I don't make mistakes,' Hudson responded confidently.

'You might think you've done the right thing in getting Sam off the streets, but I guarantee you, whoever he was after deserved it.'

'Maybe so.' Hudson smiled. 'Yet, my services were employed by a man who deemed it a necessity. Now, I could have painted the walls of your office with the inside of his skull, but I find that a little tacky. See, now, he gets to live out the rest of his days in a concrete cell. But he gets to live. As do you.'

Martin shuffled uncomfortably.

'Is that it?' he asked, clearly still shaken.

'Do you know my name beyond what I gave you? Do you know where I came from, who employed me or where I'm going now?'

Martin shook his head.

'No. Not at all.'

'Then that's it. I see no reason to kill a man who is of little use to anyone. Oh, and Martin, let me make it perfectly clear. If you do try to deviate from the story when the police come back, I will kill you. But first, I will kill Jane, Jimmy and Drew and I will make you watch. Take care.'

Hudson stepped out of the office and disappeared from sight, as Martin felt the colour drain from his face. His knees buckled and he stumbled through to the customer toilet. Before he had even dropped to his knees, the vomit climbed his throat, and he just about managed to direct most of it into the toilet. The mere mention of his family's names had brought the seriousness of the entire situation into full view, and as he finished emptying the contents of his stomach, he felt the tears flooding down his cheeks.

He knew Sam wouldn't hold him responsible, nor would he judge him for putting his family first.

But as he collapsed back against the cubicle wall, Martin wiped away the tears and realised just how dangerous a world it was that Sam operated in.

And how important it was to have Sam Pope in it.

Sam didn't believe in no-win situations.

Over a decade ago, when he was still under the respected command of the late Sergeant Carl Marsden, it had been a point of contention between the two of them.

After his good friend, Paul Etheridge, had stumbled down a cliff face during a tour of Afghanistan, Sam had sprung into action. As Marsden tried to rally the troops to rescue the man, Sam had engaged in a firefight with the oncoming Taliban soldiers. Despite providing enough covering fire for them to pull Etheridge to safety, Sam had been chastised for looking for trouble.

For heading into a no-win situation.

Sam hadn't believed they were possible, and as he sat in the back of the police car, with the sirens wailing and offering the city of Glasgow a citywide wake up call, he began to wonder if he was wrong.

He'd been in similar situations before.

Over two and half years ago, as the police surrounded the abandoned High Rise where both General Wallace and Ahmad Farukh had been killed, Sam had known the jig was up. DI Amara Singh, whose life he had just saved, tried her best to get him to run, but to keep her career intact, he allowed her to arrest him. To march him out and hand him over to the authorities.

She had done so with a heavy heart, but Sam should have spent the rest of his life in a box. Instead, with a little help from Paul Etheridge, he had been transferred to Ashcroft Maximum Security Prison.

Better known as 'The Grid', the barbaric structure was built underground in the middle of the countryside and was on a strictly need-to-know basis. Within, the worst and most dangerous men were housed and while Sam knew it was probably where he belonged, he willingly went there to hunt down one of the most powerful men in the country.

Harry Chapman.

After slaying the crime boss and inciting a riot, Sam was able to escape to freedom.

But back then, he had Etheridge to help.

Had Amara Singh to ride to his rescue.

They were both gone now and Sam couldn't reach them even if he wanted to. Singh had seen her stock rise to the point where she was recruited to a covert police team, and Etheridge, after his hand in helping Sam escape custody, had joined him on the most-wanted list.

Etheridge was in the wind, and Sam was saddened at the fact that he hadn't heard from the man since he had left him at the airport two and half years ago. Generously, he had left Sam a small fortune to fund his war on crime, but it paled in comparison to what having Etheridge around offered him.

Beyond his incomparable computer skills, the man offered Sam genuine friendship.

And as he sat in the back of the police car as it whipped through the Glaswegian streets, he began to believe that there was such a thing as a no-win situation after all. The two officers were deathly quiet, clearly understanding the gravity of the prisoner they held in the back of their car. The driver was considerably older than his partner, who looked like he was fresh out of the academy. They controlled themselves differently, with the veteran keeping his steely gaze on the road ahead, while the younger officer kept anxiously looking around or tapping his hand on his thigh.

Sam sighed and looked out of the window, drawing the attention of the younger officer.

'Feeling pretty shit, eh?' he heckled, drawing an elbow from the driver.

'Keep it quiet, Ricky.'

'What? It's not every day you have the most dangerous man in your car.' He turned and looked at Sam. 'Not so dangerous now, are ya lad?'

'Take the cuffs off and find out if you like?'

'Leave it,' the driver said, cutting in with his thick Scottish voice before the younger officer could react. The warning fell on deaf ears.

'For a man who apparently fights for justice, it's a shame to see you knocking off a local business.' The young officer turned to Sam and shook his head. 'I guess you're just full of shit like the rest of them.'

'What do you think was going on back there?' Sam asked, his hands cuffed behind his back. 'Do you honestly think I need to hold innocent people at gunpoint to steal a car?'

'Stop talking,' the driver spat to both men.

'Well, it ain't looking good for you, buddy. Considering all the other shit you've been up to, I'd say you're pretty fucked.'

'That man who was pretending to be a customer, he is a hired killer, paid for by Dale Munroe to try to take me out.'

'Dale Munroe?' The young officer shrugged. 'Oh yeah, that's right. You threatened his son, didn't you?'

'I did. Do you know why? Because I spoke to the girl who he raped. She told me how he beat her and forced her to do things that will live with her for the rest of her life, while Jasper Munroe will walk free because the justice system you guys represent allowed him to.'

The older officer shuffled in discomfort, and the younger one frowned.

'Don't tarnish us Scots with the shit your police do. They've been searching for you for years and then like that' – he clicked his fingers – 'we got you.'

'You're either blind or an idiot. Or both,' Sam said as he sat back in his chair. 'That man wasn't a customer. Those men didn't work there and when you hand me over to whatever authority, they're going to keep me from Jasper Munroe. So, well done. You just let a serial rapist of young women loose on the streets. Excellent police work.'

'Enough!' the driver yelled, and the young officer started in his seat. Sam turned and looked out of the window, watching as the beautiful city of Glasgow slowly brought itself awake. More cars were beginning to appear on the roads, and the streets were littered with joggers, all pushing themselves through the cold in their high-vis clothing. The two police cars ahead of them turned right at the lights, but the driver didn't follow and carried on. His younger passenger looked at the cars disappearing from view before turning back to his partner in confusion.

'Station's that way.'

'We're not going to the station.'

Sam's ears pricked up, and the driver shot him a glance in the mirror. Sam frowned in confusion.

'Orders were to escort him back to the station immediately.'

'Do you honestly think they want the most wanted man in the country sitting in such an easily accessible place?' The man shot Sam another glance. 'He escaped once. Not again.'

The young officer turned with a cocky smirk on his face.

'Shit morning for you, eh?'

'Shit company can do that.'

As the police car veered off at the next left turning, Sam kept his eyes on the street signs to try to piece together where they were going. As the urban jungle of Glasgow soon gave way to more trees and fields, he realised wherever they were going wasn't for the public eye. And by the way the driver kept shooting him glances in the rear-view mirror, Sam had a bad feeling that whatever was really going on wasn't for the public eye either.

As they sped away from the city of Glasgow, Sam was beginning to realise what a no-win situation truly felt like.

CHAPTER EIGHTEEN

After driving for over half an hour, Sam could see the younger officer starting to get agitated. Shuffling in his seat and uncomfortably tapping the dashboard, the young man kept looking to the driver for more information.

There was none forthcoming.

As they sped through country lanes, whizzing by fields and dead trees, Sam began to contemplate the reality of the situation.

It was clear that something was amiss.

Whatever the explanation the older officer had given, it certainly didn't seem like his partner was clued in. Which meant one of two things. Either they were heading to a location so remote only a few knew of it, or the driver had an entirely different motivation.

Sam had made a lot of enemies over the years, and it wasn't lost on him how many of those enemies had links to the police. He'd been waging war on organised crime for over three and a half years, and along the way, he had seen how many criminal organisations had filtered into the police service like a plague. The idea of a corrupt officer was something that turned Sam's stomach, but his good friend, Adrian Pearce had managed to shed a little light on it. Pearce had been a detective for nearly thirty years, over half of which were spent working for the Department of Professional Standards for the Metropolitan Police.

The DPS.

Effectively, he investigated his own police officers, and the tactics used within investigations to ensure they were on the right side of the law. Sam saw corruption as incredibly black and white.

You were either on the right side or the wrong side of justice. Wearing a badge should have been akin to pinning your colours to the mass, but Pearce knew there were other shades to the thin blue line.

Some officers were, in fact, criminals. Happy to take a backhander, or were on the payroll of a crime boss. Others were desperate, reaching to cover expenses greater than the moderate police salary.

Others were blackmailed.

Sam only had to think about Jack Townsend, the undercover police officer who had saved his life from a burning building to know that the path taken by a copper could be a long and winding one. Townsend had been a devoted family man, but due to his upbringing and his profile, he was sent undercover into a gang in his local Liverpool. From there, his handler, Inspector Reece Sanders, had cut a deal with Slaven Kovac, and in a pathetic attempt to garner leverage with his new employer, Sanders thrust Townsend further into the firing line. For two years, Townsend had been part of Kovac's gang, walking a tightrope that very nearly got him killed.

All because of the selfish actions of others.

Which meant that whatever was racing through the driver's mind as he turned onto another desolate road, Sam knew that there was likely a long and arduous road for him to get there.

Eventually, the palpable tension in the car reached its boiling point.

'Right. Where the fuck are we going?' the young officer asked.

'I said be quiet.'

'I'm radioing in…' As the younger officer reached for his radio, the driver's hand swung up and snatched it from his jacket. 'What the fuck?'

'Don't make me do something I will regret.'

The warning was laced in certainty, and for the first time since they'd sat in the car, Sam saw a little fear in the younger officer's eyes. It wasn't uncommon for younger, greener officers to have a more hopeful outlook on the work they do, nor was it a surprise to see the young man carry himself with an unearned swagger.

Sam had seen it before.

Before his entire one-man war on crime had started, he had worked in the archive office at Scotland Yard, where he was privy to a multitude of officers, all of whom had varying levels of experience. The newbies often acted like the 'cock of the walk', arms out and chests puffed, as if they were the first officer to ever be given a badge and a stab-proof vest. Over time, that exuberance was replaced with apathy, and the realisation that no matter how hard you worked, or how many hours you put in, the world was still a cesspool and would continue to rotate as it did the day before.

Officers like the driver were what such a career produced, with the relentless exposure to the dregs of society ebbing away at the hope and happiness.

Sam knew it then, and he knew it when the driver pulled the car into a train station car park.

The driver had reached his tipping point.

There were no other cars parked, and the train that

ran once an hour was unlikely to pick anyone up from the platform.

They were in the middle of nowhere, a good forty-five minutes from Glasgow and Sam found himself cuffed in the back of the car.

'Out.' The driver demanded of the younger officer, who looked just as scared as Sam felt.

'What the hell are you doing?'

'I said get out.'

The driver pushed open the door and stepped out, the bitter cold immediately latching onto him and trying its best to snake beneath his clothing. The younger officer shook his head in disbelief and then did as he was told. Sam watched as the two of them met at the front of the car, the younger one remonstrating dramatically as the driver kept his arms folded.

Whatever they were discussing, Sam knew he was the subject, and the driver turned and walked back to the driver's door of the car, threw it open and leant in, in mid-discussion.

'I left it in here…'

He wasn't talking to Sam, but he then flashed Sam a look, and with his hand concealed under his body as he leant into the vehicle, he tossed something between the seats and onto Sam's lap.

It was the handcuff key.

Sam looked down at it, then back up at the officer, who had already stepped back from the car, waving the radio to the younger officer, who quickly snatched back his equipment. Quickly, he jostled until the key fell between his legs and he then lifted himself in the chair, allowing the key to slide down the seat until he could reach it with his cuffed hands.

Confusion was flooding through his mind, but Sam had been trained his entire life to act on a second's notice, and as he gritted his teeth, he managed to twist his wrists enough to jam the key in the lock and turn it.

He was free.

Sam swiftly drew his hands round to his front and stretched out the aching in his shoulder. The position had been uncomfortable since his arrest, and the stab and bullet wounds he had suffered over the years didn't help. He rubbed the tenderness from his wrists and then glanced ahead.

The two officers were deep in conversation, with the older one clearly explaining something to his younger colleague. With his back to the car, the younger officer didn't notice Sam silently climb through to the front of the vehicle into the passenger seat, where the young man had left the door open. The bitter cold nipped at Sam as he stepped out of the car. Like a coiled snake pouncing, Sam drove forward onto his foot and wrapped his muscular arms around the young man's neck. Instantly, the officer began to struggle, but Sam hooked one of the man's arms and locked him in place, his other slowly cutting off the man's air supply.

After a few moments, the man faded and dropped to his knees, and then seconds later he was unconscious. With extra care, Sam lowered the young man onto the ground and then turned to the older officer with his eyebrow arched.

'Explain.'

The still conscious copper shuffled past Sam and quickly checked his partner's pulse. Once he found it, he nodded, removed the young man's radio and his own and dropped them on the ground.

'Name's Hugh. Hugh Boyd,' he said with a sigh. 'You know, I've been doing this for over twenty years.'

Boyd lifted his boot and then stomped as hard as he

could on the radios, smashing them to pieces. Sam stood stoically, trying his best to figure out the officer's motives.

'Hell of a career,' Sam eventually offered. 'So why do this?'

'Because, Sam, I have a teenage daughter.' Boyd shook his head in disgust. 'You spend your whole life trying to make this place a bit safer, you know? Every day, you're out on the streets, doing whatever you can to leave this world in a better place for your kids. But how can you do that when some people are above it all?'

Sam stood, his fists clenched. He let the man continue his clear battle with his conscience.

'My daughter is seventeen in a few weeks. Seventeen. And the thought of someone doing something to her fills me with dread. So while I know you should be behind bars, Sam, I keep thinking about the poor girls that this Jasper Munroe has raped.'

'They're broken,' Sam said coldly. 'The girl I spoke to, her name is Hayley Baker. She's a strong kid, but what he did to her will live with her forever.'

The officer drew his lips into a thin line of frustration and then he took a deep breath.

'Then go and fucking nail the bastard.' Boyd turned to Sam with his inner turmoil painted across his face. He reached into his pocket and tossed him the keys to the car. 'You've probably got about thirty minutes till they start tracking us.'

'Thank you.'

'Let's just be clear. I think you should be locked up for the things you've done. But if you're the only one who can get justice for that girl, then you're better off on the streets.' Boyd took a deep breath. 'Now, punch me in the face.'

'Excuse me?' Sam startled.

'It needs to look like you jumped us and smashed our radios. They'll ask questions if I'm unharmed so…'

Sam swung his right hand, cracking the officer flush on the jaw and sending him spiralling to his knees. Boyd caught himself before he collided with the ground and he leant over, his palms pressed on the ground as he struggled to control his desire to retaliate. Sam shook his hand off.

'You good?'

Boyd lifted his hand and gave Sam a middle finger, drawing a smile from him. With blood trickling from Boyd's lip and his younger partner still out cold, Sam dropped into the driver's seat, brought the engine to life, and within minutes, he was rushing back to Glasgow.

'I'm so sorry, Mel.'

Martin was slumped in one of the chairs of the Carnival bar, his forearms resting on the table and his eyes red with tears. Mel sipped her tea and allowed herself a few moments to absorb what she'd just heard. She knew Sam's life was one full of peril, and she hadn't slept at all the night before due to the pounding ache of her broken heart. That and the adrenaline and fear that had been elicited from her meeting with Mr Hudson. Coming face to face with such a terrifying man put into perspective just how dangerous Sam's world was, and that being a part of it was putting herself and Cassie at risk.

Sam had seen that and was walking away for their own good, despite the heartache.

Cassie had been distraught after Hudson's threat with the boiling water, and after a few hours of consoling, she eventually fell asleep next to her mum. Mel hadn't the heart to tell her that Sam wasn't coming back.

Sam's leaving would devastate her just as much, especially as her useless father was the furthest thing from a role model.

Sam had proven to be a stabilising influence in her daughter's life, and Mel dreaded the idea of her losing that.

Foolishly, she had tricked herself into believing that once Sam had finished his fight, he'd stride back in like a knight in shining armour, ready to whisk her off her feet and they could move on and be happy together.

He'd told her that he didn't miss the life, and it was only because of his love for Mel and Cassie that he decided to look into the Munroe story with any real interest.

But now he was gone.

Locked away in a prison cell somewhere and unlikely to ever see the free world again.

It made her lip tremble and her heart shiver, but she took a breath, composed herself, and then reached out a hand and placed it on Martin's shoulder.

'It's not your fault, Martin. That same man came here last night.'

'What?' Martin's eyes widened with horror. 'Are you okay?'

'I'm fine. Nothing happened, although he did threaten to pour boiling water over Cassie.'

Martin shuddered.

'I tell you what, Mel. I've met some nasty people in my time. The number of ex-cons who've passed through the haulage yard over the years. You wouldn't believe some of the shit they've done. But this Hudson fella? He's on another level.'

'I know.' Mel took the seat opposite. 'He's terrifying. Told me he'd kill Cassie as slowly as possible and make me watch.'

'The bastard. Threatened my family, too.'

'Look, you didn't do anything wrong. Sam is a good

man, but we both knew who he was and what he'd done. At some point, if you keep looking for trouble, eventually, you'll find it.' Mel reached out and held Martin's hand. 'This isn't on you?'

'But I called him in—'

'Because the man had a gun to your head. Because he threatened your family.'

'Aye. You're right.' The two of them sitting in silence at the table, sipping their warm tea. The bar wasn't open for business, and the rest of the tables were topped with overturned chairs. As he finished his tea, Martin let out a satisfied sigh. 'I best be getting on.'

'Look, Martin. If you ever need to talk…'

'Thanks, Mel.' He stood and pulled his hat over his head. 'You, too. I know you really cared about him.'

The straw finally landed on the camel's back, and Mel felt her tears flood forward. Martin stepped towards her and wrapped his arms around her, and she buried her head in his burly frame. The devastation of losing Sam, not just from hers and Cassie's life, but knowing that he'd been marched out of Martin's office in cuffs flooded over her and she couldn't stem the wave of sadness. As she finally let her heartbreak consume her and accepted the kindness of her friend, she didn't know that through the door and sat on the stairs was Cassie, battling through her own tears as she discovered that Sam had gone.

CHAPTER NINETEEN

Commissioner Bruce McEwen knew what he was getting into when he took the top job in the Metropolitan Police Service, but it was laid out in no uncertain terms by his predecessor, Michael Stout at their final meeting.

'Prepare yourself for a myriad of shit.'

McEwen had laughed it off at the time, knowing that Stout had been in the hot seat when the focus on the police's inability to both catch Sam Pope and deliver the same amount of justice as the vigilante was at an all-time high. Stout had been looking to retire and promote Deputy Commissioner Ruth Ashton into his seat, but her behaviour around the attempted terrorist attack at University College Hospital London in Euston, and her supposed links to the disgraced General Ervin Wallace, had made her position untenable. With her forced removal from the Met, Stout had agreed to stay on until a new successor could be found.

McEwen fit the bill, and his extensive experience and involvement in famous operations, such as Operation Pear Tree made him a widely respected candidate.

With so many years of experience to draw upon,

McEwen truly believed he would be able to facilitate change within the Met, along with helping to rebuild London as a safe haven for its inhabitants and thriving businesses. The disconnect between the public and the police needed to be fixed, and with Sam Pope dead, the spectre of his supposed "good deeds" would no longer be an issue.

But Stout had been right.

Inexplicably, Sam Pope returned from the dead, nearly two years after he had been identified as the body of a man found in the smouldering remains of a dilapidated warehouse in South Carolina. The most wanted man in the country had returned to his city and had unleashed his own brand of violent justice against the criminal underworld.

What was worse was that public opinion was in his favour. People believed that the likes of Daniel Bowker and Slaven Kovac, men believed to have been murdered by Sam, were better off dead.

To the working-class public, a man like Sam Pope was a guardian angel, fighting the good fight for the people who didn't have the means to.

He was the voice of the voiceless, yet he let his actions speak for him.

To them, he was a hero.

To the rich and powerful, and those especially with something to hide, he was a menace.

Which is why, with the taste of sick building at the back of his throat, he had agreed to a meeting with Dale Munroe. The billionaire was one of the most powerful men in the country, and as part of the public image he had cultivated, he was a keen supporter of the police and had been instrumental in a number of their outreach programmes and initiatives. The man had donated millions to the cause, all of it as a tax writeoff, but McEwen knew the game the man was playing.

It had given Munroe a direct line to him, and while McEwen was keen to re-emphasise their roles in life, there was no doubting in both men's minds who was answering to who.

If Dale Munroe wanted a meeting with the Commissioner of the Metropolitan Police, it was a request that was granted.

It sickened McEwen to his very core, but like Stout had warned, there was a lot of shit that came with being the most powerful man in the Met, and he knew he had to humour Dale.

Sam Pope had been apprehended less than an hour ago in McEwen's hometown of Glasgow, and coincidentally, within minutes of it happening, Dale Munroe requested an audience.

McEwen didn't need his decades of police experience to connect those dots.

He stood, his tall frame clad in his pristine police tunic, with his medals and lapels pinned proudly to it. He walked across the spacious office in the New Scotland Yard building and stood in front of the mirror. As he was adjusting his tie, the door opened, and in walked McEwen's secretary, followed closely by a smiling Dale Munroe. McEwen turned and forced a smile.

'Mr Munroe.'

'Commissioner.'

The two shared a firm handshake, both of them trying to convey a sense of control. McEwen showed Dale to the seat opposite his desk.

'Please sit.'

As Dale obliged, McEwen rounded his desk and lowered himself into his own leather chair. Thoughtfully, he placed the tips of his fingers together and regarded the bullish billionaire carefully.

'So, what's the plan?'

'The plan?' Commissioner McEwen raised his eyebrows. 'I assume you mean what will happen to Sam Pope?'

'Well, I wasn't asking about your Christmas party, was I?'

McEwen ignored the antagonisation. He wouldn't rise to it.

'He will be held in a secure location in Glasgow until he can be transferred back under the control of the Metropolitan Police. He'll be tried, he'll be sentenced, and then he will spend the rest of his life in prison.' McEwen held his hands up. 'Simple.'

Dale Munroe leant forward; his eyebrows furrowed. He adjusted his expensive suit and then spoke.

'Considering he escaped from police custody, not once, but twice, you can understand my lack of confidence in your ability to make that happen.'

'I think your lack of confidence is your own business. As Commissioner of the Met Police, I don't have to assure you of anything.'

McEwen cleared his throat and lifted his chin, trying to assert his authority. Dale smirked.

'Come on now, Bruce.'

'Commissioner.'

'Bruce.' Dale's tone shifted, and he scowled. 'It took me one day to have Sam Pope delivered to you on a fucking platter. I need assurances that he won't be able to move, let alone escape.'

'I don't know what you're implying—'

'Surely, you have enough sway to know people who know people who handle things like this in prison.' Dale's eyes glistened with excitement. 'Otherwise, I do know people who can organise such a thing. But if I have to make that phone call myself, Bruce, then I will make it very clear that you didn't want to cooperate, and as you know, I have some very capable people solving my problems.'

'Are you threatening me?' McEwen stood, his tall, spindly frame towering over Dale who remained relaxed in his chair.

'I wouldn't say threatening.' He smirked. 'Informing you.'

Before McEwen could respond, his phone rang. He kept his eyes locked on the imposing glare of Dale Munroe and lifted the receiver.

'McEwen.' Very quickly, his bravado faded, and his eyebrows lifted in shock. 'You're kidding me? Get them on the phone right now.'

McEwen slammed the receiver down and massaged the bridge of his nose with frustration. Dale sat back in his chair and itched his chin.

'Everything okay, Bruce?'

'He's gone.'

'Excuse me?' Dale sat forward.

'Pope. He assaulted the arresting officers and escaped.' McEwen sighed and shook his head. 'I need you to back off, Dale. Do you understand me?'

Without responding, Dale Munroe stood, buttoned his blazer and nodded a goodbye to the commissioner. He stomped across the office and threw the door open, but before he stepped through, he turned back to the desperate man for the last word.

'Like I said, I have capable people solving my problems. And I need you to understand that.'

The door slammed shut behind him, and McEwen dropped into his seat. The phone began to ring, and he slammed his fist against the desk in frustration before recomposing himself, lifting the receiver and trying to wrestle control of a situation that was spiralling out of his usually authoritative control.

Sam had dumped the police car the second the call over the radio came out. With Sam's arrest the hottest topic on the channel, panic had begun to spread across the Glasgow Police Service when he hadn't been delivered. Officer Boyd had obviously done his best to keep them at bay, but he was right.

They were now searching for him.

As soon as the call came through that they'd traced his car to the outside of the city, Sam pulled over and left it for them to find. He popped the boot and took out his sports bag which they'd confiscated, and then made his way as quickly as he could through the city, keeping to the back-streets and then once he approached the centre, he disappeared among the sea of people who were flooding the streets to begin their Christmas shopping. The festive season hadn't been something he had even entertained since his son had died, and the memories of Jamie excitedly exclaiming that Santa had been, were beginning to fade.

Time heals all wounds, but it does so by erasing the memories associated with them.

Every shop window promised an avalanche of lights and decoration, with many displaying posters for their incredible Christmas discounts. Eventually, he made his way through the town centre, where the open shops were eagerly awaiting the deluge of Christmas shoppers. Sam knew that the longer he stayed visible, the more likely he would be spotted.

He ducked into a coffee shop, smiling a greeting to the young man behind the till.

'Busy morning?' the barista asked, his fluffy beard telling Sam he was barely into his twenties.

'You wouldn't believe.' Sam shrugged. He ordered his coffee and took a seat in the far corner, keeping himself out of sight of the high street beyond the window. The internet café was a few streets away, but Sam doubted it was likely to open exactly at nine, so he drank his coffee at a leisurely pace and contemplated his next move.

He needed one.

There were few absolutes in life, beyond death and taxes, but one of them was that men like Dale Munroe refuse to fail. Once word spread that Sam had escaped custody, there was no doubt in Sam's mind that the enraged billionaire would throw more money at the problem. The man known as Mr Hudson had tried to do things as peacefully as possible, with no bloodshed. If he had taken Sam off the streets without a hint of Munroe's intervention, then the trail would end with Sam himself.

But Dale wouldn't accept that.

There was still one more day until Jasper needed to make his confession, and with that hanging over them both, the senior Munroe would respond.

There would be bloodshed.

There was a chance that Mel or Cassie would be in danger.

The only shot Sam had at bringing this whole episode to a close was to strike first. Make himself a bigger problem to Dale and follow through on the promise he made.

Jasper Munroe would be held accountable for his crimes.

But now, so would Dale.

As the morning rush hour began to calm, Sam thanked the barista, dropped some change in the tip jar, and left the premises. He turned and walked through the hordes of shoppers, passing numerous high street brands and eateries until he reached the internet café. As he stepped through, the same girl he'd spoken to a few days ago greeted him with a pearly white grin and a twinkle in her eye.

'Morning, you,' she said, bordering on flirtation.

'Morning,' Sam replied gruffly, setting the tone. 'I just need ten minutes…'

The young girl nodded, handed Sam the password to the same computer he had used before, and then brought her finger playfully to her lips.

'On the house. But don't tell anyone.'

'Thank you.'

Sam nodded to her and then rushed to the computer. He accessed the computer and then pulled up the search engine.

Sure Fire Inc.

Pages of articles flooded the screen, and after scanning the title of a number of them, he refined his search and scolded himself for not doing it sooner. He picked up a sheet of paper from the desk and wrote down the address he needed.

Then, he booked a train ticket.

He took a deep breath.

Considering the vast resources the Munroe family had, and that Dale Munroe had already flexed, Sam knew there was no going back from this.

Once he did what he was about to do, then it could only end in one way.

With a thankful nod to the woman behind the counter, Sam headed for the door, already plotting his route to the train station via another shot of caffeine.

He was about to go to war.

CHAPTER TWENTY

Dale Munroe stood in his private hangar, which was on the far end of Gatwick Airport's North Terminal. He had acquired it, along with the jet, for a substantial amount of money. The status it commanded was worth the investment alone, but he had found being able to charter a luxury flight to any of his overseas properties at the snap of his fingers was one of the greatest perks of his wealth.

There was nowhere he couldn't go.

Nowhere was out of reach.

The bitter, winter morning had already soured when he'd spoken to Commissioner McEwen and the revelation that Sam Pope had been able to escape custody in Glasgow had unlocked the part of Dale's mind that had made him such a ruthless business mogul to begin with.

The sheer refusal of failure.

When he had built Sure Fire Inc., he had seen opportunities to not only bully his way into a market that was just beginning to prosper, but a way to completely monopolise it. As harsh as it was, the majority of the start-up companies that were providing network solutions were usually under the control of tech wizards or university graduates with more academic knowledge than business savvy.

As soon as he became the gravy train, they would sell to him for what they would assume was a small fortune, not realising that he was creating a business worth millions more.

For those who were willing, he paid a fair price.

For those who resisted, he crushed.

There was no compromise in the mind of Dale Munroe, and it was how he'd lived his life since he'd failed at school and was forced to make ends meet through jobs he saw as beneath him. It was why he was so bloodthirsty when it came to the boardroom, and why his reputation in the press as a billionaire was one of terrifying power. His PR team had tried to offset that with multiple charity creations and philanthropic endeavours, but the cold truth was, if Dale Munroe needed or wanted something, there was nothing and no one who could stop him.

Not the Commissioner of the Met.

Not Sam Pope.

No one.

The fight had originally been to keep his son out of prison, more so for the good of his company as opposed to his own flesh and blood's safety. As far as he was concerned, Jasper was a disappointment, and was unfit and, more importantly, undeserving of his respect. He loved Jasper; he was his only child. But the young man's life choices and continuous bad behaviour had eroded any chance for them to have a relationship.

Dale Munroe had a standard of excellence, and his son was nowhere near it.

But it still didn't give Sam Pope the right to question his authority. By refusing to back down from his threat to Jasper, Sam had effectively called Dale's bluff, and now, action needed to be taken. Hudson was the best there was, and Dale always appreciated the man's careful plotting. He had posted Hudson in the direction of over ten people over the years, and Hudson had worked tirelessly to ensure their deaths were never traced back to the Munroe name.

Hudson had tried it his way.

Now it was time for Dale's.

He watched with a weird sense of pride as his jet cut through the clouds and fog of the murky day, and approached the runway, the wheels popping out from beneath and squealing wildly as they touched down. The pilot and cabin crew were some of the best in the business, and Dale ensured they were healthily compensated for being at his beck and call and turning a blind eye.

As the jet slowly rolled into the hangar and came to a stop, Munroe gave a small clap of appreciation.

The best money could buy.

After a few moments, the door to the jet opened and then lowered to the ground, offering the passengers a safe exit from the plane down the steps. As one of the beautiful cabin crew motioned to the door, Hudson stepped through, buttoning his crisp suit and then he stopped as he saw Munroe. The man was too calm to show any element of surprise, but Munroe knew the man was confused by the welcoming party. Descending the steps, Hudson approached Dale with his back straight and his chin up.

'Mr Munroe. To what do I owe the pleasure?'

'Nice flight?'

'As always, your jet is exemplary.' Hudson turned and motioned to it with his hand. 'Yet, I hardly believe you have taken the effort to come here for my review of your private jet.'

'It didn't work,' Munroe said, his fist clenched.

'Excuse me?'

Before Hudson could react, Dale reached out and grabbed him by the lapel of his suit and shunted him back a few steps. The mercenaries who were exiting the plane gasped.

Dale instantly knew it was a bad idea and let go.

'I'm sorry,' Dale eventually spat, hating the idea of an apology.

'Mr Munroe, I appreciate this is an emotional time for you' – Hudson straightened his suit and stared at his employer – 'but my fee does not include abuse. Remember that the next time you lay a finger on me, as I will be forced to react.'

The two men stared at each other for a few moments, and Dale tried to maintain eye contact. Hudson's stare was mesmerising, with his body motionless and his fear absent. Eventually, to save face, Dale ran a hand through his hair and turned away.

'He escaped. Pope fucking escaped.'

'Impossible.'

'Oh, it's very fucking possible. I was lucky enough to be with the commissioner when he got the good news.'

'But he was unarmed, with multiple police cars—'

'Yeah, well, what can I tell you? The guy's pretty good.' Dale shrugged and then pointed his finger at Hudson. '*You* told me you would handle it. Now, I'm assuming, at some point in time, you had the man in front of you.'

'I did.'

'Then you should have put a bullet through his fucking skull.'

Dale's anger boiled to the surface once more, and he pressed his finger viciously into Hudson's forehead. Instinctively, Hudson snatched the man's wrist, twisted it maniacally, and rendered the man to his knees on the floor. Dale howled in pain, and Hudson held the grip expertly, bending the tendons and bone just a few centimetres from breaking point.

'I did warn you, Mr Munroe.'

'Fuck. I'm sorry. I'm sorry.'

Hudson relinquished his grip. Dale dropped back onto his haunches and rubbed his wrist, looking up at Hudson in submission.

'For that outburst, my fee has now doubled. I appreciate, I have yet to solve the problem you hired me for, so I will of course ensure a resolution as soon as possible.'

Dale struggled to his feet, his wrist red and aching.

'I need you to finish this. Okay? Situations getting out of hand is not something I am comfortable with, especially when—'

'They are to do with your son?' Hudson offered.

'When they could be public.'

'I understand.'

'I just need this done. Money is no object. Resources are not a problem. You…' Munroe pointed to the mercenaries. 'Make a list of whatever weapons you need. I just want this taken care of.'

The three men behind Hudson smiled with excitement, and Hudson nodded.

'Understood.'

Dale took a few steps towards Hudson, who didn't flinch at all. He'd already asserted his dominance of the situation, and the tentative steps Dale took were evidence that he knew it too.

'Don't let me down, Hudson.'

Hudson flashed his immaculate smile.

'When have I ever?'

The temperature dropped to minus degrees that evening, and Sam was a little disappointed that the same bone-chilling weather wasn't just exclusive to north of the border. As the train had pulled into Birmingham New

Street Station, he had disembarked and then made his way to the town centre.

It was a long time since he'd been to Birmingham, and he was impressed with the level of investment the 'second city' had received since then. Gone was the dreary collection of shops now replaced with a buzzing city centre, complete with the usual shopping centres and activity establishments, along with a parade of bars and clubs to usher a night scene. With multiple universities nearby, he was in no doubt that a Friday night in the centre of Birmingham was a hive of activity.

Which meant the police would be on high alert.

Sam spent the day hiding in plain sight, even taking a walk through the Botanical Garden, which was still open despite the inclement weather. With the sun missing in action, the display wasn't as impressive as he would have hoped, and when the darkness of another freezing December night descended upon the city, Sam found a quiet, family-run restaurant on the outskirts of town for dinner.

He was the only customer during his visit, and while the owners didn't speak a lot of English, they continuously shot him confused looks from the bar.

They knew who he was.

But as he was starting to realise, a lot of people were okay with that.

It was a strange feeling. Throughout his war on organised crime, Sam had never felt like he was in the wrong. He understood that he'd broken the law, and when he was standing in front of a judge, he himself had accepted that his actions came at a cost. To himself, he felt justified.

He didn't realise that so many of the public felt the same.

As the first groups of students and friends began to spring up around town, the entire atmosphere changed, and despite the British weather, many were dressed to impress. Sam had stopped in one of the shops within the town centre, which specialised in outdoor wear, and he had purchased a few items.

A sweatshirt, cargo trousers, boots, woollen hat and leather gloves. All of them jet black.

He also bought a black rucksack, and while he believed he looked like someone who was up to no good, the young cashier simply smiled and accepted payment. A student just working for a little extra pocket money probably wasn't too fussed what their customers were buying.

Sam found a public toilet and changed into his new clothes. He stuffed his into his sports bag, along with the those he didn't need anymore, and he handed it to a homeless man who was shivering on the street. The man gratefully accepted the gift, and Sam made his way towards the outskirts of the town, his new rucksack pulled tight.

It contained his Glock 17, the lighter fluid matches and some binoculars.

Sam travelled light, and the last thing he needed was a big sports bag weighing him down. He wasn't extravagant with his spending but donating a few sets of clothes was hardly splashing the cash.

With his head down against the cold, protected by the thick wool of his new hat, Sam made his way across the city, until he arrived at the final bus stop before the country roads. Nobody was waiting for the bus, and he checked the electronic notice board.

Three minutes until the next bus arrived.

By the time it did, Sam was thankful as the bitter coldness in the air had risen, and the cold gnawed away at him like a forgotten password. It was a sixteen-mile bus journey to Dudley, and Sam took his seat and looked out at the vast darkness of the surrounding woodland as the bus trundled down the M6. By the time he got to Dudley, it was nearly ten, and Sam located the local taxi rank. Unsurprisingly, the footfall was non-existent, and the owner was more than happy for Sam's business, asking no questions as Sam asked to be taken to the industrial estate not far from Tipton. Presumably, the driver pegged Sam as a security guard arriving for a shift and he helpfully dropped Sam near the closest entrance to Sure Fire Inc's data centre. Sam paid the man and then, once the car had gone, he made his way into the darkness of the treeline that surrounded the building. Sam rounded the building, sticking close to the shadows until he was directly in front of the entranceway. Ignoring the cold, he dropped to one knee, rummaged into his rucksack, and pulled out his binoculars.

Scanning a perimeter and a location was second nature to Sam, and peering through the scope sent his mind flashing back to the countless missions he had completed behind his sniper rifle.

His connection to the weapon, and how, in his hands, it was more than just a gun.

It was a guarantee.

Sam wasn't there to kill anyone. In fact, he sat and watched for over two hours, mentally clocking the faces and the times of the security guards as they made their half hourly trip outside the building to secure it.

There were three guards.

None of them seemed particularly well-built or interested in the work, and Sam knew he would face little to no resistance if he was spotted. His only concern was that one of them would try to play the hero, and he couldn't allow his one shot to deal Dale Munroe a hammer blow to fail because of an enthusiastic tough guy. Sam sat and waited for the next check, and right on the minute, another guard came out of the main entrance, scanned the area with a torch, and then made his way around the building to the side entrance. On his way, he placed his security fob against a reader built into the wall, to electronically clock that the checkpoint had been completed.

Sam kept low to the ground as close to the shadows as possible, as he scurried across the tarmac, closing in on the security guard. The young man beeped his card and pulled open the door, just as he heard the footsteps directly behind him.

It was too late.

Sam wrapped his arms around the man's neck from behind and tightened his grip, his powerful muscles locking around the guard like a boa constrictor. As the guard fought for air and consciousness, Sam wedged his foot in the door, keeping it open as the man in his arms began to fade. As the body went limp, Sam lowered him gently to the ground and reassuringly found the man's pulse.

He took the man's security pass and stepped into the building. The data centre was one of the most nondescript buildings Sam had ever seen, and all it was, was rows upon rows of network drives, floor to ceiling, with multiple blinking lights and a tangle of cables hanging from each of them. What looked like a complete mishmash of computer equipment was actually storing and backing up numerous company networks, ensuring that data wasn't just saved, but stored securely. With the increase in cybercrime, Sure Fire Inc. had partnered with Black Out, the company Paul Etheridge had started and sold.

A lot of what Sam had read on the Sure Fire website had been indecipherable, but he did know one thing as he stared at the columns before him.

Pumping through those cables was the data networks for some of the biggest companies and banks in the world. Each one represented another pillar of Dale Munroe's vast wealth and power.

It was hard to land a blow on someone like Dale

Munroe. A man of such resource could have his son protected from rape charges and have highly skilled men track Sam in the space of a few days. There was no way an idle threat would even land on a man of such stature.

So, Sam knew the only way to hit back at Dale Munroe was to damage the one thing he held dearest.

His reputation.

It took Sam less than thirty seconds to start the fire, ensuring he hit the fire alarm as soon as the blaze began to take. The high, shrill ring would not only trigger the security guards to evacuate but also alert the emergency services.

Sam would be long gone before anyone knew what had happened, so to ensure Dale Munroe knew it was a deliberate arson attack, Sam left the fluid and the matches alongside the prone body of the security who he dragged across the tarmac. As the thick, black smoke began to pour from the building, and the odd flicker of an orange flame could be seen through the window, Sam retreated to the shadows once more.

Moments later, the two security guards rushed around the side of the building, clearly relieved as they found their unconscious friend on the outside. They raced to his aid, and as he slowly came to and the sound of sirens began to puncture the quiet of the night sky, Sam disappeared into the darkness.

CHAPTER TWENTY-ONE

'I can assure you. I have already spoken to our overseas centres and there is no damage to any of the networks.'

Dale forced himself to smile at the camera, taking every ounce of energy to conceal the fury within him. It had been a long time since he had to work a Saturday morning, but the events of the night before had forced his hand. An arson attack at one of the Sure Fire data centres had been big news, and as soon as it flooded the internet, his phone was awash with concerned stakeholders, all of whom were threatening to cancel their contracts with his monopoly. To them, Sure Fire was supposed to be the safest place to store their data and with the handsome sums of money they made off the back of his network, they were willing to turn a blind eye to the odd deal he made under the table.

Share prices had never been higher, and as Dale looked at the grid of webcams on his laptop, he felt a twinge of disgust at what he saw.

Old, fat, rich, white men. Each sitting at their personal desks, all of them swimming in more wealth than they knew what to do with. They were a mirror of himself, scrambling to ensure that they were the buffer between the elite and the 'sort of' rich. Sure Fire was a key cog in their machines, and although there was no lasting damage to the customer data, the significant damage done was to the stock prices.

From being the highest they had ever been to almost cutting in half, the arson attack and the ongoing public issues with Dale's son meant that the value of Sure Fire was tumbling.

People were worried.

He'd have never admitted it to anyone, but so was Dale. And he knew exactly who did it.

Sam Pope.

The disgruntled reaction from the camera feeds told Dale his words were falling on deaf ears, and then the CEO of one of the most prestigious high street banks spoke up.

'You can understand our hesitancy to believe that when the issue is still not under control.'

'Like I said, there is no issue.' Dale rubbed his eyes in irritation.

'The name Sam Pope makes a lot of people nervous, Dale.'

'It was an empty threat to my son.'

'And this attack has nothing to do with it?' The CEO chuckled. '*Come on, Dale. We might not know the intricacies of data networks, but we are all smart men. We can put two and two together—'*

'And you're getting five.' Dale slammed his fist on the table. 'Let me make something very clear to you all. You all rely on my networks. Not the other way round. In the years you've worked with Sure Fire, there has never been an issue like this. So, if you're all sitting there with tight arseholes because of a little fire, then by all means, take your data to another platform. But just remember, you all signed over certain rights to me. Which means if you so much as renege on those terms, then I will bury you in legal fees.'

'Don't threaten us, Mr Munroe—' another voice piped up. Before he could react, Hudson opened the door to Dale's office and walked in, his urgency piquing Dale's interest.

'I have to go,' Dale said firmly. 'Remember, I have more money than you. So play it smart.'

Before any of the powerful men could respond, Dale disconnected the video conference and slammed his laptop shut. It had been a hell of a morning, and despite the disparaging eye of Hudson, he stomped across the room to fix himself a Scotch. He knocked it back in one and then gasped, a brief moment of relief in the eye of the storm. Dale closed his eyes and tried to gather his thoughts. For decades, he had been the most powerful player at every table at which he sat. Through sheer force of will and cutthroat business acumen, he had terrified anyone who had ever opposed him.

To not be in full control, or know that it was being taken care of, was an alien feeling, and with Hudson's eyes locked onto him, Dale did his best to maintain his calm.

But Hudson knew.

The man knew everything.

Blowing out his cheeks, he turned to Hudson, hands on his hips, and shrugged.

'What do you want?'

'I have a message from Sam,' Hudson said, holding up his phone. Dale stomped across and snatched it from his hand, and stared at the screen.

Call me.

It was the number that Sam had called from a few days before. The phone had originally belonged to a Glaswegian heavy who Hudson had seriously overestimated, and had since been arrested by the Glasgow Police once he'd been treated for the severe beating he had received from Sam.

Dale's eyes bulged with anger.

'Do it then.'

Hudson tapped the *call* button, set the phone to speaker and then rested it on the table beside the sofa. He unbuttoned his crisp, grey, pinstripe jacket, to reveal a similar patterned waistcoat and freshly ironed white shirt. As he sat, he adjusted his bow tie.

The call connected.

'Sam? Are you there?' Dale spat angrily, saliva foaming at the side of his mouth.

'I am.'

'You've made a massive mistake, my friend. Massive. Do you think I haven't dealt with shit like this my whole career? Do you—'

'First off, I'm not your friend.' Sam interrupted. *'Second, you've never dealt with me, Mr Munroe. You have no idea what will happen if you do not hand your son over to the police so he can confess to what he did.'*

'Fuck my son. You've come after my business. My empire. My legacy.'

'And you've sent your little lap dog after people I care about. I'm assuming he's on the call too?'

Dale flashed a glance towards Hudson who leant forward.

'I assume you're referring to me.'

'See, Mr Munroe. You've never fought fair. You've bullied and betrayed people because you have the means to do so. The thing is, I can't be bullied. I have no interest in your money or your legacy. I made it very clear…your son has until the end of today to hand himself into the police and confess to what he did.'

'Fuck you,' Dale spat, drawing an exasperated eye roll from Hudson.

'If he doesn't…' Sam continued, ignoring the outburst.

'Then I will keep going. Building by building. Brick by brick. I will bring everything down until you don't have the means or the resources to protect him anymore.'

Dale leant down and snatched up the phone, taking it off speaker and then walked to the window.

'Listen to me, Sam, and listen good. You are treading on very dangerous ground. Do you hear me? So far, I've allowed Mr Hudson to do things his way, but now we're going to do things my way—'

'Your son has until the end of the day.'

Sam disconnected the call. Dale tried to continue talking, then, in a blur of red mist, launched the phone against the wall of his office, and watched as it shattered into a shower of cracked plastic and glass. Without a word, he stomped back to his cabinet, sunk another Scotch, and then began to fill the glass up again.

'I want him dead.'

Dale's words were cold, and he turned to Hudson, glass in hand. Hudson stood, nodded, and then marched to the door. As Dale watched him leave, he knew what he had just done. Hudson, while being the politest man he'd ever met, was also the most dangerous. They knew there were people Sam cared about, and if needed, Hudson would put them in the ground to draw Sam out.

Dale hoped he did.

He wanted Sam to suffer as much as possible.

But, as he drank the Scotch, the ice clattered in his glass, and he realised he was shaking.

He had just gone to war with Sam Pope.

The most dangerous man in the country.

With a nervous tremble, he finished his drink, placed the glass down on the desk and then collapsed into his chair, with the horrible realisation that there was only one guarantee out of all of this.

Sam Pope was going to fight back.

With bloodshot eyes, Jasper Munroe stared at his reflection.

The usual cleanly shaven, elegantly groomed man was nowhere to be seen. A thick, patchy stubble had sprouted across his jawline and his hair was greasy and messy. The bags under his eyes aged him significantly, and he wondered when he'd last experienced a good night's sleep.

Not since Sam Pope had entered his world.

For so long, he had walked around the city of London as if he owned it. Knowing full well that his wealth would open every door and lure in most women. If things got out of hand, then his father's untouchable power would keep the wolves from the door.

It had before.

Many times before.

But not this time. As he leant over the thick porcelain sink in his bathroom, he glared at himself in the mirror. For the first time in his life, Jasper felt threatened, and the only thing he wanted was for his father to step in front of him and protect him. When the police had investigated the claims against him, his dad had made the necessary calls and signed the required cheques to ensure his son walked free.

But this was different.

In less than twenty-four hours, Jasper Munroe was expecting Sam Pope to kick down his door and drag him to the police and all he craved was for his father to be sitting with him.

Protecting him.

Instead, Dale Munroe had instructed Hudson to find Jasper a suitable babysitter, and now, a grisly looking man with a thick beard and bulging muscles sat in his living room, watching the sports channels, and grunting whenever Jasper asked him a question.

At least the man was armed.

Jasper wasn't an expert on firearms, but he knew that whatever handgun the man had tucked into the holster underneath his sculpted arm, it would blow Sam Pope away if he stormed in.

But Jasper didn't feel safe.

His body felt weak, and as he tapped out another line of cocaine onto the edge of the sink, he knew it was a bad idea. His brain was on the verge of cracking under such pressure, yet the only comfort he could find was in the instant gratification of the white power with which he'd fuelled his social life.

He'd been high on cocaine when he'd been confronted by Sam himself.

And when he had raped Hayley Baker.

Those two names rattled around his head like the last pill in his Xanax bottle. His life had been the picture of perfection before either of them had entered his orbit, and they were both now ebbing away at the fringes of his sanity. The good-looking man with the perfect life no longer stared back at him from the mirror.

The spacious penthouse apartment that his father had bought him felt like a prison, and he was certain that every hour, the walls moved an inch closer to him. In the depths of what was left of his mind, the idea that this was his comeuppance was floating, but he drowned it out with another harsh intake of cocaine.

This time, his head snapped back, and he audibly groaned, the rush burning through his senses. He stumbled back into the wall and held his nose as the tears poured down his cheeks.

This wasn't his fault.

It was Sam Pope's fault.

And it was hers.

Hayley Baker.

The thought of her caused a rumble of anger to course through his arm, and Jasper slammed his fist against the bathroom tiles. The pain was brief, as the drugs numbed his senses, and he stumbled forward, dropping against the sink once more and resting his head on the edge of it.

His tongue flicked out, and he licked the remnants of cocaine from the porcelain, salivating as the powder filled his mouth and then, slack jawed, he stood and gave himself one more glance.

He needed to get back to who he was.

He needed to be Jasper Munroe again.

Then the idea took hold. At first, the remnants of his common sense tried to bat it away, before an avalanche of cocaine flooded his mind and goaded him on. As he stumbled to the door, Jasper knew he wasn't thinking straight. He knew that the terror of his predicament, along with the scarring neglect of his father and a constant binge of drugs had left him clinging precariously to the edge of his own sanity.

But he had less than a day left.

Nothing to lose.

Everything to gain.

It all started with her. It would end with her, too.

Jasper yanked open the bathroom door and collapsed into the hallway, colliding with the wall before he steadied himself. A grunt echoed from the living room, and Jasper looked around desperately, before his hand landed on the crystal bowl on the hallway table. It was a decorative gift from a designer label, and he had received it in exchange for a social media post to promote their brand.

There was nothing in it, but it still weighed enough to catch him by surprise.

'Everything okay?'

The gruff voice grew louder, as did the footsteps, and a second later, the armed bodyguard stepped into view.

Jasper swung with all his might.

The sickening crunch of crystal on skull caught him by surprise, and he watched as the man collapsed to the ground. His body was already twitching, as blood pumped out of severe dent in his skull. His eyes were open, but they weren't watching, and Jasper took a step back in horror at what he'd done.

But then he remembered he'd done it for a reason.

Hayley Baker.

The guilt of the man's imminent death evaporated, and Jasper reached down and took the gun from the man's motionless body. As Jasper tucked it into his jeans, he threw on his coat and then stepped over the body.

The man was dead before he'd even closed the door.

With the adrenaline of murder and the copious amounts of drugs battling for supremacy, Jasper Munroe abandoned trying to hold onto his sanity.

He had a new focus now.

And she would regret ever trying to ruin his life.

CHAPTER TWENTY-TWO

Hudson had spent the rest of the morning enjoying the Christmas rush of London. With nobody to provide for, he often found the idea of lavish Christmas spending to be a garish reflection of how materialistic the country had become. While the television adverts would be awash with community spirit and the season of goodwill, all he witnessed was a barrage of irritated shoppers, clambering over each other to spend as much as they possibly could.

It made him chuckle.

After Dale Munroe's deadly command to end Sam Pope's life, Hudson had left the office and walked down the street from the Sure Fire office. Kensington was one of the more affluent parts of the city, yet with Christmas just a few weeks away, it felt like the entire world had descended upon its high streets. Hudson eventually found an expensive café and took a seat, ordering himself a strong coffee and a healthy breakfast.

He hated to admit it, but he was tired.

Things such as fatigue or fear were filtered out of his mindset when he was working. It was why he was so good and it his job and such a valuable commodity in the eyes of the elite. Due to the trauma of his upbringing, Hudson had been able to push away anything that could impinge on his mission, and then he would settle up later.

Once Sam Pope was in the ground, he would be able to get some rest. Perhaps he would spend some of the payment on a luxury holiday for some winter sun. As the waitress took away his empty plate, Hudson ordered another coffee and then, once it arrived, he pulled out his phone. Despite the foot traffic on the streets outside, the coffee shop was practically empty, with just himself and a wannabe author the only customers. The young man, who seemed deep in the flow of creativity, had his headphones on and his eyes glued to the screen. The waitress was somewhere out back.

Hudson made the call, confidently crossed one leg over the other, and took a sip of the luxurious coffee.

The call connected.

'No negotiation.'

Sam was obviously expecting the call, and Hudson smiled to himself. While his professionalism would see that he did kill the man, he was a little disappointed. Sam was an interesting and impressive opponent, and Hudson speculated that perhaps the world was a better place with men like him in it. Unashamedly, Hudson put his skills to the highest bidder. It didn't matter whether he agreed with his employer.

But Sam was a man of principal. With a strict moral code.

He was also one of the most dangerous men alive.

'There is nothing to negotiate.' Hudson spoke calmly. 'Except a time and a place.'

'I'm not the dating type.'

Hudson chuckled.

'We both know that Jasper Munroe lacks the courage to face the consequences of his actions. And we both know that I have been hired at a great cost to Dale Munroe to ensure you do not get to him.' Hudson took another sip of his coffee. 'Now, I don't particularly like either man, but I am a professional. Therefore, I wanted to give you the chance to name the time and place.'

'You know, I keep hearing people tell me that they're professionals. As if that makes a blind bit of difference. Just because you're swimming in the most expensive pool, it doesn't mean you're not swimming with sharks. You're still just a hired gun. You might have a fancy suit, but you're nothing more than a killer.'

'Oh, I feel that's a little unfair. And may I say, a little hypocritical.' Hudson's brow furrowed. 'Just because you claim to do things for the greater good, it doesn't alleviate the fact that you, too, are a cold-blooded killer, Mr Pope.'

Hudson smiled as he heard Sam pause for thought. The man was calm and calculated, and Hudson knew he wouldn't do anything rash.

'I don't intend to kill Jasper Munroe. I just want him and those like him to know that they're not above the law.'

'That's incredibly noble of you. Yet, misguided. Because they *are* above the law, Mr Pope. Dale Munroe considers Commissioner McEwen a close friend. The rich keep the police onside, and the world keeps turning. However, as pleasant as it has been to talk to you, and it has been pleasant, I have a job to do. Unless you give me a time and place, then I shall be forced to hurt people I would prefer not to. That nice lady and her daughter. Your boss and his beautiful family.'

'They have nothing to do with this,' Sam said through gritted teeth. The threat as obvious as it was understated.

'I agree,' Hudson said, finishing his coffee. 'Therefore, I am giving you the opportunity to tell me when and where, and I promise you, after you're dead, no harm will come to the people you care about. As we have already established, Mr Pope, I am a professional.'

Silence followed, and Hudson knew Sam was contemplating the very real threat he'd just laid out.

'The haulage yard. Midnight.'

'See you there.'

Hudson stood, the phone still pressed to his ear, and he buttoned his jacket. He dropped a fifty-pound note on the table, more than enough to cover the cost of his stay and a generous tip.

'You don't mind if I fight back, do you?'

Hudson felt a twinge of excitement.

'I'd be disappointed if you didn't.'

Sam hung up the call, and Hudson strode back through the streets of Kensington, weaving between the army of shoppers, until he returned to Sure Fire's building. The weekend security team was sparse, and he made his way back to Munroe's top floor office with no obstacle. As soon as he relayed the appointment to Dale, the greedy billionaire's eyes lit up, and he authorised the use of the private jet once more. Hudson contacted the three mercenaries who he'd travelled with the day before, all of whom were excited that the directive had changed from *apprehend* to *kill*.

They'd get to scratch the itch on their trigger fingers after all.

With everything set, Hudson turned to leave, but Dale Munroe stood from his desk.

'I expect you to kill this man,' Dale said firmly. 'If you fail, it will be the end of your career.'

Hudson, despite being a few inches shorter, stepped forward with purpose, and Dale suddenly felt a little smaller.

'As someone who has worked with you for many years, permit me a moment of honesty. Your son is a vile human. He should be rotting in a prison cell for the things he's done.' Hudson straightened his tie. 'With that said, you have paid a handsome fee for my services, and I have never let you down. But don't worry about my career, Mr Munroe. The only way I will fail is if Sam Pope ends my life.'

Hudson turned and marched out of the office, leaving Dale Munroe to slump into his chair as he dealt with the effects of too much Scotch at such an early time of day. It was approaching lunchtime, and Hudson wanted a few hours with the crew to discuss tactics and to ensure they knew who was in charge.

He'd never taken on someone like Sam Pope before.

And as he left the Sure Fire Inc. building, Hudson understood that there was only one way the night was going to end.

Either he or Sam Pope would die.

And he was excited to find out who.

Sam had been expecting the phone call.

After burning the data centre to the ground, he'd made his way back towards Dudley and then taken a taxi back towards Birmingham City Centre. As he was travelling down the motorway, he saw the cavalcade of police cars, followed swiftly by a few fire engines, as they rushed to attend to the damage he had caused.

If they only knew.

Dale Munroe had made it explicitly clear that he valued his business and his name far more than his own son, and that his push back to Sam was more of a matter of pride than anything else. As with most bullies, Dale wasn't accustomed to someone pushing back.

But that's what Sam did.

It's what he always did.

Once he'd returned to the town centre, he booked

himself into the cheapest Travel Lodge he could find, pleased to see that his pseudonym of Jonathan Cooper was still valid. A cunning detective had linked the identity to Sam back in Derbyshire, but as Sam was starting to discover, his own good deeds meant even the authorities were willing to look the other way sometimes. Eventually, he would be held accountable for his crimes, but while there was still a war to fight, there were people who saw the good he did.

The good he could still do.

After a reasonable night's sleep, he woke, showered, and then headed out for breakfast, bypassing the depressing offering of the hotel. A few streets away in the train station was a typical café, proud of its 'greasy spoon' aesthetic and the myriad of unhealthy options that dominated its menu.

Sam was famished, and a full English breakfast was just what his body craved. Alongside a pot of tea, Sam devoured his breakfast, drawing a knowing nod from the other customers. Local tradesmen who had stopped by for breakfast before they started work. They knew who he was, but once again, Sam felt nothing but approval.

In the top right corner of the café, a television was playing the usual early weekend nonsense before it changed to the news. Sam's eyes caught the headlines and the images.

Devastating fire outside Birmingham. Police suspect Arson.

A slideshow of the brave firefighters battling the blaze followed, and although Sam couldn't hear, he knew what was being discussed. His handiwork was headline news, and he lifted the phone he'd stolen from the thug who he'd left in a battered heap behind Mel's bar, and sent a simple message to Mr Hudson.

The call came back almost instantly.

Sam paid for his breakfast and then exited the café

before he took the call. As expected, Dale Munroe was threatening to scorch the earth to find Sam, who calmly relayed the terms of his son's surrender.

As he hung up, he knew it had fallen on deaf ears, and he zipped his coat up and took a brisk walk through the city of Birmingham. The Second City had received plenty of investment over the years, doing its best to become one of the culture destinations of the United Kingdom. Before he could enjoy any of the sights, the phone buzzed again, and Sam answered.

Mr Hudson.

There was an unease that Sam felt whenever the man spoke. The eloquent voice and the perfect articulation gave off the air of a highly educated man, and Sam knew it was a façade. It was used to catch people off guard, and he was certain that a man of Dale's power and reach would only hire the most clinical of people to solve his problems.

Which meant Hudson was dangerous. Of that, Sam had little doubt.

Hudson laid out the threat as clear as he could, and Sam told him when and where.

The haulage yard.

It was the only place he could think of where he would have an advantage. He didn't have much in the way of weapons, but he would at least be on familiar ground.

It was vast.

There was plenty of cover.

Considering Hudson travelled with company the last time they were face to face, Sam doubted he'd be coming alone. The men who'd been with Hudson stank of ex-military, which meant they were trained, lethal and unlikely to hesitate. The fact they were selling their skills for cash meant their moral compass had long been tossed out of the window.

Things would get messy.

People were likely going to die.

Sam marched back to Birmingham New Street Station and navigated his way through the ticket booking machine. He purchased a ticket to Glasgow and then made his way towards the platform where the train was due. He had half an hour to kill, so he found the nearest coffee kiosk and treated himself to one, knowing it was going to be a long day and an even longer night.

He needed to get back as soon as he could, to give himself as much time to prepare as possible.

But first, he needed to speak to Martin. The man had been running the haulage yard for years and took pride in the business he'd inherited from his father. He was a good man, willing to offer second chances to people who had paid the price for their crimes.

Second chances to men like Sam, who just wanted a fresh start.

Sam had brought trouble to his doorstep, and as he'd been marched out of Martin's office by the over-eager police officers, he could see the guilt on the man's face. Despite it all, it was Martin who felt like he'd let Sam down.

It was something Sam needed to set straight.

He wanted to apologise to the man for the problems he had caused and the likely issues that were to come.

He didn't need Martin's forgiveness.

He needed his permission.

Permission to go to war. And to use Martin's haulage yard as the battlefield.

The train to Glasgow pulled up to the platform and Sam boarded it, knowing that he was heading back to the gothic city to fight for his life.

Possibly for the last time.

CHAPTER TWENTY-THREE

Hudson sat in the black Range Rover and stared at the gates of the haulage yard. Despite the heat pumping from within the car, his breath plumed from his mouth in a faint cloud, as if his soul was trying to escape his body. A chilling drizzle had begun to fall, guaranteeing icy streets in the morning.

Hudson looked at the time.

It was ten to midnight.

The flight back to Glasgow had been uneventful, with the three mercenaries seemingly more excited as they locked and loaded, exchanging macho promises of bloodshed and fantasising about their pay day.

Hudson had ignored them, staring out at the clouds as he sipped his tea.

There was nothing exciting about it.

It was just business.

Hudson had maintained his professional calm throughout the rest of the evening, from hiring the car to grabbing some food. A few of the men joked about it being the last supper and Hudson resisted the need to urge caution. They were about to enter a dangerous game with Sam Pope, and while their history of violence was commendable, it didn't mean anything if they weren't focussed.

Sam Pope deserved their focus.

Commanded it.

They had arrived at the yard a little after ten thirty, hoping to get the jump on Sam. There was no sign of him.

No sign of anyone.

The gates were shut, with the sign that was emblazoned with the company's name attached to them. They were in the middle of nowhere, and Hudson realised another reason why Sam had picked the location.

Not only did it provide him with plenty of cover, but it was far enough from civilisation for them not to hear the inevitable gun fire.

'We doing this?' Carter spat. He was a big man, and he filled the driver's seat next to Hudson. The other two men followed his every move and despite being under Hudson's command, he acted like he was running the show.

'No time like the present,' Hudson agreed, and the four men simultaneously opened their doors and stepped out. The bitter cold greeted them instantly, and Hudson was thankful for the thick overcoat that he'd worn over his suit. The grunts with him were all dressed in black military wear, proving their manliness with exposed forearms and open collars.

Hudson shook his head with displeasure.

The three men held their Glocks in their hands, whereas Hudson kept his Desert Eagle tucked firmly in his jacket. They were there to do the dirty work, and Hudson was hoping he wouldn't need to draw his gun unless he absolutely had to. The feeling in his stomach told him it was a certainty. Carter approached the gate, stuffed his gun into the band of his trousers, and scaled it quickly. As he dropped to the other side, he motioned silently with his hand for his men to follow. Just as they were about to reach for the chain-link fence, Hudson cleared his throat, asserting his authority. As they watched on with annoyance, Hudson pushed the gate open.

It was unlocked.

They were being let in.

Hudson ushered the other two men through and then followed, walking calmly as the three men began to spread out across the gravel forecourt, their weapons raised to eye level and their brains aching for a target.

Their footsteps crunched the stones beneath.

The office that they'd invaded the day before was pitch-black, as was the vast yard itself, with a few pathways among the piles of scrap metal visible before it was enveloped by the darkness.

Sam Pope was here.

Somewhere.

One of the men took a few steps towards the walkway into the yard, while Carter moved towards the closed metal doors of the garage to the side of the office. The third man stayed near Hudson, as if he needed protecting, which Hudson found amusing.

A bright light exploded into life.

From high above the office, the floodlight illuminated the entire forecourt, catching all four men by surprise. Hudson did well the avert his eyes in time, but the other three allowed themselves to naturally turn and look at it, temporarily blinding them.

A figure emerged from the office door.

Hudson couldn't see who it was, but before any of the men could train their guns on him, a gunshot echoed out.

But not from the office.

Before they realised it had come from the darkness of the haulage yard itself, a bullet ripped through the cold, relentless drizzle and embedded into the neck of one of the mercenaries. An audible panic broke out among the rest of them, and Hudson demanded they take cover. They all rushed towards different parts of the forecourt as their comrade struggled for breath, choking on the blood that was pumping from the bullet hole in his throat.

Hudson withdrew his Desert Eagle.

The man by the office had gone.

Somewhere in the darkness, Sam Pope had them in his sights.

And one of Hudson's men was dead.

Sam had watched carefully from the shadows, shielded by the remains of an old, broken fridge. One of Hudson's men had scaled the fence before Hudson had discovered the gate to be open. The four men had accepted the invitation, and each of them, bar Hudson, were expertly holding their guns. Sam knew they couldn't see him, and along with the all black clothes he'd worn to infiltrate and burn down the Sure Fire data centre the night before, he had also smeared boot polish across his face to conceal himself further.

He watched.

He waited.

When he'd reached out to Martin to explain what was happening, he had been shocked at the response. He was bringing nothing but trouble to the man's front door, and if things went as expected, Martin would have a lot of police hassle to deal with. But Martin's guilt for letting Sam be arrested seemed too heavy to move past and not only did he give Sam permission to wage war on his property, he insisted on helping. According to him, being held at gunpoint and having his family threatened wasn't something he was willing to forget.

With the four men spreading out across the gravel forecourt, Sam lifted his Glock, his finger resting steadily on the trigger. One of the men was venturing towards the walkway that would lead him towards Sam, but the darkness proved a fabulous shield.

A light exploded onto the concourse, catching the men by surprise. As planned, Martin had waited until they were all within the yard, meaning the sudden illumination would not only blind them temporarily, but would also provide Sam with a clear view of where they were.

To add to the distraction, Martin bravely stepped out of the office, drawing the eyes and the guns of Hudson and his crew in his direction.

Split-second timing was something Sam had lived by. His years as an elite sniper meant that he knew that life or death could hang by a millisecond.

As the men turned their attention to the office, and the shadowy figure of Martin bathed in the light, Sam's instinct kicked in.

He lifted his gun, squeezed the trigger and sent a bullet ripping through the drizzle. It blew through the nearest mercenary's neck, sending him spiralling to the gravel below. The other men scattered for cover, and the only noise for a few moments were the gasps of air as the mercenary choked on his own blood.

Sam had made the first move, and keeping low, he quickly scurried from his spot and further into the maze. Hudson was a talented tracker, that much was clear, and it wouldn't take him long to discover where the bullet came from. Sam rounded a large pile of metal grates until he came by the side of an old oven. The hob atop it was coated in rust, and he crouched down beside it. Hudson had given the order for the remaining two men to hunt him, and Sam could hear the footsteps of one of them a few metres ahead.

They grew louder.

Closer.

Carter took a few more tentative steps into the darkness, his eyes trained down the sight of his pistol. His finger was one twitch away from firing, and he trained the pistol on the pathway ahead. He could see the stack of metal grates, and as he rounded the battered oven, Sam launched upward and wrapped his hand around Carter's wrist. Deflecting the gun upwards, Sam violently twisted Carter's wrist, wrenching the tendons and loosening his grip, causing the gun to clatter into the stack of metal.

The audible clang would draw attention, and Sam tried to end it swiftly. He drove a knee up towards Carter's stomach, but the man was skilled enough to deflect it. With his free hand, Carter cracked Sam with a nasty right hook, sending him stumbling back, before he swiftly pulled a knife from his belt. He gripped it with the blade facing downward, the serrated edge built to maim, and then he dived at Sam, slashing wildly into the darkness. Sam evaded a few swipes before the man skimmed the edge of his arm.

Sam grimaced, feeling the skin on his arm opening slightly and the warmth of the blood that began to dribble from the wound.

The sound of distant footsteps became clearer, as another mercenary followed the noise of their fight, ready to outnumber Sam and most likely, put a bullet in his skull.

Carter tossed the knife back and forth between his hands as he sized Sam up before he lunged again. Sam evaded the blow, drilled his elbow into the man's temple, and then gripped his arm. A violent wrench caused the man to drop the knife, and Sam dropped to his knee and caught it with his free hand before it hit the ground.

He spun it by the handle, gripped it tight, and then drove it full force through the leather of the man's boot, crunching through his metatarsal and obliterating his foot completely.

Carter screamed in agony, just as his crew member rounded the corner, his gun by his side.

'Mother fucker!' the man cried out, lifting the gun in Sam's direction.

Sam wrenched the blade from the top of Carter's foot, and then, with every modicum of power in his body, he twisted and launched it. The blade spun through the air, slicing the droplets of drizzle that was peppering them all, and ripped into the mercenary's chest. The sound was sickening, taking the man off his feet and he crashed to the ground, gasping for life as the blade invaded his lung, filling it with blood and drawing the air from his body.

The man gave a few short, sharp breaths but was dead before Sam got to his feet.

'Sam!' Hudson's calm voice rattled loudly through the darkness, echoing off the plethora of metal surfaces. 'Let's do this quickly, shall we?'

Sam stepped over the body of the dead man and carefully followed the pathway back until the courtyard became visible again. Although he was shielded by the darkness, the courtyard was glowing under the floodlights, and in the centre of it was Hudson.

In his left hand, he had a Desert Eagle.

His right arm was wrapped around Martin's neck, and the portly man looked terrified as the weapon was pressed to his temple. Sam cursed under his breath, leant back against the shell of a car beside him, and responded.

'Let him go,' Sam yelled.

'Come and take him,' Hudson goaded. 'You have three seconds before I put a bullet through his skull. One.'

Sam knew walking out into the light would give Hudson a clear shot.

'Two.'

Sam checked once more. There was no way to cleanly make the shot from where he stood. Not without risking Martin's life.

'Three.'

Without hesitation, Sam stepped out from the shadows, his hands held high. He stepped onto the gravel and towards Hudson, who greeted him with a smile and a loaded weapon.

It wasn't long after midnight that Jasper Munroe drove through the dark, country roads of Harefield until he came to a stop. It hadn't taken him long to find Hayley Baker's address. Although her friends would claim to be loyal as dogs, one of them very quickly changed her tune when Jasper Munroe offered her ten thousand pounds.

To him, it was loose change.

He'd typed out a nonsensical story of wanting to put things right, of helping to pay for Hayley's university and legal fees, as he didn't want their misunderstanding to be a black mark against Hayley. The story sort of worked, but as with everything in life, money talks loudest.

As he pulled up in front of her family home, he scoffed.

It was a quaint street, with a lovely canal running alongside the main road. But it was still a world away from the glitz and glamour of his own life, and it became evident that she didn't belong in his world.

She had brought enough trouble with her.

Driving had been tricky with the copious amount of

cocaine in his blood, but he'd arrived with little trouble. Now, he glared up at the dark house and knew that within slept the cause of his problems.

She had spoken to Sam Pope personally and explained everything he'd done to her. The things he'd said.

She'd set Sam on his path of destruction, causing his father to pile even more hate upon their relationship and drive thousands of followers from his account. Potential sponsorship collaborations were being pulled and the hard work and dedication he'd put into building his own brand was filtering through his fingertips.

All because of her.

The rage was uncontrollable, and Jasper slammed his fist against the solid leather steering wheel. With his hand shaking, he tipped a little more cocaine onto the wheel, leant forward, and inhaled it greedily.

His mind was shaking.

His entire body convulsed with adrenaline and fury.

'Fuck it.'

Jasper cruelly spat as he threw open the car door, retrieved the gun from the passenger seat, and then marched up the garden path to the front door. Not wanting to alert the neighbours, Jasper rang the doorbell. A moment or two later, a light flicked on upstairs, followed by the unmistakable sound of someone racing down them. As the figure approached the door, Jasper lifted the gun.

The door flew open, and an exasperated man angrily stepped out.

That anger quickly dissolved into fear, and Jasper lifted his finger to his lips.

'Angela, call the police,' Henry Baker yelled back to the house, and as he turned back to Jasper, he was greeted with the full force of the butt of the gun. The metal smashed into the man's skull, knocking the consciousness from his body. As he slumped back into the house, Jasper stepped in and closed the door.

A few minutes later, he emerged with Hayley, marching her to the car and with the gun trained on her, told her to drive away. With her father unconscious with his hands and feet bound like her mother, Hayley brought the car to life with shaking hands, and pulled off into the night, terrified of what was to come next.

CHAPTER TWENTY-FOUR

As Sam's boots crunched across the gravel, he saw Hudson's eyes sparkle with excitement. The last time they'd been face to face, Hudson had surprised him. The man who the country had dubbed its most dangerous criminal had walked into a trap that he'd sprung, and that should have been the end of it. But Sam had a proclivity for upsetting the apple cart, and Hudson had appreciated it. His reputation was staked on bringing the wanted vigilante to his end, and Sam had put that in jeopardy.

But not now.

Sam knew it and Hudson knew it.

With a resigned sigh, Sam stepped closer, stopping a good ten feet from Hudson with his arms in the air. He took a deep breath, which puffed from his mouth in an icy white cloud. The drizzle bathed both men in the cold, as well as Martin, who stared at Sam in desperation.

'This is a predicament, isn't it?' Hudson goaded, enjoying the position he was in.

'Just let him go,' Sam demanded. 'He's a good man. He has nothing to do with this.'

'See, I would disagree.' Hudson tapped the barrel of

the gun against Martin's temple. 'As brave as he may have been, he did help you kill some of my men. Now, I say that loosely as they were hired guns, but still. Principles.'

'You have me.' Sam held his hands out. 'Bang to rights. Nowhere for me to run. Nowhere to hide. Let him go, point that gun at me, and let's get this over with.'

Hudson chuckled.

'My, you are impressive.' Hudson ran his tongue against the inside of his bottom lip. 'Even now, you're fighting for what you believe to be the right thing. As you wish.'

Hudson released his grip on Martin and let him drop to the ground. Martin scrambled quickly away and headed towards the office, flashing a worried look back at Sam. Despite the imminent certainty of death, Sam offered him an assured nod.

Permission to run.

Martin obliged, and as he disappeared into the darkness, Hudson turned his attention back to Sam.

'I assume you killed those men.'

'We have to do what we have to do,' Sam replied coldly.

'True.' Hudson lowered the gun and held it by his side. 'Before I kill you, I wanted to commend you. As far as I can see, Jasper Munroe is a repugnant human being who doesn't deserve the protection his wealth affords him. The world would be a better place if men like you were allowed to win.'

'Then let me.' Sam shrugged. 'Step aside and let me do what's necessary.'

'But the world isn't a better place, Sam. And I've been paid a lot of money to keep it that way.' Hudson frowned. 'It's a shame, because I really have found you to be quite the target.'

Hudson slowly raised the gun, looking at it tentatively.

Sam had no doubts that the man was as dangerous as he appeared. If people like Dale Munroe were willing to pay Hudson millions for his services, it was evidence that the man was highly skilled. Strip away the expensive suits and the articulate vocabulary and Sam was certain that Hudson was a stone-cold killer.

And judging by the disappointment he seemed to have at shooting Sam, there was one chance Sam had for survival.

Ego.

Hudson sighed as he pulled the gun up to his eye level.

'Is that it?' Sam asked. 'You're just going to shoot me?'

'Go on…' Hudson raised his eyebrow.

'You could pull that trigger, put me in the ground and collect your money. Sure. Life goes on and you continue doing this sort of thing for the elite scum who run this world.' Sam lowered his hands and balled them into fists. 'Or you can toss the weapon and prove that you're as good as you think you are.'

Hudson began to chuckle and shook his head.

'That is tempting.' Hudson reasserted his grip. 'But ultimately, I am a professional and…'

The sound of an engine roaring into life echoed through the courtyard, followed by the blinding headlights of a forklift truck. Hudson spun on his heel and faced it as Martin pressed his foot on the accelerator and it burst forward, ripping across the wet gravel towards the armed man. Hudson fired a shot in the direction of the vehicle, the blinding lights not telling him if he hit his target.

Sam launched forward, covering the distance between the two of them, and Hudson turned back.

He aimed the gun at Sam.

But Sam dived forward, driving his shoulder into the man's stomach and taking both of them off their feet and spiralling to the hard ground beneath them. Hudson lost his weapon in the collision, and he drove his foot into Sam's chest and rolled backwards, quickly getting to his feet and straightening his jacket. He looked dressed for an expensive dinner, but with a frown across his face, Hudson slowly began to remove the jacket.

'So be it.'

Sam stood, cracked his neck and then raised his fists, and Hudson burst forward with a flurry of fists, each one of them connecting with a surprising power. Sam absorbed the blows with his arms, until Hudson expertly drove a knee into Sam's ribs, followed swiftly with a right hook that sent him stumbling backwards. Sam shook the wooziness away, and then deflected the driving kick that Hudson threw his way, and then caught the man with a right hook of his own. With an obvious height and strength advantage, Sam's punch took Hudson to the floor, and the hitman pushed himself back up with clear frustration.

He lifted a hand to his lip and felt the blood and then glared at Sam.

Their section of the courtyard was lit by the full beams of the forklift, and Martin watched from the driver's seat, frozen in a mixture of fear and wonderment.

Sam and Hudson lifted their fists once more and edged towards each other, two highly skilled fighters ready to fight to their final breath. They exchanged blows, with both men deflecting them away, before Hudson connected with a left jab, followed by a vicious elbow that struck Sam's jaw and sent him to one knee. Hudson switched his balance to the other foot and then drove forward, cracking Sam in the cheek with a brutal knee that sent him sprawling back across the gravel.

'Is this good enough for you, Sam?' Hudson asked. He stalked Sam as he got on all fours, and then drove his expensive Italian leather shoe into Sam's rib. Sam grunted with pain, and as Hudson swung another foot, Sam hooked his arm over the man's ankle and wrenched, dragging him to the ground. Hudson tried to wriggle free, showing an impressive knowledge of Brazilian Jiu Jitsu movement to shift his body weight, and he managed to drive his sharp elbow into Sam's biceps, deadening the arm and loosening his grip. With a swift shift of bodyweight, Hudson swung his foot forward, drilling Sam in the eyebrow and splitting it open and sending him rolling backwards. Both men scrambled to their feet once more, and Sam could feel the blood pouring down the side of his face.

Hudson smirked as he unbuttoned his shirt cuffs and began to roll them up his arms. The bitter chill of the evening had become an afterthought, and Hudson and Sam seized each other up once more. Hudson propelled forward with a flurry of hard strikes, but Sam managed to evade them, before absorbing one blow into his ribs but locking his arm over Hudson's. With his nimbler opponent trapped, Sam wrenched the man's shoulder back, before driving his skull viciously into the man's face. Hudson's nose exploded and an avalanche of blood gushed down his pristine white shirt. Blinded by the pain, Hudson took a few steps back, and Sam bounced forward onto one foot and then leapt into the air, before driving down with a sickening punch.

He knew it had broken Hudson's cheekbone as soon as it connected, and the now disfigured man collapsed to the gravel, his brain rattled and his fight over.

Sam took a breath and dabbed at the gash across his eyebrow. With Hudson slowly crawling into his final moments, Sam readied himself to finally end the fight.

Clunk!

The hard metal struck the back of Sam's skull, and he stumbled forward, his vision blurring as the gravel sliced away at the palms of his hands. Behind him, Carter limped forward, his foot a bloodied mess and his skin pale. He'd lost a lot of blood, but the desire to kill Sam had been enough to pick him up from his dark, cold death bed and retrieve his fallen comrade's gun. He had managed to conjure enough power to drive the handle into Sam's skull, and now, with their target lying prone on the ground, he was ready to finish the job.

Sam rolled over onto his back. His skull was still reverberating from the brutal blow and his brain vibrating within.

He could just about make out the silhouette of the man standing over him.

The man lifted the gun.

Everything suddenly became illuminated in bright white lights.

Just as the ringing in Sam's ears subsided, it was overwhelmed by the roar of an engine. Carter turned wearily towards the increasingly powerful light, but before he could pull the trigger, the forklift truck ploughed into him, dragging him beneath the mighty vehicle and crushing him to death with an agonised scream.

Sam sat up with disbelief as the engine of the forklift died, and Martin scrambled down from the driver's seat. He looked haunted by what he'd done, but he turned to Sam and offered him a hand up.

'We need to get you out of here,' Martin said sternly, helping Sam to his feet and draping Sam's arm over his shoulders.

'Thank you,' Sam muttered, the pain of the battle beginning to set in.

'I will find you, Sam.' A voice echoed behind them. Both men turned, and Hudson was trying to pull himself to his feet via a pile of scrap metal. The man had been beaten to the point of delirium, and Sam knew what he was witnessing.

The last stand of defiance.

The man's ego wouldn't allow him to just lie down and let Sam walk away.

'Don't listen to him,' Martin said. 'I'll call the police the second we're in the car. I'm sure they'll have some questions for him.'

'He'll get out,' Sam responded with a resounding sigh. 'He's got too much money behind him.'

'And then, I will come for you and everyone you care about,' Hudson spat, his words disjointed from the brutal disfigurement of his face. 'I'll kill every one of them. Him. The woman in the bar. Her daughter…'

Sam stepped away from Martin and bent down beside the forklift truck, his fingers wrapped around the Glock that had rattled his skull moments ago. Hudson had managed to get to his feet, and he turned to face Sam with a blood-stained grin.

His nose was crooked.

His left cheek was fractured.

He was beaten.

With a vicious grin, he looked Sam dead in the eye.

'You are impressive,' Hudson offered.

Sam lifted the gun, held it a few inches from the man's forehead, and pulled the trigger. Hudson's head snapped backwards, and he collapsed into the scrap metal, along with a visceral spray of blood, brain and bone. Sam's hand fell to his side, his finger still on the trigger, and he stared down at the man he had killed.

Hudson was dead.

But this was far from over.

'Come on, Sam.' Martin stepped forward and rested his hand on Sam's shoulder. 'Let's get out of here.'

'I'm sorry, Martin,' Sam offered, his eyes still on the dead body of Hudson that was strewn across the metal. 'I've brought you nothing but trouble.'

'For the right reason, though.' Martin offered a smile, shivering in the cold. 'Someone has to fight for this young lass you told me about. So you need to keep going. Yeah, I've got a fucking mess to clean up here. But don't make it for nothing, you understand?'

Sam turned to Martin and a slight smile cracked across his bloody face.

'Thank you, Martin. For everything.'

'Well, you can thank me tomorrow.' Martin slid Sam's arm over his shoulder again. 'Let's let Jane have a look at you and then do me a favour…'

'What's that?' Sam said as he obediently limped next to Martin.

'Make sure you see this through to the end.'

Sam chuckled and then grimaced with pain. The two men shuffled across the gravel towards the exit, and down the side road where Martin had parked his car.

Sam knew he would do just that.

See it through to the end.

He didn't know any other way.

CHAPTER TWENTY-FIVE

Two paracetamol didn't seem enough.

Commissioner McEwen was sitting at the island in his pristine kitchen, rubbing his temples as another migraine threatened to take control of his day. When he'd replaced Commissioner Stout as the top dog within the Met, he knew it would be the catalyst to finally move out of the city and towards a more rural location. Farnham wasn't deep in the countryside, but it was a quaint enough little village that he and his wife, Leanne, could enjoy the limited time off he had. Their two sons had both finished university, and with neither of them living at home, it had seemed like the perfect move to make.

McEwen had four years left before retirement, and although he physically was fit as a fiddle, he knew he was mentally reaching that point.

Becoming commissioner had been a dream come true, and the ability to help shape and guide the Metropolitan Police Service in a new direction had appealed to him. Stout had begun some incredible work before he stepped down, and McEwen was grateful for the blueprint left behind.

But now, the only thing that Stout left was the words of warning.

'Prepare yourself for a myriad of shit.'

McEwen finished his glass of water and then stepped off the stool. He rounded the island and approached the black marble work top and kicked his luxury coffee machine into action. As it went to work, frothing the milk and grinding his coffee beans, he turned his attention to the television. The BBC news reporter looked frozen, visibly shaking against the Glaswegian cold, and McEwen took a strange sense of pride. He was a proud Scotsman, and at times, he felt a twinge of guilt that his ambition had outstripped what his hometown could offer.

But that wasn't what was troubling him that morning. It wasn't the catalyst of the dull, gnawing pain in the back of his skull.

Four men had been found dead at the McGinn Haulage Centre on the outskirts of town. Three of them had been shot. One of them had been found with a serrated knife embedded in his chest.

It didn't take years of police experience to connect the dots, especially with what had happened over the past few days.

Sam Pope had killed them.

And, worryingly, it was likely that Dale Munroe had sent them.

The billionaire's thinly veiled threat of handling Sam Pope himself was born out of the need to protect his vile son. As much as McEwen despised Jasper Munroe and his clear, constant flouting of the law, he could understand why Dale Munroe threw his vast fortune and weight in front of him. There was nothing that McEwen wouldn't do for his sons, and while he would hope that if his boys ever did something wrong, he would hold them accountable for it, he understood Dale's need to protect.

It was what fathers did.

As the coffee machine rumbled to a stop, McEwen turned his attention away from the television and back to his beverage, tipping the milk in before taking a thankful gulp.

It was going to be a long day.

He walked across his kitchen to the conservatory, where he peered out onto the vast garden that was covered with frost. A few tasteful Christmas decorations lined the windowsill, and he knew that Leanne was looking forward to welcoming the boys home for a few days over the festive season. He wished he was as excited, but the situation was spiralling out of control.

Questions would be asked.

Fingers would be pointed.

And the buck, quite rightly, stopped with him.

'You okay, love?'

Leanne's voice echoed from the kitchen, and McEwen turned and offered her a smile. Leanne was a few years younger than McEwen, and like himself, she took great care to ensure she lived a healthy lifestyle. A cold Sunday morning was usually a good excuse to stay in bed, but Leanne was dressed in her gym gear and was clearly ready for her morning class.

'Aye. Just another shit storm.'

McEwen nodded towards the television, which Leanne looked at as she fiddled with the coffee machine.

'Oh dear.' She frowned. 'I assume you'll be working today.'

'I'm working every day,' McEwen said glumly, sipping his coffee as he stared out at the icy river that ran across the back of their garden. 'Someone needs to take charge of this situation.'

Leanne took a few more moments before she joined him with a coffee of her own. Lovingly, she rested a hand on the small of his back and rested her cheek on his shoulder.

'Well, that's why they have you, isn't it?'

'I haven't been good enough.' McEwen scolded himself.

'Bruce! That's not true.'

'No, it is.' McEwen turned and looked at his wife. 'This job…it wasn't what I thought it was. I wanted to be an agent for change. To make things better. But there are some things that you can't just change. The politics of it all are so inbuilt into the very structure of the Met that you have to play the game to survive. Michael told me that on his way out, but I was naïve enough to think I could change it.'

McEwen finished his coffee and then shook his head. Leanne took a sip of hers and then looked up at her husband with nothing but love. He was a good man who worked harder than anyone she had ever known.

He was a wonderful husband.

A brilliant father.

'Well, what are you going to do about it?' Leanne asked with a shrug.

'What do you mean?'

'Well, if things are so bad right now, what are you going to do to change them?'

'It's not that simple—'

'Isn't it? If this situation is getting out of control, and there are people stepping out of line, then someone needs to take back that control. Someone needs to take charge.' Leanne leant up on her tiptoes to kiss her husband on the cheek. 'You've never backed down from anything in your life, Bruce. You're one of the good guys. So do the right thing and change it.'

McEwen took a few moments to register the words, and then he scoffed.

'Behind every good man is a great woman.' He smiled at his wife.

'I try.'

'I'm going to upset some powerful people.' McEwen looked out over their picturesque garden once more. 'People who won't want me sitting in the seat anymore.'

Leanne put her coffee down and took his hand.

'Fuck em.' They both smiled. 'If that's the case, they don't deserve you, anyway.'

McEwen lifted Leanne's hand to his mouth and kissed the back of her fingers.

'What would I do without you?'

Leanne shrugged playfully and then let go of his hand. She walked back to the kitchen to put their mugs in the sink and, as she did, she turned her attention back to the television. A few reporters were speculating on the involvement of Sam Pope and the threat to Jasper Munroe. She looked back at her husband, who was staring out the window, deep in thought.

'I'm assuming a lot of this has to do with Sam Pope.'

'Mostly.' McEwen didn't turn back. 'But there are other snakes in the grass.'

'Well, far be it from me to condone the man's actions, but what would he do?'

McEwen turned back to his wife with a furrowed brow.

'Excuse me?'

'I know he's a criminal. But he always does what he believes is the right thing. It's why the public love him.' Leanne mused. 'Maybe, Bruce, just maybe…doing the right thing is always the way to go. No matter the consequences.'

McEwen turned back to the window and sighed as his wife left and headed to their car. As had been the case throughout their marriage, she'd cut through the noise surrounding every problem he was facing and dropped a seed of wisdom into his brain.

It was why he loved her.

Needed her.

And as he heard the car pulling off the drive, he took a deep breath and knew she was right.

It was time Bruce McEwen began acting like the Commissioner of the Metropolitan Police.

It was time to do the right thing.

Having to defrost his car while the rest of the street was sleeping was just another added frustration to Dale Munroe's ever-growing list. As he waited for his luxury vehicle to warm up and melt the thick, frosty layer across the windscreen, Dale sipped the travel mug that was filled with piping hot coffee and frowned. Most Sunday mornings were spent with a casual lie-in with Beatrice, plotting out the day where nothing was out of their grasp. Sometimes, they would take the private jet for a day trip to Paris.

Other times, they would visit the exclusive sports club just outside of Chelsea where they would rub shoulders with celebrities and other elite members.

Good food.

Better wine.

But this was unlike most Sundays and being awoken by yet another call from his son was the last thing he'd wanted. A few nights before, it had been the panicked voice of his boy that had set off the chain of events that had brought Dale to the edge of his patience, and yet another whining, snivelling phone call was unlikely to curtail his mood.

Jasper had phoned in a panic, his voice slurring, and Dale pondered what drugs were coursing through his son's veins. He was equally angry at the man Hudson had assigned to watch Jasper, and why he hadn't stepped in to ensure the phone call never came through.

That triggered Dale's concern and having not heard from Hudson, who had ventured up to Scotland the afternoon before to bring their Sam Pope problem to an end. A man of meticulous manners and professionalism, Hudson would have updated Dale the moment the deed was done.

Unless Sam had skipped town?

Unlikely, but it was a better option than the other possibility.

Once his car was fit to drive, Dale guided the Aston Martin DBS out of the gates and into the foggy streets of London, the light from the lampposts causing the frost across the black paintwork to sparkle.

There was little traffic, and Dale cruised through the streets of the sleeping city, heading for the Sure Fire Inc. offices. He had spent over half of his life in that building, watching as he took more control and wealth from the data protection industry and amassed such power that it had become his ivory tower.

He did look down on people.

All of them.

Especially his son.

Despite the love a father has for his child, Dale had never warmed to Jasper as a person. Where he'd built a legacy on hard work, his son had been happy to eat every treat from the silver spoon he was born with. He found such behaviour embarrassing, and when his son decided to build a career around showing off the massive wealth his father had garnered, he lost all respect for him.

Jasper Munroe was an embarrassment to the Munroe name.

Dale pulled into the Sure Fire Inc. private car park and stopped in his designated parking space. He stepped out of the car, zipping the black bomber jacket to protect him from the cold. He marched to the lift and stepped in, wondering how exactly his son would be.

Sam's deadline had passed, which meant if Hudson had failed to deliver, then Jasper's time as a free man would be coming to an end. Dale had already made the decision, that if Jasper was forced to confess to the crimes Sam had held him accountable for, then he would disown his son and put as much distance between him and his company as possible.

He would strong-arm McEwen into stating how he had helped with the enquiry, and how even when it came to his own son, Dale Munroe held the law in high regard.

It would at least lessen the hit on the share prices.

The impact on the bottom line.

The lift doors opened, and Dale looked up and directly down the barrel of a gun.

Behind the shaking fist holding it, Jasper glared at his father with bloodshot eyes.

Dale lifted his hands in surrender and frowned.

'Jesus Christ, Jasper. Lower the fucking weapon.'

After a few moments of intense hesitation, Jasper stepped back and beckoned his father out of the lift and onto the landing. Dale looked around. There was no sign of anyone else, although the door to his office at the end of the hall was open. The corridor was lined with locked doors, all of them expensively decorated meeting rooms.

Dale stepped further into the waiting area of the top floor and looked back at his son. The one thing he did approve of, was the pristine condition his son always kept himself in. Clean shaven with a neat haircut. Well-tailored clothes.

Although he didn't particularly deserve it, Jasper Munroe often looked like he had money.

But not today.

A shabby stubble had sprouted across his strong jaw, and his hair was a greasy mess. The bags under his bloodshot eyes told Dale his son wasn't sleeping, and whether that was fear, guilt, or the drugs, he couldn't tell.

But Jasper was clearly on the edge, and as he looked at his son, he wondered how authoritative he should be.

'Whatever it is, son. I can help.'

'Help?' Jasper stammered. 'Help? By throwing money at it?'

'I've spent a lot of money trying to fix this problem—'

'But you haven't done anything to try to fix me, have you? It's all for the business. All for your precious legacy.'

Dale refrained from losing his temper.

'You are my legacy. For Christ's sake, son, why do you think I'm trying to keep you out of prison? Or why I've sent Hudson to kill Sam? Because you are my son. And I want to, no…*have* to protect you.'

'Well, I decided to protect myself,' Jasper spat. Dale raised an eyebrow, and Jasper nodded to his office. Briskly, Dale marched down the corridor and pushed open the door to his plush office. Sat on the sofa, with tears rolling down her cheeks, was a young lady he'd seen at one of Jasper's initial court hearings.

'Jasper, what have you done?'

'I didn't rape her, if that's what you're implying.' Jasper stood in the door, his hand twitching as it clasped the gun.

'Whatever you think you're doing, it isn't helping. It's just going to make things worse.'

'No. NO!' Jasper's volume spiked erratically as he waved the gun. 'This bitch told Sam Pope that I raped her, and now I want her to tell the world that she was lying. I want you to get your news people. I want them to bring their cameras and I want her to tell the world I did nothing wrong.'

Dale looked at his deranged son, and then back at the

terrified woman. From the desperate plea of her watery eyes, he knew it was a true.

Jasper did rape her.

But he wanted the world to think differently. He wanted to get off scot-free.

'I'll have to make some calls,' Dale said firmly. 'But I need you to give me the gun.'

Jasper stomped forward and pressed the gun to his father's forehead.

'You're not in control this time.'

Dale nodded that he understood and then walked to his desk. The situation had spiralled so far out of hand, he had no idea how he would reign it back in.

He needed to placate his son.

He needed to protect the young woman who was crying on his sofa.

He needed to hear from Hudson that Sam Pope was dead.

As he sat at his desk, he blew out his cheeks in annoyance and opened his laptop. Moments later, as the breaking news flashed onto his screen, Dale Munroe's jaw tightened, and he looked up at Jasper.

Without knowing it, Jasper's actions may have just handed the Munroes their only way out of the mess Jasper had created.

The headline read *Four Dead in Brutal Glasgow Gangland Killing*

But Dale knew the truth.

Hudson was dead. So was his crew.

Which meant Sam Pope was heading to them to make good on his word.

And unbeknownst to him, Jasper had just secured himself a bargaining chip.

CHAPTER TWENTY-SIX

'Sir. You're not supposed to be here today?'

Assistant Commissioner Henrietta Sarrett stood to attention as McEwen stepped through the door. A fierce and driven woman, Sarrett had knocked down multiple doors of inequality and diversity to become a figurehead within the Met and a shining example to Black women in the city. McEwen trusted her explicitly and had already told her he expected her to kick him from his seat before he retired. McEwen nodded for her to relax, and she quickly gathered some notes from her desk.

'Busy day?' McEwen asked dryly.

'Ha. Ha. You've seen the news I take it?'

'It's why I'm here.'

'Well, I'm just about to jump onto a call with the CC from Glasgow and a few other people from your task force.' Sarrett rolled her eyes. 'I think we have some serious boot licking to do.'

'I can imagine.' McEwen took a seat at the desk. 'Fill me in when you get back. I know the CC pretty well, so he should be somewhat on our side.'

Sarrett opened the door, her arms wrapped around folders, and she raised her eyebrows.

'Four dead in his city by a guy we've let go a number of times?' She shrugged. 'I doubt it.'

McEwen chuckled as she disappeared, and he looked around the office. Sarrett's desk was as neat as a pin, and he was surprisingly calm about the inevitable backlash that would be coming their way from north of the border. His second in command was a sterling officer and a hell of a politician, and she seemed tailormade for the role.

As much as he tried, McEwen couldn't get his wife's words out of his head.

He'd allowed himself to hide behind the bureaucracy of the role as Commissioner of the Metropolitan Police, ensuring every party was as satisfied as could be and the city of London at least felt safe. But they hadn't done enough.

He hadn't done enough.

He had cosied up next to the city's most elite and powerful and curried their favour, ensuring he had support for his role by anyone who harboured any influence.

McEwen had played the game so many had before him, and he was on easy street.

But it wasn't enough.

He turned to the locked computer screen on the desk and tapped in his credentials. As soon as he arrived on the network, he pulled every digital file that was on record for Jasper Munroe.

Reading back the accusations and the statements caused his stomach to flip, and McEwen found himself reading each report with a balled fist.

Although he believed staunchly in the law, he couldn't believe the clear pattern of injustice that had fallen to these victims. Sexual assault and rape was an under-reported crime as it was, but for the women who had been brave enough to speak up, he felt sick at how he and the Met had let them down.

Had let Jasper Munroe, with his unlimited wealth and zero regard for the human condition, continue to live a life of luxury while these poor women would have to deal with the scars of trauma for the rest of their life.

Not just from Jasper.

But by the law itself.

For its failure to protect them.

As he finished reading the final report, he shook his head in disbelief and sat back in his chair. It was the final write up of Hayley Baker's case against Jasper, which had been dismissed due to a lack of corroborating evidence. The bottomless pockets of the Munroes had clearly been used to ensure Jasper's freedom, but without the paper trail to prove it, it was just a theory. One that was spouted in the comment section of any tabloid newspaper that gave Jasper Munroe an ounce of publicity.

To the public, it was clear what Jasper Munroe was.

But the influence of his father, and the extraordinary wealth at their disposal, meant that he would never be held to account for it.

It made the justice system look broken.

The Metropolitan Police look weak.

McEwen slammed his fist down with frustration, rattling the desk and causing a few pencils to roll onto the floor.

The irony of the situation was that he now found himself agreeing with Sam Pope.

The man he had publicly shamed in front of the cameras and had invested a lot of taxpayer's money into capturing. Instead of fighting the very true and obvious evil in front of their faces, the Met, and the media had allowed Sam to become the focus, while men like Jasper Munroe walked free.

Even with the weight of a nationwide police hunt bearing down his neck, Sam had marched through the Met's back garden and threatened Jasper. The popularity-craving public captured it on their phones and McEwen himself had seen the footage.

When he had first seen it, he had seen a criminal assaulting a few people and threatening the health and safety of a powerful ally's son.

Now, as he watched it back, he saw a good man, willing to put his own safety on the line, to fight for the right thing.

He saw bravery.

Conviction.

Integrity.

McEwen shook his mind clear, knowing he was verging into dangerous territory, as siding with the most wanted vigilante in the country was a death knoll for his career. Stout had told him how people like DI Adrian Pearce and DI Amara Singh were quietly shuffled out the door to pastures new.

It cleared up the headache of senior officers siding against their employer.

He couldn't in good conscience condone the killings of the four men in Glasgow, even if Sam was just fighting back against what McEwen assumed were Munroe's forces. The billionaire had told him that he'd handle it, but with none of the men being confirmed as Sam, McEwen assumed that Munroe hadn't got his money's worth. McEwen was certain that once the men had been identified, he'd be able to link them back to Dale Munroe.

Then he'd be able to apply the pressure on the powerful man and threaten not only his public image, but the integrity of his business. Considering it was built on trust with his clients, he was certain Dale would budge.

For the first time since he'd come into office, Bruce McEwen finally felt like he was in a position of power. All he needed was enough to implicate Dale, and then he'd be able to get to Jasper and deliver justice for all the women who'd been let down.

By him and the entire broken system.

McEwen dipped his hand into his jacket to retrieve his phone, wanting to send a message to Sarrett to request the autopsy reports of the four deceased when they were ready, when it buzzed in his hand.

An incoming call.

Dale Munroe.

With confusion spread across his brow, McEwen answered the call, unaware of the deal he was about to be offered and the dilemma he would be facing.

As Sam's eyes blinked the final remnants of sleep from his eyes, he looked up at the unfamiliar ceiling. It took a few moments before clarity set in and he remembered he was on Martin's sofa. It had been a long night, and the pain from his showdown with Hudson and his men had begun to set in. After they'd stumbled into the house in the early hours of the morning, Jane, Martin's wife, had tended to Sam's wounds. As a nurse, her first priority was her duty of care to the man, but after she patched Sam up, he could hear her scold Martin in the other room for the trouble he had brought to their doorstep. Their two boys were asleep in their beds, yet Martin had brought a bloodied vigilante into their home.

Martin explained the threat made against her and their kids and how Sam had put an end to it.

How Sam had effectively saved their lives.

Begrudgingly, Jane allowed Sam to spend the night under the strict condition that he'd be gone in the morning.

Sam had duly agreed and thanked her for her hospitality. His muscular body was beginning to bruise from the heavy body shots, and his eyebrow stung from the gash that Jane had carefully stitched back together. With a grunt of pain, Sam lifted himself from the sofa and slid his feet into his boots, before he stepped across the modest living room to look into the circular mirror on the wall.

He looked rough.

The few hour's sleep were enough for a brief recharge, but the mayhem of the last four days had begun to take its toll. His powerful jaw was now thick with greying stubble, and the eye beneath the stitching was beginning to darken with bruising. The constant travelling back and forth across the border had begun to etch its way onto his face, and exhausted bags hung under his eyes.

His lip was cut, and as he lifted his hand to dab at it, his ribs screamed with agony.

He was beat up.

But not broken.

Beyond the closed door, he could hear the jovial chatter of Martin's kids as they tucked into their breakfast, discussing their Christmas presents and not wanting to go to school tomorrow. The unmistakable smell of bacon wafted through the house, causing Sam's stomach to rumble, and he glanced at the photo tree hanging on the wall next to the mirror.

It was a display of happiness. Martin and Jane were in most pictures, either smiling or cuddling, along with multiple pictures of their sons pulling funny faces and enjoying life. Cherished memories of a happy family.

In the years gone by, Sam would have found the McGinn's photo display too difficult to look at. It would have triggered the pain and guilt of Jamie's death and sent his mind spiralling back towards a darker place. But Sam had made peace with the loss of his son, knowing that in his honour, he had continued to fight for the people who needed help. Sam was far from concrete, and that dark place was still lurking between the cracks, but the fight was what had put him back on a better path.

Had kept him going.

As he looked over the photos, he didn't feel one ounce of jealousy.

All he felt was happiness, and a smile crept across his beaten face, and he took pride in bringing Martin home alive.

'The faces they pull, eh?'

Martin's thick Scottish accent filled the room, and Sam turned. Martin was standing in the doorway, his dressing gown wrapped around his portly body and two mugs of coffee in his hand. He stepped into the room and handed one to Sam, who gratefully accepted.

'You have a nice family, Martin.'

'And thanks to you, I get to spend the day with them.' Martin took a sip of his coffee. 'You stepped out in front of a loaded gun, and a man who was more than willing to pull the trigger, to save me. I can't begin to tell you how grateful I am.'

'Well, I owed you one.' Sam shrugged. 'I brought that trouble to your door.'

'Aye.' Martin agreed. 'With that in mind, I'll be heading back to the yard shortly. Call it in, you know? So you better…'

'I better be gone.' Sam nodded and finished his coffee. 'Thank you for everything. And please, thank Jane for me. She didn't have to do that for me.'

'Good people help good people, Sam.' Martin retrieved the mug from Sam and smiled. 'You don't always have to do everything on your own.'

Sam slowly bent down and picked up his jacket and

slid it tentatively over his powerful frame, and then extended his hand to Martin.

'Thank you, Martin.'

Martin took it and shook firmly.

'Stay safe, Sam.'

Sam nodded, and then quietly stepped out of the living room. The hallway was narrow and proudly lined with the smiling faces of Jimmy and Drew in their school uniforms. The kitchen door was ajar, and the magnificent smell of cooked meat filtered through, along with the giggle of the two pictured boys. Sam pulled open the front door, and the bitter cold of the Sunday morning welcomed him with an icy slap to the face. The street was covered in frost and the walk promised to be a treacherous one. Just as Sam stepped through the door and down the step, a voice called out to him.

'Wait.'

It was Jane, and Sam turned around in surprise as Martin's wife rushed to the door. Sam braced himself, as the woman had been far from welcoming the night before, despite patching him up. He'd put her husband in danger, and quite rightly, he turned to face the music. To his surprise, she threw her arms around his neck and hugged him, burying her head into his shoulder. Taken aback, Sam eventually reciprocated and hugged her back, and when she pulled away, she smiled at him.

'Thank you for keeping him safe. He told me what you did.'

'I didn't have a choice.'

'You always have a choice.' Jane pressed the palm of her hand tenderly to Sam's face, offering him some comfort in the midst of another war. 'It's just you always make the selfless one.'

She stepped back and handed him an object wrapped in kitchen roll. Sam pulled away the edges to see two bacon sandwiches, and his eyes lit up as his stomach growled. Overwhelmed by his gratitude, Sam could only muster a nod of appreciation.

'Thank you.'

'You're a good man, Sam,' Jane offered as she stepped back into the house and stood next to Martin. 'Now go do what you have to do.'

Sam took a few moments and then turned and headed down their front garden and out onto the icy street. His purpose had been renewed, and he knew, now that the deadline had passed, he needed to hold Jasper Munroe to account.

He had to keep his word.

As he marched down the street and devoured his sandwich, his phone buzzed in his pocket and Sam was thankful that Martin had lent him a charger for the night. Sam fiddled with his jacket to answer it, he had no idea that the balance of power was about to shift so drastically.

CHAPTER TWENTY-SEVEN

As a billionaire who dominated the cyber security space, Dale Munroe was able to unpick locks that nobody knew existed. By creating a monopoly over the industry, he had cherry-picked the best analysts and coders in the business, had engulfed numerous rival companies and run every trace of competition into the ground. It meant that when he needed something done; it was at the click of his fingers.

He needed to contact Sam.

And he knew just how to do it.

Sam still had the phone he'd taken from the first failed attempt to bring him in, and had since been contactable on one of their phones.

A phone he had contacted Hudson on.

Although Hudson was now clearly dead, Dale had his number, which he was able to pass on to one of the top analysts in his company, who was able to provide him with all the incoming numbers over the past few days.

Within minutes, Dale had the number he needed, and he smirked as he hoped the incoming call would interrupt Sam's Sunday morning.

The phone rang a few times before it finally answered.

'Hello?'

'Sam.'

'Dale.' Sam's voice was laced with venom. *'I assume you're not calling to tell me your son has handed himself in.'*

Dale stood from his desk, phone clasped to his ear.

'I don't know how many times you need to be told, but nobody threatens me or my family.'

'Or your business, right? Because that's what you're really protecting isn't it?'

'You're damn right it is!' Dale yelled, slamming his fist against the wall. 'Just because you're on some bullshit crusade to try to clear your conscience doesn't mean you understand what fighting for something is. What I've built, Sam, it goes beyond just my company. Hundreds of companies survive off what my company provides for them. If I go down, they go down and that is pressure you will never understand.'

Dale took a few deep breaths and tried to collect himself. There was an audible pause before Sam's voice crackled through.

'Pressure? You have no idea about pressure.' Wherever Sam was, he was outside, and the howling wind echoed behind him. *'You sit in boardrooms all day, or behind an oak desk in an expensive suit, deciding how to share your wealth. You've never been in the heart of combat. You've never been trapped in a situation knowing one false move, and that would be it. Everything would be taken away from you. You've never known pressure, but you do now, Dale.'*

'Fuck you,' Dale spat, his voice rising with his anger. 'Do you know how many people have come after me? After my business? Do you know how many people have tried to bring me down? You don't scare me, Sam. I've been fighting for as long as you've been born.'

'Not like this, you haven't. The men you sent after me, even they think your son should be rotting in a prison cell.'

'I don't give a flying fuck about my son,' Dale yelled in a blind rage. 'That useless shit has been a stain on my name for as long as I can remember, but the impact of you taking him down and the aftermath of what I've done to stop that happening would have too big an impact on my company. On my true legacy.'

'Then there's nothing left to say.'

'I wouldn't be so sure.' Dale marched across the office to the sofa and held the phone out. 'Speak.'

'Sam? It's Hayley.' Her voice was shaking with fear and judging by Sam's silence, it had caught him completely off-guard.

'You're on speaker, Sam,' Dale said smugly.

'Hayley, have they hurt you?'

'N-no.'

'Not yet,' Dale corrected.

'You've made a very dangerous mistake, Dale.'

'No, Sam. I just made, what we call in business, a bold move. So here is what's going to happen. You are to come to this office at exactly six this evening. You come unarmed. You come alone. Follow these instructions, and Hayley will be returned to her family safe and sound.'

'Or what?'

'Or I will let my bastard of a son loose on her once more and this time, Sam, it will be you who failed to save her.' Dale glared at a terrified Hayley. 'See you at six.'

Dale hung up the phone and then tossed it onto his desk. He felt sick to his stomach, and the idea of threatening a harmless young woman with a sickening sexual assault rattled him. The fact that he knew he was protecting his son for his own selfish reasons offered little comfort, and despite his tendency for a morning drink becoming worryingly regular, he lifted the decanter of Scotch with a shaking hand and poured himself a glass.

Sam Pope wasn't the villain of this piece, and Dale

knew that. For what it was worth, he understood why Hudson had found him so impressive, but the fact was, he was threatening everything Dale had worked for. As a man who'd dominated the world before him, Dale couldn't let that happen, and while his disdain for his son was palpable, he wasn't going to allow someone to come into his life and turn it upside down. Not even if it was justice.

Not even if his son deserved it.

Dale Munroe would be credited as the man who orchestrated Sam Pope's downfall, and it would only add to the aura he'd created as one of the most powerful businessmen in the world.

He'd still be able to walk out of this entire situation as the winner.

With his plan set in motion, his useless son sleeping off his coke binge in one of the meeting rooms, and with his leverage crying on his sofa, Dale lifted the glass and took a sip, gazing out of the top-floor window and berating himself for letting it get this far.

At six o'clock that evening, it would all be over, and Dale Munroe would be sitting atop the world once more.

Jasper knew, as he looked down at the line of cocaine on the meeting room table, that he had lost his grip on his mental state. It was a strange feeling, knowing that he wasn't in control of his actions but not being able to rectify it, and he stared at the white powder in confusion. It felt like a permanent state of drunkenness, that he knew he needed to lean forward to snort the drug but didn't know how to connect his brain to the action and make it happen.

Somehow, it did, and his head dropped forward, and he inhaled the powder into his nose, the rush smacking the back of his skull like a torpedo and sending him shooting backwards in his chair.

There was no coming back from it.

It wasn't just the past few days that had taken him to breaking point; it had been years of living in an enormous shadow and struggling under the pressure the shade provided.

Everything he had done was to try to forge his own path and be his own man, but having grown up with no limits, he'd never had the correct guidance.

Never had the lines drawn for him.

With the world treating him like he owned it, Jasper had basked in the privilege of his wealth and had allowed it to corrupt his mind. The rules didn't apply to him and when he broke them it didn't matter.

His overbearing father would be there to make it go away.

As the cocaine rattled through his body, Jasper stumbled from the chair and nearly collided with another. The table shook, with the last remnants of his cocaine spilling next to the loaded handgun he'd pointed at his father.

His own flesh and blood.

A wave of desperation crashed across his mind, and Jasper felt his eyes watering. For so long, he had craved his father's approval, yet here he was, abducting women and binging on drugs while his father tried his best to clean up the mess he was leaving behind.

That desperation burst forward and as he wept, Jasper stumbled towards the door, ready to embrace his father for the first time in years and finally succumb to whatever his father wished.

He could be the son his father had wanted, and they could rebuild the Munroe family name.

Together.

Jasper's errant hand finally found the doorhandle, and

he yanked it down, pulling open the door and instantly, he could hear his father's booming, authoritative voice.

'Fuck you. Do you know how many people have come after me? After my business? Do you know how many people have tried to bring me down? You don't scare me, Sam. I've been fighting for as long as you've been born.'

His father was on the phone to Sam Pope, the man who'd threatened his freedom and the man his father had spent the last few days tracking down. A plan had clearly entered his father's mind when he demanded Hayley stay in the office with him, while Jasper slept off whatever drug he had been abusing, and Jasper, as he always had, obliged weakly.

Hearing his father threaten a man like Sam Pope filled Jasper with pride, and his broken mind was trying its best to keep him on track.

To get him to his father.

Just as he was about to step foot into the corridor, his father responded to Sam once more.

'I don't give a flying fuck about my son. That useless shit has been a stain on my name for as long as I can remember, but the impact of you taking him down and the aftermath of what I've done to stop that happening would have too big an impact on my company. On my true legacy.'

Jasper froze.

He blinked a few tears from his eyelids, and they slithered down his cheek and into his scruffy stubble. Every muscle in his body ached and the devastating words collided with the memories that his brain was thrusting to the forefront of his mind.

All the disappointed scowls.

All the spiteful comments.

All the disparaging remarks about the "career" he'd tried to build for himself when it was apparent he wasn't the business mogul his father was.

The times at family get-togethers or business events, where his father would belittle him for his and his friends' amusement.

All of it played out through cracked memories, struggling to form against the excessive drug use and the painful words.

'I don't give a flying fuck about my son.'

It replayed over and over in his mind as he shuffled back into the meeting room, barely registering the environment as he bumped into the table. With a feeble, shaking arm, he reached across the table and limply lifted the handgun.

He had used it to break into Hayley Baker's house, where he had assaulted her father and then forced her mother to tie him up before he'd threatened Hayley to do the same to her mother.

They would be lying there, unable to move, not knowing where their child was.

But unlike his own father, at least they would care.

'I don't give a flying fuck about my son.'

With his feet dragging across the floor like a lost zombie, Jasper shuffled out of the meeting room and headed down the corridor, following the sound of his father's voice as he hung up the call, followed by the unmistakable sound of him fixing a drink.

Nothing registered firmly in his mind.

Jasper knew he was crying but made no effort to stop or figure out why.

There was a door before him, that was all he could muster, and he felt the weight of the gun in his hand. Just as he reached out to push it open, it swung backwards, and his father almost collided with him.

'Jasper.' His father startled. 'You look like shit.'

Dale Munroe studied the vacant expression across his son's face and frowned. The young man was a sickly pale, and as always, displaying his weakness. The tears were sliding from his eyes and Dale tutted as he followed them down his cheek. His eyes continued down and he noticed the gun.

Dale's eyes widened in fear.

'Jasper, I need you to put the gun down.' Dale took a step back into his office, his hands held up in surrender. 'Come on, son. We're almost through this now.'

His father was saying something to him, but the words were muffled. Somewhere in the room, Hayley squealed with fear.

He didn't care.

Jasper knew his father was speaking, but he heard only one thing.

'I don't give a flying fuck about my son.'

Jasper felt his mind snap.

He lifted the gun and pulled the trigger.

The gunshot was deafeningly loud.

The following scream from Hayley was rife with terror.

Then, all Jasper could hear was the sound of his father stumbling to the ground, blood pumping from the bullet wound in his stomach and gurgling up through his throat. With his hand still shaking from the impact, Jasper began to feel a sense of calm.

A weight had been lifted from his shoulders, and at that moment, the finer details of the room began to return to his vision.

There was no going back now.

Whatever had broken in his mind was unfixable.

He watched as his father choked on his own blood and stared at his son with pleading eyes.

Jasper watched.

And he smiled.

CHAPTER TWENTY-EIGHT

A young child stared across the train at Sam until his mother hurriedly diverted his eyes away. Sam understood.

He'd looked better.

The black boots, trousers and jacket he'd bought before he'd burnt the Sure Fire building to the ground were thick with mud and grime, a result of his battle with Hudson and his crew. Sam knew that if he got down and dealt with the mud of society, he'd get dirty, but there was no denying he looked rough.

The gash across his eyebrow, split lip and bruised eye didn't help either.

It was no surprise to him that the surrounding seats of the train to London Euston had been left untouched, with nobody wanting to sit next to a man who clearly looked like he was having a bad day.

Who could be trouble.

It was a sobering moment for him. He posed no threat to the public, despite what the media and the police said. Yet not one of them had even questioned whether he was okay. Nobody had offered him more than a disgusted glance before deciding on a different seat for their journey. Some had even chosen to stand.

The public he fought so valiantly for, where the same people who didn't have the courtesy to check on someone they deemed unruly. It was why the homeless felt invisible.

It didn't annoy him that somebody couldn't help him; it annoyed him that nobody even offered. The world was a closed off place, yet the tech companies claimed that it had never been more connected. Social media platforms had allowed people to fabricate a reality where their life was perfect, and their value was ascertained through the number of likes or views they garnered.

It was how someone like Jasper Munroe, a repugnant human being with no empathy for anyone, was able to amass a cultlike following.

How he was able to be seen as someone to aspire to, as opposed to someone the world despised.

Sam had shed blood, sweat and tears for people he didn't know, fighting back against people who made the world a dark and dangerous place and yet over two hours into the near five-hour train journey, not one person had reached out.

He didn't need them to.

But he'd have liked them to.

Were they worth fighting for?

Sam knew the answer to that question before he even asked it of himself. Despite the selfishness of the world, he knew that he would keep fighting. People like Hayley Baker, who had done nothing wrong other than accept an invitation to an elite party, were counting on him. Now, she found herself being held captive by a dangerous billionaire and his worthless son, all because she had the courage to stand up against them.

The justice system had let her down.

The press and media had let her down.

Sam wouldn't.

He couldn't.

There was no escaping the fact that he was walking into a trap. For all he knew, Dale Munroe had fifty men with assault rifles waiting for him at his office, ready to unload every single bullet into him the moment he stepped through the door. Or Hayley might not even be there when he arrived.

But Dale had sent him the address.

He'd named the time.

Despite not knowing what he was walking into, Sam had no other choice.

He had to keep going.

Even if the world wasn't worth fighting for at times, someone had to fight for it.

For Hayley.

For anyone who had been betrayed by the mechanisms put in place to protect them.

Someone had to fight back.

With two hours left of his journey, Sam crossed his arms, slouched slightly in his chair and rested his head against the window, hoping to catch a bit of rest before walking into a suspected ambush.

As he did, he knew that that someone had to be him.

Until the final beat in his chest, he'd keep fighting.

As the sun set in the early Sunday evening, McEwen felt the temperature drop with it. He'd been sitting in his car for over an hour, watching the entrance to the Sure Fire Inc. headquarters with an unbreakable stare.

Not one person came or went.

It wasn't entirely surprising, and by nine o'clock the following morning, the building would be alive with high-paid analysts and manipulative senior managers all scurrying over themselves at the behest of Dale Munroe. After Dale had offered McEwen his proposition, he'd spiralled into a moral quandary that had irritated him.

As a police officer of twenty-five years, and the most senior figure in the entire Metropolitan Police, McEwen believed his understanding of right and wrong should have been as clear cut as his smart hair style.

But things existed in shades of grey, and it was a place he never thought he would be.

He'd thought about calling his wife, hopeful that she'd be able to provide another nugget of wisdom, but he didn't want to intrude on her day. They'd worked hard, both professionally and personally, to build their perfect life together, and he didn't want to take away her calm Sunday, especially in the lead up to the holidays.

Besides, this wasn't her problem.

Not her problem to solve.

After everything that had transpired in Glasgow, from his miraculous escape from police custody to the bloody war zone of Martin McGinn's haulage yard, Sam had become a perplexing figure in McEwen's mind. Going by the facts, the man was a known and violent vigilante, who in the last week, had threatened the son of a prominent London figure, assaulted a few of his friends, escaped from and assaulted two police officers, seemingly killed four men and was now on the run.

As a felony list, Sam had done a pretty impressive job.

What was grinding McEwen's gears was that despite the overwhelming evidence of Sam's crimes, all of them were tinged in the shades of grey that he despised.

Jasper Munroe most likely did assault that young woman, yet power and money equalled influence, and his father had a reputation for using both in equal measure. The men Sam had killed were likely hired guns, trying to put him in the ground before he could make good on his promise to hold Jasper accountable for his heinous actions.

Sam's actions were criminal. His motives? Not so much.

'Shades of grey,' McEwen uttered to himself before he checked the clock on his illuminated dashboard.

Two minutes to five.

It was time to decide.

That morning, after his wife had set him straight, had convinced him to do the right thing. When he'd headed to his office, he was adamant in his mind that he would risk the wrath of the billionaire and finally take Jasper Munroe to task for his actions. It sent his mind racing with the likely scenario of losing his job, or at least having to fight like hell to keep his seat.

Dale would come after him.

His elite level friends, too.

They would undoubtedly use their influence to turn the heads of politicians and senior figures, all of whom depended on their backing, to ensure he was ushered out of the Met with his pension paid, but his reputation tarnished.

But he'd have done his job.

He'd have put the safety of the public first and he'd have upheld the law, something he had sworn to do over two decades before.

But then Dale had called him, and offered him the opportunity of his career, something that would have eclipsed taking the top job and something that would have cemented his own legacy for years to come.

He had offered him Sam Pope.

Dale hadn't gone into specifics, but he admitted to trying to tackle Sam the same way the vigilante himself went about his business.

Outside the explicit lines of the law.

Although he was admitting to a crime, Dale did give McEwen a compelling reminder of exactly what Sam Pope, to the watching world, truly was.

A criminal.

A dangerous vigilante.

A stone-cold killer.

Dale had posed the question, which had rattled through McEwen's brain all day.

'What would make the bigger difference? Arresting a pointless loser like his son, or bringing down the most wanted man in the United Kingdom?'

As the clock on his dashboard hit five, McEwen threw open his door and stepped out into the freezing London evening. The road was clear, illuminated by the streetlights and he marched across to thc building and went inside.

He still didn't know what he was there to do.

Shades of grey.

As he rode the lift all the way to the top floor, he stepped out into the hallway, where he had expected to be greeted by Dale. At the far end of the corridor, the door to the billionaire's office was ajar, and he strode purposefully towards it, hoping that inspiration would find its way to him and he'd have his answer before he reached the office.

With his mind elsewhere, he didn't see as Jasper Munroe emerged from the door to the office.

When he did, all he saw was the young man raising the gun.

The gunshot echoed down the hallway.

As he sat, watching his father slowly bleed to death, Jasper could feel a gnawing in his brain. Like an insect scuttling from one side of his skull to the other there was an annoying notion floating through his mind that he should call an ambulance.

That if he didn't, his father would die.

But he sat and watched.

Somewhere behind him, he could hear Hayley crying.

But his focus was on his father, who stared at him with wide, fearful eyes, begging for help. He had turned a ghastly pale, as the puddle of blood around him grew and spread across the floor of his office, where for decades, he'd ruled over so many people with an iron fist in an even heavier glove.

The same office where he'd closed deals potentially worth billions.

The same office where he'd belittled Jasper, time after time after time.

And the same office where he'd struck Jasper a few days ago.

Now, it would be the place where he died.

There were no final words from the man. Dale Munroe lay back, his eyes fixed firmly on his son and even in his last breaths, Jasper didn't detect any sense of guilt or love from the man.

Just disgust.

He had never been able to live up to the man's expectations, but now he didn't have to. He tried to envisage what would happen to the Munroe empire with Dale gone, but his brain wouldn't allow it. All he could focus on were cracked memories of his father showing little affection and the last thing he could remember him saying.

'I don't give a flying fuck about my son.'

Jasper moaned loudly and bashed the side of his head with the gun, trying to break it open and take the words out. Hayley pulled her knees to her chest in terror and wept silently. Somewhere among Jasper's self-torment,

Dale breathed his last breath and passed away, his eyes locked on his murderous son.

Jasper needed some air.

The windows of the building were locked shut, a standard safety practice in most high-rise buildings in the city to ensure nobody could end their day or life early by leaping through them. Jasper imagined it would be tempting. It would close off all the problems that had been worming their way towards him and it would shut down the rapid breaking of his mind.

There were still things to take care of.

Hayley.

Sam Pope.

The thought of being charged with his father's murder hadn't even entered his brain and, while muttering to himself, he stared at the door to the office with vacant, bloodshot eyes. Hayley squirmed on the sofa, terrified of the man that was rapidly disintegrating before her.

He'd done unspeakable things to her when he was of a clear mind. She was terrified of what would happen when he turned his attention to her now.

Jasper stepped forward and yanked open the office door and his eyes illuminated in shock as the tall, imposing figure of Commissioner Bruce McEwen blocked his path. The man started and lifted his hands in surrender, but Jasper lifted the gun instinctively.

McEwen turned as if to run, but Jasper pulled the trigger and he saw the bullet rip through the man's hip and send him spiralling back into the hallway. Hayley screamed at the second gunshot of the evening, and she looked out over the dark city of London, wondering what had happened to her parents.

There was no one coming to rescue her now.

Through gritted teeth, and with a trail of blood behind him, McEwen began to pull himself across the corridor floor, a feeble attempt to get away from Jasper, who casually walked behind him, the gun hanging sloppily by his side. Halfway between the office and the lift, Jasper pressed his boot down on McEwen's gunshot wound, causing the most powerful police officer in London to roar with agony.

'What are you doing here?' Jasper asked, his eyes crazed.

'Your father called me,' McEwen said through heavy breaths. 'He said he'd made an arrangement for me to arrest Sam Pope.'

'Bullshit,' Jasper spat angrily.

'I swear, Jasper. He told me that he'd invited Pope here and I was to arrest him.' McEwen grimaced as Jasper lifted his foot off the bullet wound. 'Ask him if you don't believe me.'

'I can't.' Jasper shrugged. 'He's dead.'

'What?' McEwen struggled to a seating position and pressed his hand to the gunshot wound. 'How?'

Jasper wiggled the gun and smirked.

'Families. Am I right?'

'Jesus, Jasper,' McEwen yelled. 'What have you done?'

'I took control. All I've been hearing my whole life was that I was never good enough. That I was a disappointment. Then, when I made something of myself, woman after woman tried to take it away from me. For what? Because I took what I wanted from them?'

'You raped them,' McEwen said firmly, as if confirming the fact to himself. Jasper rolled his eyes.

'Then one of them tells a man like Sam Pope about it and once again, I'm the disappointment. I'm the target of the abuse. Well, not anymore, Commissioner. Ha ha ha. Not anymore.'

McEwen winced in pain as he clung to his hip, and he looked into the vacant, broken eyes of Jasper. Whether it was the situation, the drug abuse or his father's neglect, the pressure had built too much and burst.

The man was gone.

'Jasper, you need to put the gun down and…'

Jasper lifted the gun and aimed it at McEwen.

'Or what?' Jasper cackled. 'You're going to arrest me? Do me a favour, cuff yourself to the radiator.'

'Excuse me?'

'Do it.' Jasper bent down and pressed the gun to his head. 'Now.'

McEwen struggled as he adjusted himself and then winced as he momentarily lifted the pressure on his gunshot wound. As he did, the blood pumped out quicker and he knew that he needed medical attention otherwise he'd suffer the same fate as Dale Munroe.

He'd bleed out.

As the cuff clasped onto the radiator behind him, McEwen pressed his hand back to the hole in his hip and then groaned in pain as Jasper rooted into the man's pocket and pulled out his phone. He tossed it further down the corridor, out of reach, and then stood with a grin.

'My father said Sam Pope was coming here?'

'Yes.' McEwen was in agony. 'We can still work this out, Jasper.'

'Oh, I will.' Jasper grinned and waved the gun again. 'But first, I have one more person who I need to settle up with.'

'Jasper, I haven't done anything to hurt you…'McEwen began.

'Oh, I'm not talking about you.' Jasper's eyes shot back to the office. 'I'm talking about her.'

McEwen's eyes followed Jasper's gaze to the office door, and standing in the doorway, with a look of sheer terror, was Hayley Baker. Jasper began to march back to the room where his father died, and Hayley screamed and dashed back inside. McEwen yanked his arm as hard as he could against his binds, but it was no use. He screamed at Jasper to stop what he was doing.

But it was too late.

There was nothing he could do.

With the young lady trapped inside the office, he could only watch as the crazed and armed rapist approached the door, ready to end her life.

CHAPTER TWENTY-NINE

The whole day had been a blur for Hayley.

When the sound of her father being assaulted echoed up the stairwell of her family home, she had rushed down the stairs along with her mother to help. While her mother made it to the bottom, Hayley froze when she saw Jasper Munroe. Memories of what he'd done to her came flooding back, paralysing her, and she could only watch as he held her parents at gunpoint. With her father on the ground, groaning and bleeding, Jasper had closed the door and then demanded Hayley find some duct tape otherwise he would kill them both. Throughout the panic, her mother remained a pillar of calm, assuring Hayley everything was fine, even when she was ordered to tape her mother's wrists and feet together, and bind each of her parents to separate chairs.

Jasper had demanded their phones, too, and after he had smashed them to pieces, he wrenched Hayley by the arm, warned her not to scream and then marched her to his car. With the gun pointed at her, she was instructed to drive, and considering she had only passed her driving test a few months before, she did a surprisingly good job under the pressure.

She was certain he was going to assault her again.

Or worse, kill her.

But the man just kept snorting drugs and arguing with himself, seemingly adamant that he was going to fix the situation.

Prove his dad wrong.

Prove the world wrong.

She didn't sleep at all, but when Jasper's father arrived at the office, she felt a small semblance of safety. The senior Munroe was a terrifying man in his own right, but he exuded an authority over his son that seemed to wrestle control of the situation. Jasper was sent to sleep off his cocktail of drugs, while Dale made a threatening call to Sam Pope.

Dale assured her, once Sam arrived, she would be free to go. In fact, he'd hand her over to the Commissioner of the Metropolitan Police himself.

That all changed when Jasper put a bullet through the man's stomach, and then, later that afternoon, as the winter night had descended upon the city, shot the head of the police through the hip.

Any chance she had of survival seemed to have evaporated when the commissioner was handcuffed to the radiator in the corridor and Jasper turned and faced her, his eyes wide with rage.

Hayley screamed and dashed back into the office, looking around frantically for anything she could use for protection. On the near wall of the office, Dale had a number of framed photos and certificates, all to show his importance and plump his now useless ego. Beyond the door, she could hear the commissioner begging Jasper to stop, doing his level best to reason with the unreasonable.

The door flew open and Hayley slid behind it, providing herself with some cover.

Jasper stepped in.

Her hand clasped the nearest object.

'Where are you, you little bitch?' Jasper spat crudely, erratically flicking his head from side to side.

Hayley stepped forward and hit her hip on the door. The sound alerted Jasper, who turned, only for the thick, metal frame of a photo to crack viciously into his cheekbone. Already woozy on his feet, Jasper fell to the side, landing on one knee and screaming in agony.

'My fucking face!'

As his anger filled the room, Hayley dropped the broken frame and ran through the door, rushing to the fallen McEwen.

'Where are the keys?' she asked, as McEwen took deep breaths through the pain.

'He took them. You need to get out of here.'

'I can't leave you.'

'Just go.'

McEwen stared into Hayley's eyes and nodded, and she understood. Quickly, she pushed herself up and rushed down the hallway towards the lift. She pressed the button, but just as she did, the lift began to descend the building, and she cursed under her breath. She tried the stairwell door.

Locked.

'Oh, you're gonna fuck pay for that.'

Jasper's threat boomed out of the office, and in a panic, Hayley pushed open the nearest meeting room door and stepped in, closing it as quietly as possible. As her door closed, Jasper emerged, his cheek hanging open, revealing the muscles beneath and a stream of blood that was falling down his jaw.

'It's over, Jasper,' McEwen yelled. 'She's long gone.'

Jasper ignored him and rushed down the corridor to the lift. It was on the ground floor and just as he was about to scream in rage, he stopped himself. After a few moments of quiet reflection, he turned to McEwen and smirked.

'I didn't hear the doors open.'

Jasper's attention turned to the meeting room doors along the corridor and he pulled his gun up and approached the first one.

'You're going to go to prison for a long time. Do you hear me?' McEwen spat, trying to divert his attention. 'You think you'll get away with this? With killing your own father?'

Jasper stopped, and his eye twitched.

'Shut up.'

McEwen knew he was kicking the hornet's nest, but there was no other play.

'You've pretty much admitted you're a rapist. And now, you're a killer.'

'I said shut up!'

'Your father was right. You are a disappointment.'

Jasper stepped away from the meeting room door and marched over to McEwen, knelt down, and pushed the gun as hard as he could into McEwen's forehead. He slammed the commissioner's skull against the radiator and leant in close, his red eyes wild.

The man was completely gone.

'Say another word,' Jasper threatened. 'And I will blow your fucking brains out.'

McEwen grunted with discomfort. His head was pounding.

'You'll rot in prison for the things you've done.'

Jasper stood, and a vile smirk fell across his face.

'Well, maybe I'll just have some fun while I still have my freedom, then.'

Cruelly, Jasper stamped on McEwen's bullet wound,

causing the commissioner to double over in agony. With desperate calls for the young man to stop, Jasper returned to the meeting room door and booted it open. This time, Hayley's attempt at a blindside was thwarted and Jasper slapped her with the back of his hand, sending her spiralling onto the table.

Outside the room, the lift reached the top floor once again.

There had been no welcoming committee when he'd arrived at the building, and Sam cautiously entered. The grand lobby was deathly quiet, and Sam walked through, keeping his eyes on any potential dark corner someone could be watching him from. The last time he'd been in a building as decadent, he had been faced with a barrage of bullets by Dana Kovalenko's henchmen.

Dale's instructions had been to come alone and unarmed, and Sam knew that the man didn't make idle threats.

Hayley's life was on the line, and Sam would make sure she got home.

Whatever the cost.

He pressed the button for the lift and waited. The screen above the door confirmed it was moving down from the top floor, and Sam thought of Mel. It had been a long time since he'd felt a connection with anyone and walking away from her had broken what little of his heart was left. The last time he'd fallen for someone, Amara Singh had decided to take a job with a shady government agency, something that Sam just couldn't do.

He willingly went to prison, meaning their connection had been severed and in the near three years since, he hadn't heard a word about her.

Then he'd met Mel.

It had moved fast, but it had been worth it.

But the world wasn't a perfect place and when people like the Munroes did as they pleased with no comeuppance, someone had to do something. It was a compulsion within him, and Sam had tried his best to step away from the fight.

To try to have a normal life.

But he was who he was.

The fight was in him.

He'd broken Mel's heart.

He'd broken his promise to Cassie.

But he knew he was doing the right thing, and when the lift doors opened, Sam stepped in without hesitation. He took a deep breath, pressed the button to the penthouse, and waited for the doors to close. As he rode up the building, he wondered what was waiting for him on the other side of the doors.

The police?

A loaded gun?

It didn't matter. Dale Munroe was a vile, nasty man, but he was a businessman. He'd laid out the terms of the deal to Sam, and Sam was certain he'd honour them.

Sam for Hayley.

If this was the end of the road for Sam, at least he knew he'd done right by another girl the justice system hadn't.

He'd done the right thing.

The doors opened and Sam was greeted by nothing. The sound of a struggle drew him from the doors and into the hallway, and that was when he saw Commissioner McEwen. The senior officer was pale, clutching at his hip that was bleeding onto the floor from an obvious bullet wound. Somewhere else on the floor, Sam could hear the thrashing sound of a struggle, along with a shrill shriek of pain.

Hayley.

Sam stepped forward and drew McEwen's gaze. He expected the commissioner to bore a hole straight through him, such was the vitriol with which he'd regarded Sam on the news. But Sam saw something that surprised him.

Hope.

Sam lifted his finger to his lips and stepped silently down the hallway, his eyes trained on the nearest door. He looked to McEwen for confirmation and got it.

'You're fucking dead, bitch!'

The words echoed through the crack in the door, and Sam gently pushed it open to reveal Jasper Munroe looming over the table. Pinned to the surface was Hayley, struggling for life, as Jasper clasped his hands around her throat. The young lady clawed and scratched as she gasped for life, and she managed to grab at the exposed muscle of his ripped cheek. Jasper howled in pain and then drew his hand up to drive his fist down into the young woman.

He threw it down with all his might.

But it stopped a few inches from her face. Jasper's mind raced with panic as he saw the fingers clasped around his wrist and despite his best efforts, he felt his arm being wrenched back until he turned and came face to face with the man who'd sat across from him three nights ago.

Sam Pope.

There were no words to say, and before Jasper could even utter anything, Sam hauled him away from the table and then swung a right hook with every ounce of his power. The fist cracked into Jasper's jaw and sent him stumbling out of the door into the hallway, where he slammed into the wall and cried in fear.

Sam turned to Hayley and offered his hand, helping her off the table as she rubbed her throat.

'Did he hurt you?' Sam asked.

'I'll live.'

Sam nodded and stepped through the doorway, just as Jasper was pushing himself off the wall, drawing the gun from the back of his trousers. Sam sent him flying back into it with a stiff boot to the chest and, as Jasper rebounded back, he took him off his feet with a brutal uppercut.

Jasper hit the ground hard, a few feet from McEwen and dropped his gun as fell. He was clinging to consciousness, and Sam picked up the weapon, stood over Jasper and aimed the gun directly at him.

'Don't do it, Sam.'

McEwen piped up, grimacing as he sat up straight.

'The man's a rapist,' Sam replied, not taking his eyes off the mutilated and blood-covered face of Jasper Munroe.

'Then leave him to us.'

'Your way didn't work before,' Sam snapped. 'It allowed him to hurt more women. Hayley.'

'I know. I know. And I'm sorry,' McEwen said through gritted teeth. 'We will do better. I will do better. But trust me, he's not worth the bullet.'

'It will keep him down for good.'

'He's already put a bullet in me. He killed his own father, for Christ's sake.'

'Dale Munroe is dead?'

'Yup.' McEwen nodded. 'I take it that means you're off the hook?'

'I don't know. Am I?' Sam shot a glance at McEwen and waited for his answer. The man had made Sam public enemy number one for the past few months, and yet here he was, trying to reason with him. McEwen sighed.

'Get my phone from his pocket and toss it to me, will you?'

Sam looked at Hayley and then handed the gun to her.

'If he moves, put a bullet in him.' Hayley held the gun out as Sam bent down, pulling the phone from Jasper's pocket, and tossed it to McEwen. He also pulled out the cuff keys. 'I'm keeping these.'

'Fair enough.' McEwen unlocked his phone. 'I'm going to call this in, Sam. What with me being handcuffed and all, I guess you better get out of here. It's the best I can do.'

'Understood.' Sam nodded respectfully to the commissioner and then stood up. He took the gun from Hayley and placed his hand on her shoulder. 'You stay here. He'll get you home safe.'

Hayley buried her head into Sam's shoulder and hugged him. He ignored the burning pain in his ribs and reciprocated, wrapping his muscular arms around her.

'Thank you.' Hayley stepped back, wiping away a tear. 'Thank you for believing me.'

Sam smiled and then placed the handcuff key in her hand.

'When the lift gets to the ground floor, un-cuff him.' He looked back at McEwen. 'He's one of the good ones.'

McEwen nodded his thanks to Sam, and then Sam marched back to the lift. The door opened and as he stepped in, Hayley stepped back into view. With tears in her eyes, she waved to Sam.

Sam waved back, and the doors closed, and as soon as he left the building, Sam zipped his jacket up and headed back towards the city centre.

McEwen had given him a head start, but the hunt would never end.

Neither would the fight.

Which meant Sam had to move, as someone had to keep everyone safe. As the darkness of the night sky fell all around him, Sam stuffed his hands into his pockets, dipped his head to shield it from the cold and the drizzle, and headed towards the nearest dark alley.

CHAPTER THIRTY

The conference room was full to capacity, with the British media cramming in as closely as they could, some even sharing seats. Men and women lined the walls, holding expensive cameras, and everyone was staring straight ahead at the table on the raised platform. Behind it was Commissioner Bruce McEwen, who had just lowered himself into his seat with a lot of discomfort.

It had been a hectic morning.

The news of Dale Munroe's death and the subsequent arrest of Jasper Munroe had quickly become headline news, with every outlet playing it on repeat throughout the night. McEwen had been questioned outside the hospital that morning by a few brave journalists, who had learnt that he had been wounded in the process.

Everyone had theories.

Speculation was rife.

But now, flanked by some of the Met's finest media experts, McEwen proudly took his seat under the huge banner emblazoned with the crest of the Metropolitan Police.

'How you doing, sir?' one of the reporters called out.

'Oh, I've been better.' McEwen chuckled. 'Thought I was a few years away from a hip replacement, but there you go.'

Laughs filled the room, and the authoritative charm that had made him such a popular senior figure had begun to shine through. One of his employees slid him a sheet of paper and McEwen looked down at it.

A perfectly worded statement, talking about the diligent work of the Met and their commitment to justice, no matter who it is.

All of it written by a team of experts, all to tick boxes and win backing from the same influential people as before.

McEwen shook his head as he read it, and a few murmurs began to spread through the room. All he could think about was Sam Pope, stood over the prone body of Jasper Munroe and the meaningful hug that Hayley Baker had given him.

The image flashed in his mind, and he knew what he'd witnessed. Someone had gone to the bitter end for her, and she knew it. They had risked life and limb to protect her, and to seek the justice that he and everyone associated with the entire legal system had failed to do.

'Prepare yourself for a myriad of shit.'

McEwen slid the paper back to the perplexed media expert, who looked around the room for help. The journalists sat forward, literally on the edge of their seats.

'You know, taking this job was a dream. I worked hard when I was out on the streets, and I worked damn hard when I came off the beat. There is a pride that comes with wearing this uniform. With wearing this badge. But what people don't admit is that they don't do it to make this world a better place. Or to give back to the community. They do it for themselves. They might do it for different reasons, but they do it for selfish ones.'

The media expert leant across to whisper in McEwen's ear, but he waved her off and continued.

'Yeah, it feels good when you take bad people off the streets, but it's all to boost your own stats. Your own record. It opens up doors that you walk through, and if you work as hard as I did, they open all the way to this seat right here. I'm not saying we haven't done some excellent work, because we have. I appreciate every single officer who steps out of Hendon, puts on this badge, and puts their life on the line. But somewhere along the way, we failed.'

Audible gasps and whispers filled the room. Camera flashes flickered like a broken light bulb and journalists scribbled in their notepads. McEwen took a sip of water, adjusted himself in his seat, and continued.

'For too long, we have segmented who qualifies for punishment and who doesn't. How much or how little. But the law is the law, and we have allowed that to be used as a political tool or a bargaining chip. But I am here to tell you that that changes *now*. Last night, Jasper Munroe was arrested for the murder of his father, Dale Munroe, and the attempted murder of myself. Not only that, but we *will* be reopening every sexual assault case held against the man and this time, there will be no segmentation. There will be no favours or blind eyes. The man will pay for the crimes he's committed and let me be *very* clear. The law is the law, and the Metropolitan Police Service will come down on *anyone* who believes they are above it or thinks that their pockets are deep enough to beat us. Thank you and I will not be taking any questions.'

As expected, the room erupted into a chorus of questions as McEwen eased himself up from his chair. The media expert tried to force a smile as he walked past her and as he shuffled to the door, Lynsey Beckett managed to catch him. An officer went to step in, but McEwen stood him down and ushered her through the door to the privacy of the corridor outside. Once they were alone, McEwen leant uncomfortably against the wall for support.

'You all right?' Lynsey asked with genuine concern.

'I'll survive.'

'All that in there…' Lynsey nodded back to the room. 'How much of that was the pain medication and how much of it was bullshit?'

McEwen chuckled. He admired the young woman. She was a fine journalist, and the BBC could do with more people with such gumption.

'None of it.' McEwen looked her dead in the eye. 'I meant every word.'

'Really?' Lynsey pulled a concerned face. 'You'll piss off a lot of people.'

'That's the point. Too many people have had it too easy. Things need to change. Someone has to do the right thing.'

'Sounds like *someone* got through to you.' Lynsey smiled and leant in. 'It wasn't me, was it?'

'No. But let's just say a mutual associate showed me that *nobody* is out of reach.'

Lynsey took the message loud and clear. The rumours of her association with Sam Pope still whirled around the office from time to time, and McEwen himself had even questioned her once the Sam Pope Task Force was resuscitated. McEwen gave her a friendly nod goodbye and then ambled down the corridor, heading towards the inevitable backlash of his press conference. Lynsey watched him walk for a few moments and then called out to him.

'And Hayley Baker? Is she going to be okay?'

'I hope so,' McEwen said, turning back. 'I hope so.'

The two exchanged a pained smile and then went their separate ways, knowing the fallout of the last week would echo for years.

'Prepare yourself for a myriad of shit.'

McEwen chuckled to himself as he headed to his office. He had never been so prepared.

The press conference became big news and was played on repeat across all the news channels. Henry and Angela Baker had been watching intently as the commissioner laid out a stern warning to the rich and powerful, as well as the corrupt and criminal, that a new era had dawned. While Angela congratulated the man for finally showing some backbone, Henry was more sceptical.

Hayley had returned home to them the night before, along with a team of police officers and paramedics. They were still bound and gagged when the door opened, and after the medics checked them over and the officers took their statements, they were left to be reunited as a family.

Hayley told them everything.

How she had witnessed the death of a man, shot in the stomach by his own flesh and blood. How she had attacked Jasper with the metal photo frame, ripping his face open before he had hunted her through the office.

How he had struck her.

How he had tried to strangle her to death.

As she recounted the story to her parents, her father broke down in tears, begging for her forgiveness for failing to protect her. Her mother wrapped her arms around her, telling her how much her heart swelled with pride at the strong, fearless women she had become.

After a good night's sleep, the three of them watched the news conference, and Hayley audibly gasped when McEwen stated the charges brought against Jasper.

Justice at last.

But she remained quiet.

Her parents wanted to go for a celebratory lunch at the

local pub, just the three of them. They wanted to spend time as a family and appreciate how close they'd come to losing what they treasured most.

Hayley excused herself and went to her room, just wanting the solitary company of herself.

She had justice, but she also had scars.

Scars that would ripple across her psyche for the rest of her life. Flashes of the brutal assault by Jasper, as well as the attempted murder, would sneak up on her when she least expected it and despite showing immense courage and strength throughout the past twenty-four hours, she knew that fear would be a likely companion for the rest of her life.

Jasper Munroe might be spending the rest of his pitiful existence behind bars, but he would spend it with a piece of Hayley that she would never get back.

One day soon, she would tell her parents how she felt, and what she would need from them, but not yet. They were too thrilled at the verdict and to have her home for her to tell them just how broken she felt.

There was only one glimmer of hope she saw in the world, and that was Sam Pope.

Good people did exist.

People who would go above and beyond the lines of right and wrong to do what was necessary.

Without someone like Sam, she'd have been lost forever.

But now, she at least had a little hope that she would be able to get through it and live her life.

Live with what happened.

Live with her scars.

As she looked out of the window of her room, Hayley knew there was a chance that she could be happy.

It would just take time.

'The man will pay for the crimes that he's committed and let me be very clear. The law is the law, and the Metropolitan Police Service will come down on anyone who believes they are above it or thinks that their pockets are deep enough to beat us. Thank you and I will not be taking any questions.'

'He did it, ' Mel muttered under her breath as she stared at the small TV in the kitchen of her flat. The Commissioner of the Met stood and walked out, as the news reporter continued the sensational story of the Munroe murder and McEwen's supposed tirade at the state of the justice system. Considering all the coverage it was getting, it looked like something had rocked the entire country to its core.

Sam.

Mel felt a small swell of pride in her heart and didn't realise she was smiling.

'You okay, Mum?'

Cassie looked up from her textbooks, which were strewn around the kitchen table. She had a bowl of cereal in front of her, and her young, wrinkle-free face was frowning at the rows of text before her.

'Aye.' Mel flicked the TV off. 'Just some good news, is all.'

'I'll tell you what would be good news. If a bomb threat was called into my school and I didn't have to sit the exam.' Cassie looked up at her mum. 'Can I borrow your phone?'

'Very funny.' Mel took a seat next to Cassie and looked at the books. 'You know all this stuff, Cass. You're a smart kid.'

'I know, but I hate exams. I just don't feel ready?'

'You've been revising for weeks.'

'Look, Mum. I know you think these are *just* mocks, but they matter, okay?' Cassie shook her head and Mel stood, hands up in surrender. Mel wasn't an academic, but she appreciated her daughter's appetite for schoolwork. While she didn't agree with the pressure put on the kids about these exams, she certainly wasn't going to discourage her daughter from taking them seriously. A good education meant a good job, and although she knew she was a good mother, she felt that once Cassie was an adult with a decent career, she could then stop holding her breath and pat herself on the back.

It was just the two of them.

And that's all they needed.

Before the usual twang of heartbreak could kick in, the sound of the backdoor of the bar closing echoed up the stairwell. Both Mel and Cassie looked at each other with confusion, and Mel protectively took a step towards the door to the kitchen. The footsteps up the stairs grew louder, and after the confrontation with Mr Hudson a few nights before, Mel was on edge.

The door to the kitchen opened.

Sam stepped in.

It was twenty to eight in the morning, and the man looked dead on his feet. The last time she'd seen him, standing in the cold wind of the Necropolis, he'd been fine. Now, he was covered in dirt and his face was a picture of pain. His eye was bruised and swollen, and a nasty gash was pulled together with a few stitches.

He offered Mel a smile, and then turned to Cassie, who looked up at him with teary eyes. Mel rushed forward and wrapped her hands around him and Sam winced with the pain but held her tightly.

Cassie joined them.

Then Mel instinctively flicked the kettle on, and Sam lowered himself into the seat next to Cassie.

‘Right…Monday morning you said…’ Sam lifted her book and Cassie smiled. ‘Let’s do this, shall we?’

The teenage girl smiled, and Mel brought Sam a cup of tea as he helped Cassie with her final revision.

That was one promise he was determined to keep.

EPILOGUE

ONE WEEK LATER…

'When do you get your results?'

Sam looked at Cassie as she finished her bottle of water.

'I don't know yet. Soon I hope.'

'You'll ace it.' Sam tapped his temple. 'You're a smart kid.'

'That's what I keep telling her.'

Mel elbowed her daughter's arm, causing the last of the water to dribble down her chin. It drew the usual teenage ire, but they soon laughed it off. They were all laughing as much as they could, especially as the clock ticked down. As the joy died down, Sam looked tentatively at his mug of coffee. The Costa in Glasgow Central Train Station was vast, but surprisingly empty considering the footfall. Sam had spent the last seven days with Mel, enjoying her company for as long as they knew was possible before the inevitable conversation happened.

There was no way he could stay.

Not just because he'd eventually find another problem that needed sorting out, but because he couldn't put them in danger again.

The two of them meant too much to him.

As the silence began to hang, Cassie felt her lip quivering.

'Do you want to go?' Cassie asked, looking up at Sam. Her eyes were watering. Sam reached over and held her hand.

'Not one bit.'

'Then don't.'

'Cass…' Mel began.

'No, Mum. I don't want him to go.' Cassie turned back to Sam. 'You can get your old job back and—'

'Cass. Cass.' Sam spoke, barely louder than a whisper. 'It's okay. Trust me, if I could stay and be a part of yours and your mum's life, I would in a heartbeat.'

'Then just stay.'

Cassie began weeping, and Sam stood. He walked around the table and helped her to her feet, and then wrapped his arms around her.

'The things I've done, Cass. There's always the possibility that someone will come looking for me. Just like the other night. And I can't put you or your mum in that danger. I just…' Sam looked at Mel and smiled. 'I just love you both too much for that to happen.'

Cassie wept for a few more moments, while Mel took a few deep, calming breaths. Sam knew they were heartbroken, but he kept his own decimated heart to himself.

'Just don't forget us, okay?' Cassie said, looking up at Sam with a modicum of hope. Sam lifted her chin with her hand and smiled.

'Even if I tried.'

Cassie hugged him once more and then stepped away. Mel squeezed her daughter's hand as she walked past and she and Sam watched as Cassie marched off through the station.

'Teenagers,' Mel said dryly.

'She's a good kid,' Sam said. 'She's got a hell of a role model.'

Mel turned back to Sam, surprising him with the tears flowing down her cheeks.

'Damn you, Sam Pope,' she said playfully. 'This was never meant to become something, was it?'

Sam pulled her in and kissed her, and she planted her hands on his face. The bruising on his eye had calmed down, and the stitches had left an impressive scar that sliced through his eyebrow. As they embraced for a few minutes, Sam could feel her tears against his cheek. He pulled away and looked her in the eyes.

'I want you to know that this is the happiest I have been in a long time. I'm sorry I put you and Cass in danger and—'

Mel lifted her hand to cut him off. She dabbed her eyes and composed herself and then reached out and held his hand. She took one more look at him and smiled heart-breakingly at him. Sam did his best to memorise every single centimetre of her face.

'Go and be you, Sam,' she said with words filled with love. 'The world needs you.'

Mel let go of Sam's hand and turned and walked out of the coffee shop, her hands reaching to her eyes as she wiped the tears away. Sam felt the lump in his throat, and he watched as she followed after her daughter, and as always, threw a protective, loving arm around her. The two of them walked through the station concourse towards the exit and as they approached the main door, Mel shot a glance back at Sam.

He smiled and nodded his goodbye.

She did likewise.

Then the two of them stepped through the door and out of his life. Sam stood for a moment, cursing himself for letting happiness slip through his fingers.

But Mel was right.

The world needed him, and Sam picked up his bag, slung it over his shoulder and walked towards the ticket gates to board a train to somewhere.

Anywhere.

Somebody needed to keep everyone safe, and Sam knew that if he went looking for trouble soon enough, he'd find it.

GET EXCLUSIVE ROBERT ENRIGHT MATERIAL

Hey there,

I really hope you enjoyed the book and hopefully, you will want to continue following Sam Pope's war on crime. If so, then why not sign up to my reader group? I send out regular updates, polls and special offers as well as some cool free stuff. Sound good?

Well, if you do sign up to the reader group I'll send you FREE copies of THE RIGHT REASON and RAIN-FALL, two thrilling Sam Pope prequel novellas. (RRP: 1.99)

You can get your FREE books by signing up at www.robertenright.co.uk

SAM POPE NOVELS

For more information about the Sam Pope series, please visit:

www.robertenright.co.uk

ABOUT THE AUTHOR

Robert lives in Buckinghamshire with his family, writing books and dreaming of getting a dog.

For more information:
www.robertenright.co.uk
robert@robertenright.co.uk

You can also connect with Robert on Social Media:

facebook.com/robenrightauthor
instagram.com/robenrightauthor

COPYRIGHT © ROBERT ENRIGHT,
2023

All rights reserved. No part of this publication may be reproduced, stored in a retrieval system, or transmitted in any form or by any means, electronic, photocopying, mechanical, recording, or otherwise, without the prior permission of the copyright owner.

All characters in this book are fictitious and any resemblance to actual persons living or dead is purely coincidental.

Cover by The Cover Collection

Edited by Emma Mitchell

Proof Read by Martin Buck

Milton Keynes UK
Ingram Content Group UK Ltd.
UKHW040816161123
432684UK00004B/207